After Annie

Sue Welfare

After Annie

Copyright © Sue Welfare 2021

All rights reserved.

ISBN: 9798728864479

Published by Castle Yard Publishing 2021

Acknowledgements

With heartfelt and huge thanks to the amazing women who have helped me get After Annie to publication.

I genuinely couldn't have done this without you, Fiona Prevett, Jane Dixon- Smith, Maureen Vincent-Northam and Rebecca Emin. Enormous thanks too, to the most fabulous group of beta readers a writer could ever wish for.

*

Please note that this is a work of fiction and the practices and timescales in this book bear little or no resemblance to those within the Police Force.

I have deliberately compressed and accelerated the time between crimes being committed and evidence being collected and processed, and detection of the culprit, to add tension to the story. In real life the necessary warrants, planning, time and legal constraints and procedures make Policework and the detection and resolution of a criminal investigation a far less cavalier operation than the one described in this book.

After Annie

After Dark

'Almost there,' he said, glancing over his shoulder. 'Won't be long now.'

The wipers on the van chopped backwards and forwards, carving out a view of the bleak fen landscape. Through the rain, picked out in the headlights, he could just make out the narrow concrete track that led across open farmland to the trees. He slowed to take the turning. 'You're going to love it,' he said. His tone was warm, conspiratorial.

He'd known it was the perfect place from the minute he'd first seen it, this great circle of trees standing all alone on a slight rise, on enough of an incline so that from the road they were picked out on the horizon, as striking as a cathedral on the empty skyline. Tonight, even in the darkness, the trees were still visible, blacker than the dark of the night sky. The circle of trees had a sense of being somewhere magical, somewhere secret, somewhere completely apart from the rest of the world, even though they were in plain sight; it was the kind of place she had always loved.

In the far distance, away to the right, a range of barns and sheds were illuminated by a couple of yard lights but there was nothing else to see, no other movement, no other cars, no one else to see them. Overhead the vast sky glowered grey and gold, heavy with rain clouds that periodically broke and scattered across a sliver of moon.

He slid their favourite album into the CD player. 'You okay back there?' he asked, but she didn't reply. He sighed. People always complained that he was a man of few words, but her? These days she barely spoke to him at all.

When was it that she had got to be so hard, so sour and so angry with him? He just wanted things to be like when they first got together. The truth was that he had always been a bad lad, and she'd known that from the get go. But her? Everyone thought that she was an angel, that butter wouldn't melt, but he knew better, no one would ever believe just how bad she could be when she put her mind to it.

He grinned, remembering the mischief playing like fire in her eyes back when they first got together, and wondered where all that had gone. How many years ago had it stopped being fun? When was it that her face started being permanently screwed into that mix of disgust and disapproval? He was always on tenterhooks, waiting for her to kick off about something that he'd done or hadn't done or something she thought he'd done, and it didn't matter how hard he tried, whatever he said, there was just no convincing her, no way back from that raw, ragged, angry edge. Maybe tonight would help; maybe it would make things better for a while.

He peered into the darkness, looking for the turning he'd seen on the satellite image. She didn't say a word. He sighed. He could really use a drink.

She used to enjoy a drink with him before they had the kids, but then again she had enjoyed a lot of things back then, back before everything else had happened and she started treating him like he was the problem, like she was his mother and disappointed by everything he did and said. She'd always known what he was like. It wasn't like he had ever lied to her about anything, but back then she had been gentle, and soft, and seen that whole bad boy thing, *seen him*, as a challenge, like she could tame him, like he was a dog that she could bring to heel. Why was it that women always wanted to change you?

The trees framed a pond. He'd looked it up on *Google Earth*. On the satellite image the pond had been a perfect blue circle, framed by a wreath of green, reflecting a cloudless summer sky - not tonight though - tonight it would reflect the darkness.

A few lights twinkled far off, away in the distance, presumably other farms or isolated houses. Behind him, back along the track, visible in the wing mirrors was the dull orange glow of the bypass and a nearby village, but nothing close by that suggested they could be seen or were being watched. They would have the place to themselves.

He grinned, then thought he could hear her moving about in the back but he didn't turn to look. They would be at the trees soon enough, and he would explain everything to her then, meanwhile he turned up the music as the opening bars of her favourite song started to play.

'Remember this?' he said. 'You used to love this one. Remember dancing-'

Ahead of him, caught in the van's headlights, the concrete road rolled out like a pale grey ribbon across the black land, tipping and rippled by the shifting soil beneath. Google Earth hadn't prepared him for the tidal roll of the road's surface. He grabbed the steering wheel tighter as the camber took him by surprise, and then listened again wondering if she might say something, might complain, but she stayed quiet, and he was glad he couldn't see her face, or her expression.

'I told you it wasn't far, didn't I?'

Still she didn't answer; this time he felt a little flicker of annoyance. This was the trouble, all she ever did was criticise him, even when he was doing something special for her, her silence let him know exactly what she was thinking. He could feel her disapproval seeping over him like a miserable, scratchy grey blanket and he was glad that they were almost done.

*

In Denham Market, Detective Sergeant Mel Daley curled up under a winter weight duvet, pulling the bedclothes tight in around her, trying to keep in the heat and keep out the noises of the weather. She was surfing out over rolling waves that took her from the deepest sleep up to wakefulness and back down again, in a bedroom that was still half full of boxes that she hadn't touched since she moved in.

It was six months since the move and Mel was still camping out in her new life in Norfolk. She turned over, away from the window where a sliver of light from a street lamp across the road crept in between the curtains and sliced the room in half. Outside the wind grew fiercer, bringing more rain with it. Having crested another wave she slipped down the other side, back into unconsciousness and a dreamless, tar black sleep.

*

Alongside the roadway on the fen a network of deep steep-sided dykes, great gouges, drained the reclaimed land. The soil was inky black, heavily furrowed and glistening like wet jet in the van's headlights. He was careful to stay on the concrete. If they once ran off the road into the plough soil or, God forbid, one of the dykes he'd never get the van out, and she would never let him hear the last of it.

'Not far now,' he said again, keeping the anxiety out of his voice. He imagined her tight-lipped expression. He needed a beer.

It would be fine. It would be fine.

He picked up speed, crawling along would only make him look suspicious.

Finally he saw the side road he'd been looking for, running at right angles to the main track, leading down to the trees and the pond. It was a lot rougher than it had looked on the satellite image, pockmarked, the surface broken and crumbling. The whole place had an air of abandonment. Away to his right was the hulk of a great

4

rusted water bowser, flanked by plastic tanks in metal cages, all covered in green slime and stacked three high in the lee of a row of scrubby bushes. He had hoped that it would be more picturesque; he didn't want to give her any more reason to be upset with him.

He pulled up, and as he sat there weighing up his options, a squall rolled in across the open land like a great wave, rocking the van, the heavy rain it was carrying lashing across the windscreen as if someone had turned on a hose. He took a breath. It would be fine there, just fine, and anyway it was too late now to change his plans without risking making a mistake.

He parked as close to the trees as he dared, making a tight three-point turn, so that when they were finished he could just drive away, and then he pulled up the hood on his disposable overalls, pulled on a second pair of gloves over the first, pulled up his mask, turned off the music, opened the van door and stepped down onto the track.

The ferocity of the wind caught him by surprise, snatching at the door, threatening to wrench it out of his hand. He steadied himself and slid the side door of the van open. He had already fixed it so that the interior light wouldn't come on. Inside, the whole interior was carefully and methodically covered with disposable drop cloths, new synthetic dust-sheets fresh out of the packet, a common make available at DIY stores the length and breadth of the country, and all taped into position. The disposable overalls and gloves he was wearing all had the same pedigree, bought from different builders' merchants at different times and looking smart enough in case he was ever stopped. He just looked like another anonymous somebody on his way to or from work.

Work - the truth was that that's what this was. She had been hard bloody work for years.

He'd made sure to leave his mobile phone on his bed, so that no one could track his progress between cell towers. His phone would suggest that he had had an early night and was safely tucked up sound asleep after a long hard day.

He waited a few moments letting his eyes adjust to the gloom, taking the time to flex his back and knees, as if he was warming up for a workout at the gym. He always wore a head torch just in case, but preferred not to use it if possible. A light moving randomly in the darkness might be spotted and remembered or reported, although it was hellish dark, the likelihood of being seen was remote but it was better not to take the chance.

Gradually things around him resolved themselves into focus - a pile of bricks, a row of discarded drums containing God only knows what, and a trailer, its tow hitch almost obscured by weeds sticking up to catch the unwary. But not him. He was far from unwary; he could feel the great flush of adrenaline coursing through his veins.

He was ready.

He took a breath, feeling the heat, feeling the surge, and then waited a few moments more, letting his breathing and heartbeat settle, tilting his head to pick out any stray sounds on the wind, and hearing nothing unsettling, leaned inside the van and gently pulled her towards him.

'Come on, my love,' he murmured. 'C'mon. It's okay. We're almost done now.' And for a moment, he thought he heard her sigh.

She didn't resist him. She slid effortlessly over the drop cloths towards him. Just like in the good old days. He bent down, and lifted her up, hefting her up over his shoulder in a fireman's lift, with one hand wrapped around her knees to steady his load. She came to him willingly, her body seeming to cling to him. And all the while he talked to her, now that it was all over, whispering soft, gentle words of encouragement to reassure her and himself. He loved her, that was the thing, he had always loved her, why had she never realised that whatever he did that would always be true?

The polythene she was wrapped in came from an

industrial sized roll he had bought for work, and to ensure that there was no chance of matching the edges if he was ever caught and the roll was ever found, he had cut another sliver off both ends of her shroud and from the remainder of the roll as an extra precaution and burnt them, and then dropped the new Stanley knife blade into a skip. It paid to be careful.

The rain ran down over the two of them, making her wrapping all the more slippery. She wasn't heavy. He had always preferred small women, but the ground underfoot, once he was off the concrete roadway, was soft and dense, each step plunging him knee deep into the plough soil, making this last part of the journey far trickier going than he had anticipated.

She moved as he moved, swaying and slipping as he tried to pick his way between the furrows, constantly changing his centre of balance. Mud clung to his legs and clung to his boots, threatening to pull him over, threatening to make him stumble and fall as her weight shifted. He began to sweat from the effort and the anxiety, every step was coating his clothes in soil that could be linked to this farm, to this furrow. He felt another surge of adrenaline, this time one triggered by panic. He was wearing a disposable paper mask but he'd seen the programmes on TV, all it took was one drop of his sweat, one hair to place him there. If they ever caught him, he reminded himself.

Thank God it was raining.

The suit, the boots, the mask, the drop cloths would all go into different bins and skips. He wondered if it wouldn't be better to burn them, and had to stop himself, to stop his mind running in different directions, and just concentrate on getting to the trees without falling, or dropping her. It would be fine. It would be fine, he murmured. All he had to do was breathe. Breathe, step. Breathe, step.

And then finally he stepped into the ring of trees, and it was just as he imagined it. He paused, feeling the tension easing as he searched out the place he had seen on the satellite image. There had been a building, a collapsed shed in the picture. In the broken moonlight the circle around the pond was even more magical, the soft ground covered in thick cushions of moss and great plaits of slick, wet ivy reflecting the silvery light. It looked other worldly. He took a minute to savour how right it was, this place. It ended here.

He moved cautiously through the greenery underfoot and then very gently he let her slip down from his shoulder, and set her down with all care so that she was framed by the low moss-covered walls of the building. Once she was safe on the ground his pulse and breathing slowed.

'See,' he said quietly. 'Didn't I tell you? It's perfect.' Looking down at his handiwork he felt a sense of relief, of joy, of something he felt was close to ecstasy. Now it was done, now finally she could rest, and for a while he could be at peace too. And he had been right, this was the most perfect spot for her. It looked as if she belonged there, out in this magical wood, under the great grey-gold sky.

Her wrapping glowed soft white in the threads of moonlight and he imagined he could smell her hair on the night air, a mix of something citrusy and sandalwood, and for once her silence filled him with a sense of calm and satisfaction.

'I knew that you would love it here,' he said tenderly. 'I just knew it.'

It was tempting to peel back the polythene sheeting and wish her one last goodbye, to touch her face, to whisper her name, but instead he made do with crouching down alongside her and turning on the head torch for a long minute so that he could take one last look at her face pressed up against the plastic sheeting, so perfect, so serene, almost as if she was asleep, trapped forever under ice. He touched his gloved fingertips briefly to her lips and whispered his goodbyes, then turned and made his way back out through the trees.

Sated, tired to the bone he stepped up into the back

of the van, carefully slipped off his boots and overalls and wrapping them up into a bundle dropped them into a paper sack, along with his mask. He looked down at his gloves – he was reluctant to remove them, but then there was no one who would question his fingerprints or DNA in his own vehicle. They were fresh on – the ones he had used on her, to finish her and wrap her were awaiting disposal elsewhere. Double gloved, always – he'd seen that on a TV programme.

Finally he peeled them off and dropped them into the bag, then carefully climbed through into the driver's seat, which he had covered with a disposable plastic cover. Once in his seat he slipped on a pair of trainers that he'd left on the passenger seat. He had done all he could, now there were other things to do and other places to be. Overhead the moon broke through the clouds and the rain eased. It felt like a sign. Putting the van into gear, he drove away, feeling a sense of calm he hadn't felt in weeks.

Chapter One
Mel Daley

The sounds of someone hammering on my front door ripped through my dreams like gunfire. I'd been deep in sleep. There was a brief moment when I wondered where the hell I was and what was going on, and then I was wide awake, clambering out of bed and dragging on my dressing gown.

'I'm coming,' I yelled, tying the belt on my robe and hurrying out onto the landing. If the station wanted me surely they would have rung? Or had I missed the call? Or had I put my phone on silent? Had I remembered to put the bloody thing back on charge? Shit, shit, shit. I ran my fingers through my hair to tidy it and took the stairs two at a time.

Whoever was at the door was banging hard enough to knock the damned thing off the hinges and, having found the bell in amongst the overgrown climbers, had their finger pressed hard down so that it rang on and on.

'Wait a minute,' I shouted, fumbling with the lock. 'I'm coming.'

It was a little after midnight according to the hall clock - so, early Wednesday morning technically then, and outside it was tipping down with rain, so whatever it was, it wasn't likely to be good news. If someone had sent uniform to wake me for a major incident then they were doing a bloody good job.

I'd been on shift all day Tuesday, twelve hours straight, and along with my own casework, had been helping put together the finishing touches to a case that was going to court the following week. That, amongst other things. A lot of other things: endless reports and an appraisal form that had come down from on high, which was two months late and as indecipherable as it was important. Admin is not my strong suit but I'd drawn the short straw. We were short-handed, and I was still the new girl and still getting more than my fair share of the shit jobs.

Wednesday was supposed to be my day off. Tuesday evening I'd come home, had a shower, ordered a pizza delivery and been in bed five minutes after I'd finished eating. It was a miracle I'd found the energy to take my clothes off.

I left the chain on and peered out through the peephole in the top panel and sucked in a sharp breath. Jimmy, my brother-in-law, was standing on the doorstep, close to the door, under the joke of a porch, trying and failing to keep himself out of the rain.

I looked again just to check that I wasn't imagining things. He put his finger back on the bell. I opened the door a sliver keeping the chain on.

'What the hell are you doing here?' I said, genuinely shocked. Last time I'd seen Jimmy had been in Ross-on-Wye, maybe six months ago, maybe longer, however long it had been it felt like a lifetime ago and at the same time not long enough.

'Kathy's chucked me out.' he said. His clothes were soaked through. In the jaundiced glow of the security light I could see the rain dripping off his hair and face, his jacket was slick and moulded across his shoulders like a second skin.

'I mean I could lie to you and say I'd left her, but truth is she says she doesn't want me back. Sent me a fucking text, a fucking text,' he said, pulling a phone out of his pocket. 'Says I can go and collect my clothes and stuff from the garage. The fucking *garage*. And she's changed the fucking locks.'

I didn't say anything.

'Mel, you have to help me.' He held out the phone towards me like it would explain everything. 'She texted me – texted.' His voice was full of indignation. 'Just let me in, will you? She's thrown me out-'

'Not my problem, Jimmy,' I said, and went to close the door. I didn't add, *not before time,* because even I could see that that wouldn't be helpful.

'Wait, please,' he said, stepping up so that his body was practically pressed against the door, his face no more than a couple of inches from mine. I could smell beer and sweat and cigarette smoke.

'You have to ring her for me, talk to her, explain. She'll listen to you.'

*

Let me tell you about Jimmy. Jimmy is married to my little sister, Kathy. He's a sleazy, manipulative little shit, and worse than that, far, far worse than that, I slept with him, and not just the once.

It had been a terrible mistake which is such an understatement that it is barely worth saying. There are no excuses, but looking at it coldly – and believe me I have looked at it many, many times, Jimmy deliberately came after me when I was vulnerable and he is the kind of evil bloody snake who knows just how to make the most of the vulnerable. But that doesn't mean I couldn't have said no to him. I could have said no, and I didn't. So, yes it had been a terrible mistake but it's one I take responsibility for, and one of the reasons, possibly if I'm honest, the main reason why I'd applied for a transfer from Mercia Police and moved across the country from the Welsh Borders back to Norfolk where I grew up.

I'd like to say it felt like coming home, but it wasn't. It was like being in one of those places that you think – in a dream – that you know and have been there before, and feels vaguely familiar but is actually uncomfortably different.

So, it's taken me a while to settle in but I'm slowly getting there. I applied to join the Major Investigations Team, a promotion of sorts but fundamentally once you stripped away the bells and whistles it was a sideways move into a specialist unit. I'd been told that they were looking to take on more women and it seemed like the ideal opportunity even if part of it was about filling their quota, but mostly I applied because Norfolk and my new squad are five hours drive away from where my sister and Jimmy live, although by the fact he was on my doorstep - it was obviously not far enough.

Jimmy was unshaven, and looked crumpled and heavy eyed.

'Are you going to let me in then?' he said again. 'It's tipping it down out here,' stating the obvious.

Across the courtyard the lights in my neighbours' kitchen had snapped on. Jimmy has the kind of voice that carries.

'Just go home Jimmy.' I hissed. 'I can't do this.'

'Can't do what?'

'Let you in or ring Kathy.'

'Please, Mel, she'll listen to you.'

Another light had gone on in the house across the way.

'She won't, Jimmy, trust me.'

Kathy and I had barely spoken since I'd made the move to Norfolk. At Christmas, before she felt obligated to invite me to their place for the festivities, I'd sent a text saying I'd lucked out and was working all over the holidays, and then made sure that that was true. We'd been busy; nothing says Merry Christmas more than stabbing your wife's fancy man and setting fire to the house with your kids in it.

Jimmy was resting his forearm on the doorframe now, leaning in to the gap between the door and the frame. His breath was enough to cut sheet steel. 'You have to help me. You owe me, Mel.'

I felt a flash of fury. 'How do you work that one out? You just need to go.'

'Or what, or you'll call the police?' he snapped, stepping back laughing to himself, and then he stopped and turned. 'Look, Mel, I'm sorry. I just didn't know what else to do or have anywhere else to go.'

For a moment I thought that he was going to cry.

A door opened at number six. 'Everything all right?' shouted a man in a dressing gown, his wife tucked in behind him, taking it all in.

'Yes, fine, thank you,' I called, raising my hand and adding a cheery wave for good measure. 'Sorry to have disturbed you.' I glared at Jimmy. 'You need to go.'

The whole street knows I'm a police officer. It makes them wary and standoffish, and at the same time curious. The wife at number six barely speaks to me when I see her out, but you just know she would love a juicy bit of gossip about men turning up all hours of the night and day. I could have gone into a section house when I transferred, but I like my own company and I'd found a house to rent on a new housing estate, where I planned to stay until I worked out whether I was going to stay in Norfolk or not and had rented out my place in Ross-on-Wye for the same reasons.

Our squad was based just outside Norwich, as part of a joint East Anglian Task Force. It's around an hour's drive each way from Denham, but, at least for the time being, I liked the familiarity of living in the town close to where I had grown up.

All the houses on the development were built around brick-paved, landscaped courtyards that probably looked homely and inviting on the architect's computer mock up, but in reality meant that parking was a nightmare and some days close to impossible, and privacy more or less non-existent, which prompted a thought.

'Where did you leave your van, Jimmy?'

For a moment he hesitated, and I could see he was considering lying, his default response to anything that put him on the spot.

'You've been drinking,' I prompted.

'Oh right, yes, officer. I've been drinking. Always the bloody copper,' he said, suppressing a wet belch behind a clenched fist. 'No need to get your knickers in a twist, Sarge. I've only had a couple.'

14

It smelt like he might have meant bottles.

'It's like a war zone here with parking, Jimmy, if you've-'

'Blocked someone in? Don't panic, I didn't drive up here, and I didn't park my van anywhere near your la-di-dah fucking neighbours, I walked, okay?'

He was making no sense.

'*Walked*? From where?'

He shifted his weight and looked away. 'From the hotel.' He didn't stop for my reaction. 'We drove over first thing Monday morning. Early. I didn't want to freak you out by letting you know I was here – and anyway I only got the text today. I was thinking what to do, weighing up my options.'

I was still hooked up on his first word; I stared at him, 'Hotel? *We*?' I re- ran what he had just said. 'What do you mean *we*, Jimmy? Did you finally run off with one of your fancy women? Is that what this is about? I hope the poor cow knows what she is letting herself in for.'

He flinched. 'No, no, it's nothing like that.'

'Then do you want to tell me what the hell you're talking about?'

Even as I was saying it I knew that I didn't really want to know the answer. It would be something complicated and messy, but there was a part of me that couldn't help myself. 'If you've been here since Monday, why come round now, after midnight, half pissed and soaked to the skin? You're not making any sense. You could have rung-'

'Oh yeah right, and you would have picked up first ring, wouldn't you? Anyway I couldn't ring you. I've left my phone back at the hotel,' he said.

None of this was adding up. 'So you ran off with someone?

He glared at me. 'Are you crazy? No, of course I didn't. If you'd just let me in then I can explain-'

'You know what? Actually, I was wrong, I don't want an explanation. Just go.'

He opened his mouth as if to say something and then thought better of it.

'Go,' I repeated.

'Mel please, you're my last hope.' He paused. I waited.

'Okay, so I've got a job over here. We've got a contract on one of the big new estates. Tile Farm? You must have seen it out on the bypass, big old farmhouse; they're converting that into apartments and then building the estate around it. Not just me, there's a gang of us here, subbying off the main contractor.'

'Here? In Denham?' I said, unable to help myself.

'Yeah, we go all over the place. Gang of us, different trades, really good money.' He grinned. 'We go all over the country. Don't you watch the TV? Country needs more homes, Mel. And when I saw we'd got a contract coming up for Denham I thought I'd see if I could get on the crew, come over, see you. Catch up. See how you're getting on. You know...' his voice trailed off.

Like we were old friends or something.

What the hell had he been expecting, that we would carry on where we left off? That I'd be lonely all on my own in a new town and just jump into bed with him? Things must be really bad between him and Kathy if he thought that I was his best option.

'God's honest,' he said, miming a cross over his miserable lying heart. 'You're looking good,' he said, changing gear, testing the waters. Bastard.

'I thought it would be nice to look you up and see how you were doing. Kathy is always saying how much she misses you, you know. I came round Monday afternoon after work, but you were out so I thought I'd come back today, but later on, you know, when you'd finished your shift. '

I glanced up at the hall clock. 'It's after midnight, Jimmy. I've been working all day. I was asleep.'

He nodded. 'Yeah, sorry about that. I would have been round sooner, but I had a few things that I needed to sort out first.' A muscle in his jaw worked like knotted

16

string. Why didn't I just close the bloody door? Why was I hanging on listening to him? Looking back, your guess is as good as mine.

'The thing is I do love her, Mel,' he said. 'I rung her and she hung up on me. All those years, and the kids and everything-'

I didn't ask what it was that he had done this time, who had he slept with, what it was that Kathy couldn't forgive him for, there were so many possibilities, so I said nothing, which he took as an invitation or maybe sympathy.

'So, are you going to let me in then?' he said, his voice dropping down to a conspiratorial whisper. He pulled out a bottle of wine from inside his jacket. 'Come on. You know you want to, Mel. We could maybe grab a little nightcap, just like the good old days. No strings. For old times' sake.'

Seriously? Once upon a time, a lifetime ago that might just have worked, but now it stoked my simmering anger. He just couldn't help himself.

'Bugger off, Jimmy,' I said. 'And don't come back.'

He shrugged and then the bastard winked at me. 'Worth a shot. You should never have left, you know that, don't you? Kathy blames me for you going. Like it was all my fault.' He paused, his gaze fixed on mine, and as his expression hardened something icy tracked down my spine, and made me wonder if the drunk thing was just an act to get me to lower my guard.

'I never did tell her about us, you know,' he said. He sounded stone cold sober now.

It felt like he had punched me. 'Fuck off, Jimmy. There was never any *us*,' I said and slammed the door shut, pressing my whole body back against it as the catch caught. Bastard.

I don't know where Jimmy went after that, and more to the point I didn't care. Seeing him there on my doorstep made me feel sick. I had moved across the country to be rid of him and it seemed that it wasn't enough. I double locked the door, slid the bolt across and went back upstairs, wondering if I'd be able to get back to sleep, but the truth was that I was so tired that even Jimmy didn't stand a chance. Curling back up under the duvet I closed my eyes and was asleep within minutes.

*

It was still dark when my phone rang and kept on ringing. There was a part of me that guessed that Jimmy wouldn't give up so easily. I rolled over and picked up the phone. The good news is I had the sense to check the caller display before letting rip.

'We've got a body,' said the voice at the end of the phone. 'Governor says he'll meet you at the scene. I'm just sending the details to your phone now.'

Chapter Two
Isaac's Fen

As the sky was lightening I pulled up on the verge close to a slip road that led to the dump site, and turned off my engine. Even though I know the Fens well it is still astonishing to see the miles and miles of flat, bleak, black land laid out under the vast sky, although today it wasn't the view that was holding my attention but the two marked police cars parked nose to nose across the entrance to a concrete track-way, their blue lights rolling lazily in the damp morning air.

Mike Carlton, a local Detective Sergeant who I'd worked with on a previous case, was standing by one of the officers from the patrol car, who appeared to be peering at his phone. Mike grinned when he saw me walking towards him.

'Well, well, well, if it isn't the cavalry,' he said. 'DS Daley, good to see you - any chance you can get someone to move the road block?'

I smiled, said my Hellos while showing the uniformed officer my ID. 'Give me a break, I'm on my day off. And anyway, aren't they your lot?'

'Great way to spend it.'

'It was this or the spa day, so I thought I'd come over and pick up some tips, see how it should be done.'

He laughed. 'Right, an audience is just what we need.'

'I'm assuming this is down to SOCO.' I indicated the parked patrol cars.

'Yep, although what they're hoping to find after last night's rain and the fact everyone else came in that way.' Mike glanced back pointedly at the PC. 'So, Collins have you worked out how we can get on site without calling in a helicopter?'

The uniformed officer had been busy working his way through an on-screen map. 'Here we go, Sarge,' he said, tipping the screen towards us. 'Head back towards Denham and take the first left onto Longbank Road and then left again onto the first concrete farm track you come to, which should bring you in over there.'

He turned and pointed towards the cluster of farm buildings in the distance. 'And then there's another roadway which should take you over to the trees.'

Isaac's Fen is thirteen miles or so from Denham Market out along the A10 towards Cambridge, through rich farmland. I'd grown up in a village a couple of miles away from where we were standing. The whole area is criss-crossed by a maze of narrow concrete farm service roads, not public highways but concrete lanes that cut the land into manageable portions and meant you can take tractors, lorries, cars and heavy plant onto the fens without sinking up to your axles.

'And so we're assuming that our man didn't use that route rather than this one?' asked Mike, not unreasonably.

I waited to hear the answer. The PC nodded. 'The gate on Longbank Road is locked at night, dykes either side, so they're thinking he had to have come this way. The farmer came and unlocked the other gate for us once SOCO said they wanted this one sealed off. This is a shared access down to a pumping station so it can't be locked. We've been told not to let anyone through without prior authorisation.'

'And who's on site now?' asked Mike.

'SOCO, Crime Scene Manager, Coroner, Forensic Pathologist and DI Foreman, all the usual-'

DI Foreman was Mike's boss, an old school detective who had been generous with manpower and support when Mike and I had worked together trying to track down a missing woman.

The PC looked at me again. 'And a murder squad

DCI is on his way.'

'Paul Tomlin?' I prompted. The PC nodded. Good news. Tomlin was my governor, and by the fact we had been invited along it meant someone had called it early. Usually I would have driven him to the crime scene when someone higher up in the food chain had decided that the death was suspicious.

Truth was, despite all the guidelines and directives more often than not, we were called in on a case when the local officers had run out of steam on an investigation, when all the simple solutions had been exhausted and often well after the crime had occurred, when everyone else had pawed over the evidence, the scene, spoken to any witnesses and come up empty. In theory we could be called in at any stage, the earlier the better, but in practise we often weren't, which meant this one was something different.

A few minutes and a couple of miles later I was driving in through the farmyard and being directed to a large concrete pad more usually used to stock pile sugar beet, that was currently being put to use as a makeshift car park for a cluster of official vehicles and police cars. A temporary command centre had been set up by one of the barns.

Someone had ringed the circle of trees, which stood a way off, with bright yellow police incident tape and beyond that there was another wider exclusion zone, marked out with metal stakes and more tape, extending well out into the ploughed field and onto the side road in a bid to preserve the scene along with any physical evidence. A couple of uniformed officers were stationed outside the outer perimeter.

I parked up, and slipped off the leather boots I'd been wearing and pulled on a pair of *Hunters* I always kept in a bag in the boot.

Once we'd been logged in Mike and I headed towards the dump site, a hundred metres or so off a secondary track that was littered with old machinery and farm rubbish. A sharp inquisitive fenland wind scuttled in across the open fields, flicking up fronds of torn plastic and fabric on the piles of debris. The police tape around the trees whistled and shuddered in the wind.

'DS Daley and DS Carlton, 'Mike said, as we approached the tape. An officer with a clipboard nodded and ticked off something on his list and added our details.

'Governor said to send you down soon as you arrived and got yourselves suited up.'

'I should wait for my boss, 'I said to Mike, although even as I was saying it I caught sight of movement in my peripheral vision and turned to see DCI Tomlin striding up the track behind us. He lifted a hand in greeting. Tomlin has the face and the build of an ex-rugby player and the slightly stiffened gait that tells you he's still feeling it. I had been assigned to his team when I first arrived in Norfolk.

'Talk of the devil,' I said. We both waited for him to catch us up. I was rota-ed on to Tomlin's team and his shift pattern so technically we were both on our day off.

'Morning Sir,' I said.

'Morning Daley. Home turf for you then?' he said, and then nodded towards Mike.

I made the introductions. I knew from a conversation I'd overheard a couple of days before that Tomlin was meant to be out shopping with his wife for a suit for his daughter's wedding. He didn't look overly unhappy to be attending a murder scene instead.

'So, let's get on with it, shall we?' he said, addressing both of us as we made our way over to a SOCO van to collect coveralls. SOCO – the scene of crime officers collect and process evidence from the crime scene, as well as helping to ensure we didn't contaminate it. I took the suit I was handed, along with a pack containing mask, gloves and bootees.

'Can you run through what we've got?' said Tomlin.

So far I'd only got the bare bones. Unidentified

female victim, discovered this morning by the farm owner, Gary Heath. Uniform were on the scene at 04.50, confirmed we'd got a body, kicked it up the food chain and secured the scene.'

Tomlin nodded. 'And do we know who the victim is?'

'No, Sir.'

Tomlin glanced round as he struggled into a *Tyvek* suit. 'Pretty hard place to find unless you knew what you were looking for,' he said. 'Do we know what brought Mr Heath out here in the wee small hours?'

I hadn't got those details and glanced across at Mike.

'He said he spotted vehicle lights on the farm CCTV.' said Mike

'And what time was that?'

'He called it in around four,' said Mike. 'I'll need to confirm the exact time.'

Tomlin nodded. I made a note to add to the timeline.

There was a path marked out across the plough soil, picked out with metal plates and duckboards, set down so we could get to the scene without disturbing, destroying or contaminating evidence. Everyone who visited the scene would be going in and out the same way, following the route that had been taken by the first officers on the scene, although with the torrential rain from the night before it was hard to imagine any tyre tracks or foot prints from whoever dumped the body had survived.

That said, away from the duckboard, here and there the top of the furrows were broken, marking the progress of what appeared to be two people, moving diagonally, taking the shortest route towards a tight circle of trees, and then back again. The wide furrows would have made it hard to step over each one unless you were particularly tall.

Isaac's Fen and the farmyard were in a desolate out of the way spot – a perfect place for a body dump. At least the light was getting better, the sun creeping through a milky white sky. The wind was keen, although not enough to dry up the standing water on the heavy land. Water sat in the troughs between the ridge and furrows of the soil and in every hollow in between, reflecting the sky. In a circle of trees early morning light picked out the white tent that was covering the body.

It was hard to imagine anyone choosing this as a spot for an early morning dog walk or a jog, and even if they had been on the track it didn't explain why anyone would have gone across the plough soil to the trees. Without Gary Heath's intervention we might never have found the body.

'Heath told uniform that he saw vehicle lights on the CCTV and came out to check on what they'd been up to,' Mike continued. 'He's had a series of break-ins on the farm over the last couple of years. Uniform have been out here half a dozen times, never caught anyone, or been able to trace any of the stolen goods. Mr Heath's insurance company insisted on cameras being installed on the buildings after someone emptied the farm's tool shed and took the stuff away in his nice new trailer.'

'And someone has already picked up the footage?' asked Tomlin, his attention still on Mike.

'As far as I am aware Sir,' he said.

'Right.'

Tomlin glanced back at me. 'I'll check,' I said. I'd clocked the cameras on the barns as we'd driven in. The sooner the film was secured the better. Lots of security systems have limited storage capacity and would re-record over old footage once they were full.

'Do you know if he was watching the CCTV in real time or was it a recording?' I asked, glancing back towards the farm. It would be hard to imagine anyone seeing anything this far from the buildings. And then another thought struck me. 'Do we know if he was on site or watching remotely?'

'Sorry can't help you with that,' Mike said.

I made another note.

'He had the CCTV footage all tee-ed up for when the officers arrived, although apparently the film quality isn't that great. You can see headlights of a vehicle, possibly a van or 4x4 approaching along the concrete road from the A10 and then turning left onto the side road here. It's digital, so we might be able to do something with it,' continued Mike.

Tomlin nodded. 'Good. Presumably there's no reason why anyone else would legitimately stop there? Doesn't strike me as lovers' lane material even in good weather.'

'He says he assumed they were fly tipping and drove over to check. At that point although it had rained heavily and the vehicle was gone, Mr Heath said he thought he could make out footprints and tread marks.'

'Don't suppose he thought to take photographs?' Tomlin asked grimly.

Mike shook his head. 'I'll check, but there's nothing in the notes I've seen,' he said.

As we got closer to the dump site I recognised the bulk of DI Foreman, deep in conversation with the Forensic Pathologist, Beau Shepherd. I'd met them both before on a previous case. Both men were dressed in white disposable suits, gloves, booties and facemasks. Everyone looked up at the sound of our approach.

Foreman nodded a welcome and came over to meet us, pulling down his mask as he approached. 'Morning, glad you found us okay.' He caught every eye in turn but addressed his remarks to DCI Tomlin. 'This one's out of our comfort zone.' Foreman said, his expression grim. 'You need to see it for yourself. From the look of it I can't imagine that this is his first outing.'

Inside the ring of trees I watched Beau Shepherd turn and go back into the tent.

By the fact DCI Tomlin and I were on site meant he'd be heading up the enquiry as Senior Investigating Officer, the SIO, with cooperation from the local force. It's not always the easiest place to find yourself. The local force can swing between feeling that we've stolen their case and relief at being able to hand it off, very few have the resources or expertise to run a full scale murder enquiry, but have invaluable local knowledge, and even when we'd bring in our team to run the investigation we'd need local manpower to do the leg work and provide us with local intelligence. It was part of the SIO's role to finesse and manage that relationship so that we got the best from everyone.

I've seen it go horribly wrong but Paul Tomlin had a talent for getting people onside. He was always direct, and at the same time listened to the officers, whatever their rank, that were working with him. They're not all like that. Currently he was giving DI Foreman and Mike Carlton his undivided attention. He was good at listening.

I glanced back over my shoulder toward the farmyard.

Who would know about this place?

'Given the weather conditions last night SOCO are doubtful we'll be able to recover anything viable in terms of tread marks,' Foreman said. 'They're working on stride length to see if we can ascertain height, from the damage to the furrows between the roadway and the trees. And they've said that there is an outside chance that they might be able to recover a boot print from one of the depressions in the plough soil.'

'Good – if we can manage to track down the boot.'

Amongst the trees another figure in a white suit appeared at the doorway of the tent and beckoned to us. We pulled up hoods and masks; Foreman turned first and led us into the circle.

Inside the ring of trees, sheltered from the weather, there was an unsettling almost claustrophobic stillness that made the hairs on the back of my neck prickle. The trees had been contorted by the prevailing wind over decades, their twisted trunks and branches choked with ivy which gave them odd, almost human shapes, their branches and the tendrils of the ivy were intertwined and linked together so that the little copse looked more like a band of swaying dancers, encircling us, all holding hands, frozen in time in the morning light. Water clung to the glistening leaves and mist hung in the air just outside the circle. I suppressed a shiver.

The ground surrounding the tent was ankle deep in ivy and moss. Here and there, there was the odd fallen branch, its outlines softened by the creeping green, and narrow animal trails leading down to the open water which reflected the pallid, milky grey sky above us. I'm not easily spooked but the place gave me the creeps.

Off to one side of the pond the large white tent sat incongruously in the shelter of the trees. White light glowed through the tent sides from the lamps SOCO had set up, so that everything inside would be illuminated with the same clear unforgiving light.

Our conversation and the recap of events faded into silence as we stepped inside the tent. All I could hear was a hum from the generators for the lamps and the rising sound of the pulse in my ears as the adrenaline kicked in, some ancient instinct preparing me for whatever I was going to see.

Don't get me wrong, I wasn't afraid of whatever was in the tent, but there is something inside of me, inside all of us I suspect, an ancient visceral apprehension of the violent unknown, that kicks in unbidden.

On the whole these days I am not undone by the things I come across in my job, but it doesn't mean I'm unaffected or unmoved by them, but unlike a lot of other people I have a chance to do something about them, a chance to redress the balance and try to put things right. I think wanting to try and make things right was why I joined the force in the first place, that and the family friendly hours, and a tendency towards a very dark humour.

By the time I was standing in the tent with Mike, DCI Tomlin and the others I'd worked eleven days straight, with more than one twelve hour day, picking up the slack and the hours because we were undermanned, under-funded and – well, you get it. Sometimes I think

I'm not so much desensitised as totally and utterly knackered.

Being a police officer makes you look at people through a sharper, cynical, less forgiving lens but it doesn't mean that I don't wish sometimes that things could be different.

Chapter Three
The Bride

Inside the tent, caught in the unforgiving glare of the lamps, was our victim. She had been placed in amongst the crumbling remains of an old shed, in amongst the ivy, pillows of moss, weathered bricks and fallen rubble, her feet pointing towards what had once been the doorway, her head towards the rear wall.

My first fleeting impression was that she was wearing a wedding dress, complete with a delicate veil that covered her face, and an instant later I realised it was because she was wrapped in plastic sheeting. She looked tiny, fragile, the arc lights reflecting off the surface giving her a strange almost ethereal glow.

Here and there tendrils of ivy had settled in over her plastic shroud. I wondered if they sprung back or whether the person who had left her there had teased them out, arranging them with care - whichever it was, it made it look like she was part of the landscape, rooted down into the earth, garlanded, and the effect was oddly, unsettlingly beautiful, like a Pre-Raphaelite painting.

I pushed the thought down. It wasn't beautiful, it was cruel and brutal and whoever had posed her had done it with careful deliberation, whether it was meant for his victim, for himself or for whoever found her.

Tomlin had had the same thought. 'Posed,' he murmured, not a question but a statement.

'Makes quite the impression, doesn't it?' Foreman said.

There was a murmur of assent.

'Let's check the database?' Tomlin glanced at me. It was standard procedure to see if this kind of MO -

Modus Operandi, or method of working - had been used before. I nodded a reply, and he then turned his attention back to the young woman.

She was white, female, small, probably no more than five feet tall, maybe five feet two at most. The plastic wrapping added an odd quality to the way she looked. My first impressions lingered – even though I knew it was polythene, to me she still resembled a bride, wrapped up all in white, her veil caught by the wind pressing up against her face, and then I noticed her hands were pressed, palms up, flat against the inside of the polythene sheeting so that she looked as if she was trying to push her way out.

'Her hands –' I said aloud.

'They have to have been arranged like that, don't they?' Mike asked, taking the words out of my mouth.

We looked at Beau Shepherd, the Forensic Pathologist. 'We won't know for certain until we get her back to the lab and unwrap her, but it seems highly unlikely they would have fallen naturally into that position.' He played a torch across her face, the effect was uncanny, as if she was surfacing.' If you look closely you can just pick out signs of lividity on her left side which would suggest she was killed elsewhere and moved here. The lividity appears fixed which would suggest that wherever she was killed she remained in the same position for some hours-'

'Which given the lack of disturbance in the area makes sense,' said Tomlin. 'So not the primary site. Can you estimate time of death?'

'We have to allow for the effects of the polythene on heat loss. But taken together with the lividity and the degree of rigor we're talking within the last twenty-four hours. Best guess between two and ten pm on Tuesday evening.' He paused. 'She's in full rigor now. Generally, it starts between two and six hours after death. This is obviously temperature dependent, and takes longer if the body is cool. Given the fact he carried her here, it would have been considerably more difficult, though obviously, given her size, not impossible if she was in full rigor.'

'There don't appear to be any signs of drag marks through the plough soil,' Mike said grimly, glancing back over his shoulder.

Tomlin nodded.

'I can tell you more later today,' said Beau, 'Once we get her out of the sheeting.'

Every inch of the polythene, once it had been carefully removed, would be scrutinised for evidence, fibres, fingerprints, plant matter and bugs – everything would be gathered up and examined, along with the wrapping itself.

'Other than establishing core temperature, doing some initial observations and photography, nothing else has been disturbed,' Beau continued, as we all stared down at the young woman. 'It'll be a while before we can move the body.'

'So, what are we looking at?' said Tomlin in an undertone. We all have our own ways of focusing our thoughts. This was Tomlin's invitation to speculate. He moved closer and crouched down, his gaze travelling back and forth and then he looked up at me - an invitation.

'It looks like she's been carefully placed and posed here. This place, the way she looks, these things are likely to mean something to him,' I said.

I used 'him' because although, given the size of the victim, it was possible that the killer was a woman, it was statistically unlikely. Most women are killed by men, most often men they know. In 2016, nine in ten women died at the hands of someone they knew. Of those, most were killed by their current or former intimate partner. The statistics really haven't helped my view on relationships.

'It might have some special significance to her or for them as a couple,' suggested Mike.

Tomlin glanced around. 'Seems like an odd spot, but yes, very little disturbance to the area, so we'll want to be looking elsewhere for the primary scene.'

'And the plastic wrapping, 'Foreman pointed. 'Beyond the obvious forensic countermeasure, it looks like he staged it so we can see her face.'

The vision of a woman in a wedding dress flashed through my mind again. This time she was laughing, ducking her head to avoid a shower of confetti, a fleeting image that I couldn't quite keep hold of.

Tomlin glanced across at Beau Shepherd for confirmation. We all know better than to touch anything.

Beau nodded. 'It certainly appears that the sheeting has been cut away at an angle although I'll need to confirm that.'

'So she can see us or we can see her,' said Mike.

'She looks like a bride,' I said, finally unable to hold the thought in. 'That almost looks like a veil.'

Tomlin nodded and straightened up. 'So he wants us to see her? To admire her?'

'In which case why put her here, in the middle of nowhere?' asked Foreman.

I moved a fraction closer. Her eyes were closed as if she was asleep, but there was something else that was scratching away at the back of my mind; the young woman reminded me of someone. I looked again to see if I had imagined it and as I did the likeness slipped away although the unsettling feeling didn't leave me.

I caught Tomlin glance at me, a question in his expression.

'Do you think he already knew about this place?' Mike was saying. 'Hard to imagine he found it by accident.

'Are we suggesting that the killer had local knowledge?' said Tomlin

'These stands of trees around ponds are not exactly uncommon on the fens or anywhere else come to that,' Foreman said. 'I could find you half a dozen more places like this within a fifteen-minute drive, probably more. Although not all are as accessible by vehicle-'

'Okay, so we need to find out if this one held any special significance for him. Any idea if it has a name?'

Mike shrugged. 'No one's mentioned one, Sir.'

'I'll find out,' I said. 'Do you think he expected her to be found so soon?' If it hadn't been for the farmer worrying about fly-tipping it makes you wonder how long would it have been before anyone discovered her? How often does anyone come in here?'

Tomlin nodded. 'Good point. Can you check up on that? And I'd like you to talk to him as soon as we're done here. What's his name again?'

'Gary Heath,' prompted Mike.

'Okay, so our first priority is getting an ID for the victim. Knowing who she is will make this a lot easier-' He glanced round at DI Foreman, Carlton and Beau Shepherd.

Beau nodded. 'Best I can currently do is young, adult female, IC 1, so white North European, around 155 cm tall and probably no more than 50 kgs, blonde hair, although we all know that can be dyed. Small frame-'

'Age?' prompted Tomlin.

Shepherd pulled a face. 'Without examining her? I'd say mid-twenties to early thirties, although I reserve the right to revise that figure once we get her back. Botox, fillers and surgery make it less obvious on a superficial examination. Pierced ears but no visible jewellery, no tattoos or scarring that I can see, but that too can change obviously.'

'We need to find out who she is; someone must be missing her,' said Tomlin. There was a murmur of agreement.

Once we had a name it made things simpler. A name would give us her family and friends, her address, her job or college, her relationships, good and bad, and access to her social media, her identity would open up a pool of suspects and possibilities. Despite what the films and TV programmes would have us believe most murder victims are killed by someone they know.

I thought fleetingly about Jimmy, about why he was

in Denham, and what had kept him so late that he couldn't get to mine until after twelve.

Behind us the tent flap opened to let in a technician. The slightest movement in the damp air dislodged a droplet of moisture on the outside of the plastic sheeting, which glittered like a crystal in the lamp light and ran down over the girl's veiled face like a single tear.

Chapter Four
Gary Heath

The farm office was overly warm and smelt of onions, damp sacks and wet dogs. The uniformed police constable who had been sitting with Gary Heath nodded a greeting as I opened the door. Heath was well over six feet tall, a great broad-shouldered slab of a man, dressed in a cream and green checked flannel shirt, and green corduroy trousers, held up by a pair of bright red braces and a thick leather belt, and had a belly that hung out over his trousers in an impressive arc. Mud-caked wellington boots stood just inside the door by a stack of cardboard boxes branded with the farm logo, a jaunty red and blue banner that promised farm fresh celery and onions. He was padding around the office in a pair of battered leather moccasins. A *Barbour* jacket was hanging over a chair by one of the radiators to dry. He was ruddy faced with a sparse thatch of white blonde hair and tiny blue-grey eyes ringed around with white lashes. I would have put him in his late forties or early fifties. He was finding it hard to tear his gaze away from the activity outside the office window.

'I've already rung and told Sandra not to come in,' he said over his shoulder, waving towards the window as I introduced myself.

'Sandra?' I repeated.

'Sandra Bailey, she's my bookkeeper, she comes in and does the accounts for me. Mornings. Most mornings just for a couple of hours. No point her coming in today, is there? Not with all you lot here.' He spoke with a strong local accent, and as he shook my hand his engulfed mine. 'Have you got any idea when they'll be finished out there?'

'I'm afraid not, Mr Heath. But I'll make sure someone keeps you informed of progress.'

'They took my clothes you know and my boots. Good job I'd got some spare clothes here.'

I nodded. 'It's just standard procedure, Mr Heath. Would you like to sit down?' I said, indicating the chair behind his desk when it looked as if he intended to have me interview him while he stared out of the window. When he finally sat down, I took the phone out of my bag. 'Do you mind if I record this, it's easier than taking notes?'

He nodded. 'If you like.'

'I'd like you to tell me what happened, and what you saw.' I set the phone down on the desk, between us, gave my name and his and where we were and the date and time. 'So, last night-'

'I've already told the other officers. Truth is I'm finding it hard to concentrate on anything at the moment,' he said getting to his feet again. 'You don't expect this sort of thing, do you? Not round here. I was thinking it was going to be building waste, bricks and plasterboard or maybe even chemicals, or just household rubbish, not a body. A body.' He paused, running his fingers back through his hair, and then said, 'We've had a lot of that sort of thing. Old mattresses, fridges. We have to pay to have it taken away, you know. The commercial tippers are worse, brick rubble, building waste, drums of God only knows what, I've seen some things over the years but nothing like this.'

I said nothing and waited.

He shook his head and then slumped back down into his chair. 'What is it you want to know?' And then added, 'Miss?' speculatively.

'Detective Sergeant Daley,' I said. 'I need to ask you a few questions about last night. Has someone been in to collect the CCTV?'

Heath shook his head. 'No – but-'

'Okay.' I nodded towards the officer by the door.

'Can you get the tech team in here to pick it up asap, please?'

The PC got to his feet and headed for the door.

Heath looked uncomfortable.

'Is there a problem, Mr Heath?'

I waited.

'There might be,' he said after a second or two more.

I waited some more.

'About the CCTV, I think I might have accidentally deleted it,' he said sheepishly. 'Not all of it - the bit with the vehicle on it. I don't know what to say. I mean I didn't mean to. It was just a slip of the finger after I'd shown it to your lot when they got here first thing.'

'You believe you may have erased some of the footage?' I repeated, keeping my tone neutral and the surprise out of my voice.

'By accident.'

Given the overnight weather conditions when the body was dumped, the film footage for the farm's CCTV cameras might well be the only solid early lead we'd got.

Anxiously Gary Heath barrelled on straight into an explanation: 'I was looking at it, after the first policemen arrived, they came in and took a look. You know, while they were waiting for the big guns to show up, and I suppose I was a bit nervous. It's not every day you find a body, is it? I was just highlighting the bit that I thought you'd be interested in. I thought I'd make a copy and stick it on a CD for you, you know, so you could take it off the computer-' he was speaking more quickly now and pointing towards a computer and monitor that stood alone on top of a row of filing cabinets. There was a label with a blue thunderbolt stuck to the side of the monitor.

'Only I was getting a bit flustered I think and I pressed delete instead. By mistake.' He shrugged and gave me an odd nervous smile. 'I mean it's easy done. It was a complete accident. I was only trying to be helpful. And then it asked me if I was sure and I said *yes*. So stupid - I couldn't believe I'd done it – pressed it just like that - and then I couldn't find a way to undo it.' His colour drained as he saw my expression. 'I'm sorry. I feel such an idiot – but like I said to the other officers, you couldn't see that much.'

'And this held the only copy?' I nodded towards the machine.

Heath nodded.

'Do you back up the footage off site? Maybe on the cloud or an external hard drive?' I asked, making another note, and wondering why Heath had been left alone in the office and for how long, once uniform had arrived to the site, and what else we might have lost by accident.

Heath's expression gave me the answer – as far as he was concerned it was gone for good - although we would need to check with whoever installed the system. Truth was very little on a hard drive is irretrievable but it takes time to recover information and it isn't always complete.

'Do you have the details of who installed your CCTV system?'

'No, but I can ask Sandra. She arranges all that kind of thing. Do you want me to give you her phone number?'

'If you could, Mr Heath, that would be helpful.'

He pulled a phone book out of the desk and passed it to me. I made more notes.

'Do you pay some kind of management fee or did you buy the system outright?'

Heath pulled another face. 'Like I said, I don't know. Sandra deals with all that kind of thing.'

'Okay. We'll get the computer bagged and tagged and I'll make sure the technicians are aware of the problem. Do you have just one computer for the cameras?'

As well as the computer on Gary Heath's desk, there was another on what I guessed was probably his bookkeeper's desk, and the third standing on top of a bank of half height filing cabinets that ran along one wall, which I had assumed from following his gaze was the machine we were talking about.

'I already told you, I've deleted the film,' he said again, more firmly this time. 'No point taking it if the film's gone, is there?'

'It's not ideal but we may well still be able to recover some of the footage,' I said.

From his expression I don't think this was the response that Gary Heath had been expecting.

'But you can't see anything except the lights anyway – and you can't take it away,' he protested. 'I need it for the farm. I mean it's for security – the insurance won't cover us if we haven't got CCTV-'

'Perhaps you could use one of the other computers as a temporary measure or give whoever installed it a ring. Maybe they might be able to lend you something? We'll get it back to you as soon as we can,' I said, and then before he could raise any further objections, continued, 'So where were you when you saw the vehicle on the CCTV?'

Heath hesitated, and then rubbed his chin.

'Were you here, Mr Heath?'

'I do use my computer at home, sometimes, that's where it goes, the film – it'd be pretty pointless having the CCTV one just in here if we're burgled again. But you can view the footage on any of the machines once you've logged in.'

'And you were logged in where? At home or in the office?'

'Here,' he said. 'In here.'

'And you deleted the images from here? Using that machine?' I pointed.

He nodded. 'Yes, I had to log into the main menu to get access. I was going to save it for you, on a CD.'

'Right, okay. What I'm asking is were you here or were you at home when you saw the vehicle on the CCTV?' There was something else, something uneasy and anxious in his body language. He glanced up at me.

'There might be a bit of a problem about that; I'm

39

not a hundred percent sure about the times. You know, what I told the other officers about what time I saw the lights, and the times I arrived, things like that. I might have been off by a bit. The whole thing was a real shock.'

I waited. There was more.

'I'm not sure what time I drove over here. Not really. I didn't expect to have to explain to anyone where I was or why, so I didn't really take any notice of the time.'

I glanced down at the notes I'd been given. 'You called the police at-'

'About four,' he said, 'But then I was here awhile before that-' he hesitated. 'I came back in the office after I found her, just to gather my thoughts, to steady my nerves before I rang your lot.'

I nodded and made another note. I wasn't sure what this was about or where he was going with this but he was deeply uneasy about something. 'And how long do you think that took, from finding her to you calling us?'

He shrugged. 'That's just it. I don't know, I was pretty shaken up.'

'Okay, well let's talk about what happened. Were you here, in the office when you saw the lights on the CCTV?'

'I was.'

'Not at home?'

He shook his head. 'No, I'm more or less certain-'

'How long had you been here, approximately?'

'I don't know, it might have been an hour, maybe longer I'd lost track of time.'

'What were you doing? I mean, do you often come here in the early hours?'

Gary Heath flushed bright red. He hesitated and then finally said, 'I was watching a film, an adult film I suppose you might call it. And I didn't want to disturb my wife. So, so-'

'You came across to your office for some privacy?' I suggested, expression neutral.

He nodded vigorously. 'That's right.'

'And how did you get here?'

'I drove. In our delivery van. It's quieter than the truck and like I said I didn't want to disturb Linda, that's my wife.'

'And then what happened?'

Gary Heath considered for a moment or two.

'I stopped the film to get myself a drink.' He caught himself and added, 'Just a small one, not so much as I'd be over the limit or anything and while I was sorting that out, I thought I'd flick through the CCTV.'

'Do you usually look at the CCTV footage?'

'Yes, every day, mostly in the evening. It's easier then, no disturbances. I put it on fast forward, double speed, and let it run through, and that was when I spotted the lights. Driving down the concrete road towards the farm.'

'And you were definitely here in the office when you saw the lights?'

'Yes.'

'Were you watching the vehicle live or was it a recording?'

He was chewing down on his lip now. 'Recording. I'm pretty sure it was a recording.' Which I guessed meant he wasn't sure at all and made me wonder what the hell he was watching that was so engrossing.

'Did you think there was a chance that the vehicle might still be on the farm?'

He glanced up at me. 'I don't know. I was just surprised to see anyone on the farm at that time of night.'

'Was there footage of the vehicle leaving?'

'I'm not sure now. I didn't get much beyond seeing the headlights. I've got two chaps that work for me but they'd have rung me if they were coming over, and why would they come here at that time of night?'

'We'll need their names and addresses.'

Heath nodded. 'Bill Partlett and Roo Holman. I've got their addresses in the files.' He got up and found them for me, then settled back behind his desk, his gaze moving back to the window before he took his seat.

'So, about the lights,' I prompted.

'First off I thought that it might be someone going down to sort out the drainage pump. That farm road off the A10 leads down to an automated pumping station at the bottom of the track, over by the big drain. They'd only come out if there was a problem - but then whoever it was turned off the track.'

'And what time was that?' I asked. 'Did you notice the time stamp on the CCTV?'

He shook his head. 'No, but it was dark.'

'And then what did you do?'

'I re- ran the film just to make sure that I hadn't made a mistake.'

'And then what?'

He looked confused.

'What did you do then, Mr Heath, when you had seen the lights?' I prompted.

'Well, I went over there and found her, didn't I? Over by the pond in that old shed. I played there when I was a kid. I can still see her. Did you see her?'

For the first time since I'd come into the office Gary Heath looked me squarely in the eyes. 'I don't know how you do your job. I wouldn't be able to sleep at night. I won't be able to forget seeing that in a hurry.' He shivered.

'Just to confirm, once you'd watched the CCTV footage you went over to take a look at where you thought the vehicle had gone?'

He paused for a second or two, as if gathering his thoughts. 'I think so, more or less. I drove over to the turn off that goes down to the trees. We store a lot of old equipment down there out of the way. I keep meaning to clear it out. It would be an easy place to dump rubbish, just reverse in, dump it and drive out. I couldn't see anything at first and then I saw the tyre tracks and it looked like someone had gone in across the plough soil. Walked, not driven – which seemed peculiar – if you were going to dump anything. Anyway I got a torch out of the van and went across to take a look.' He took a deep breath.

'You could see where they'd been, there were breaks over the ridges and furrows, then in through the trees in amongst all that ivy, where he'd been, stepping it down. I could see the plastic sheeting from the far side. First, I thought it might be an old carpet or something, although I couldn't understand why anyone would have bothered carrying it all that way, so I went in, got a bit closer, and then saw her.' He looked up at me, his colour all but drained away.

'Frightened the bloody life out of me and for a second I thought maybe it was a shop dummy, someone having a joke, but nothing could have looked that real and then-' he stopped and swallowed hard. 'I thought I was going to throw up. I ran back to the van. I can't remember doing it, but I've never been so bloody scared or moved so fast in all my born days. I thought I was going to-' he paused, reddening now, choosing his words carefully. '– soil myself.'

I nodded. 'And there was no one else there then?'

He shook his head. 'No, whoever it was, was gone. I would have seen them. There was just me, and her. No, whoever had left her there was long gone.'

'And you drove over there?'

'Yes, well as far as I could get. You couldn't drive right over to the trees in a van. It was raining and it's black as your hat out there at night so I got as close as I could and then walked. I couldn't have got across that field without using a tractor.'

'Did you see anything? Did anything particularly stick in your mind?'

He grimaced.

'Did you touch anything? Touch her maybe?'

'What do you mean *touch* her?' Heath snapped angrily.

'To check what it was or maybe to see if she was alive.'

'I didn't need to touch her to know what she was – I could see what she *was* with my torch and I knew just

43

looking at her that there weren't nothing alive in there.'

I glanced out of the window, trying to gauge how long it had taken me to walk from the trees back to the farm buildings. It had been dark when Gary Heath had found the victim, dark and raining, but driving it wouldn't have taken him more than a few minutes. 'And when you came back was that when you rang 999?'

He bit down hard on his lip; his tell. A little bubble of scarlet rose under a canine. 'No. Well, not straight away. Like I said I took a bit of time to compose myself. She wasn't going anywhere, was she?'

It seemed an odd thing to say, but people under stress say and do odd things, but there was something about him that wasn't quite right. 'How long do you think it was before you rang it in? Five minutes, ten?'

Heath shrugged.

'Longer than ten minutes?'

'Maybe – yes, probably. Longer.' He shrugged again, not meeting my gaze. 'I really don't know now. It was all a bit of a blur.'

I made a note. We should have been able to corroborate his story from the CCTV footage, which might be another reason why he had conveniently deleted it.

'So how long was it approximately between finding the body and ringing us?'

He hesitated. 'I'm not sure if I've got it clear in my head, the shock-'

'If you've forgotten to tell the other officers something-' I prompted. 'It happens all the time, it's fine. Things may come back to you later. So, was there anything else?'

He looked at me as if trying to gauge how well he'd done.

'Mr Heath we're just trying to find out what happened here-'

He reddened and looked away. 'There are a couple of other things,' he said. 'My wife doesn't know about-' he took a deep breath. 'The films. You know, she thinks

I'm over here doing bookwork for the farm or checking up on the place.'

I nodded. 'I understand, Mr Heath. She shouldn't need to know but I'm afraid I can't promise.'

He looked down at the floor like a small boy caught with his hand in the sweetie jar. 'I understand,' he said.

*

One of the technicians came in to take Gary Heath's computer and I arranged for Mr Heath to go down to the local police station to make a formal statement, and then headed for the on-site command centre. DI Foreman and Tomlin were inside looking at aerial photos of the circle of trees with the Crime Scene Manager, Jackie Marshall.

While the SOCOs worked the site the rest of the investigation would crank up. Back at the local station we'd start combing through missing persons reports looking for anyone who fitted the description of our victim. Uniformed officers would be going house to house in the immediate area to see if anyone had seen anything suspicious, which given that the copse and the farm were so isolated seemed unlikely, but stranger things had happened, and in a rural community people probably noticed things more than in the hustle and bustle of an inner city.

Over the next few hours the first pieces of what would soon be a river of information would begin to be collected, collated and indexed by receiving officers, so that everything was available to everyone on the investigating team.

Stepping up into the caravan my expression must have given me away.

'Something?' asked Tomlin.

'I don't know, Sir - Gary Heath's story and the timeline he gave uniform is all over the place. He can't remember when he found the body or how long it took him to ring it in - The kicker is he told me that he erased the footage from the CCTV – although he says it was an accident.'

Tomlin lifted an eyebrow. 'Convenient?'

'Possibly. And he's concerned about the fact that his wife might find out that he is watching porn in his office. I'd like to go and talk to her to see if we can verify what time he was at home and what time he left. I've asked uniform to take him down to the station to make a formal statement.'

'And keep him away from his wife so they can't cook something up?'

'Possibly.'

He nodded towards DI Foreman. 'I believe that you worked with DI Foreman and DS Carlton previously on the Leah Hills case?'

'Yes, Sir. I did.'

'Good. Well, we'll be working together on this one too, although everything comes through me. Okay?'

I nodded.

'And yes, Mrs Heath, go and see what she's got to say for herself.'

'One more thing, Sir, Gary Heath wanted to know when we would be done here? I told him I'd ask.'

'What did you tell him?'

'That we'd keep him informed, Sir.'

Tomlin nodded.

We both knew it could be hours before the body was removed and possibly days before the farm was handed back over to Heath.

'Do we know if he has any livestock?' asked Foreman. 'Even if we have to send an officer with him, any animals will need tending to. Don't want animal welfare on our backs.'

'Good point.' Tomlin looked across at me.

I glanced down at my notes which I'd been updating as I was interviewing Gary Heath. 'According to what he told first responders, Mr Heath is an arable farmer with two full time employees. He's given me their names and addresses, but there's no indication that there's livestock on the farm.'

'Okay. Can we arrange to interview the farm workers this morning?' Tomlin asked, glancing at Foreman, who nodded. 'Anything else?' he said, his attention moving back to me.

I scrolled down. 'Mr Heath takes on seasonal and contract help as required and employs a bookkeeper called Sandra Casey, who lives in Southery. He said that she has details of the contractors and seasonal workers if we need to speak to them.'

'No cows in need of milking?'

I shook my head. 'Not on here, Sir. But given his ability to recall facts it might be worth asking him again.'

Tomlin snorted. Outside it started to rain.

Chapter Five
Jimmy

They usually had the radio in the works van tuned to Radio 2 but the signal on the new housing estate was really bad, or maybe it was the aerial, who knew. Jimmy rolled his shoulders to ease out the kinks. All those uppity rich bastards buying homes off plan wouldn't like it if their new executive homes couldn't get all their favourite stations, although most likely it was all fibre optics, and Wi-Fi this and Bluetooth that given the spec of the build.

He flicked through a great rolling sea of static looking for a station, any station, trying to find something that didn't snag on his hangover. He hadn't started drinking seriously until he left Mel's, which had been a real mistake on a school night. God, he felt rough.

He hadn't mentioned anything about Kathy to the other lads, not that they'd take the piss or anything, but compared to him, or at least the way they talked they were bloody saints, one's missus had just had their first baby and he was cooing over pictures and Skyping his missus all the time, and one of the Polish lads was homesick for some woman he'd left back at home and he didn't so much as look at another woman, so the truth was they might not be sympathetic to the situation he found himself in.

He felt a little bubble of nausea rising from his churning gut and swallowed hard. He hadn't told Mel the reason Kathy had thrown him out, because she would have gone ballistic. The waitress in the last place they'd been working had only been a fling. He thought she knew that. How the hell was he to know her biological clock was set to kill? The thought of her going round to confront Kathy made him feel physically sick. She was meant to be a bit of fun, that was all. She knew that. She knew. She was just meant to be fun. Simple. Fucking hell, he ran his hand over his face, some fun she had turned out to be.

He had tried ringing Kathy when he first got up, at a time when he knew she would be at home, busy with the kids, getting breakfast, finding swimming kit and panicking over last night's homework. The truth was that despite everything she had said, and that he had said in anger, he really wanted to hear their voices. *Her voice.* He wanted to hear her voice even if she was snippy as fuck with him, but she hadn't picked up, hadn't answered either her mobile or the house phone. *'If you'd like to leave a message after the tone.'* Except he didn't want to leave a message because he didn't know what to say. What a bloody mess.

The road network for the whole of the new estate was already laid out, all soft curves and little cul de sacs with the plots arranged around communal courtyards. At the far side of the site was a Victorian farm house surrounded by old farm buildings, all of it fenced off, all earmarked for some kind of a serious trendy make-over. The rest of the estate, the new houses, were in various stages of construction across the site, some were barely out of the ground, no more than footings, while others were stylish roofed boxes with no interior fittings, just waiting for their new owners to decide on the spec and how much they wanted to blow on a kitchen, and then there was the section that Jimmy and his gang were currently working on.

The gang Jimmy was in had been brought in to work on the first phase – the high end houses, that looked handsome and inviting even in the rain, and were arranged around what would be a communal garden in a nice little cul de sac where someone had been smart enough to leave in a few mature trees. The new road, named for some obscure Norfolk hero, was ringed with two and three storey houses, all high spec, all different, at least on the outside, like they had developed organically over time, not been thrown up over the course of the miserable wet winter. The trees added to the sense of the houses having been there a while. This was the end where the show homes were, show homes and those new homes that had already been sold off plan and were now ready for their second fix. Around and behind each house landscapers had already transformed churned up waste ground, heavy with brick rubble, re-bar and assorted site debris into neat suburban gardens. These homes would be the shop window for the rest of the estate.

Behind him the men in the van were getting restless, everyone was waiting for Lennie to show up with the bacon sandwiches from a little bakery that he'd found in Denham high street; an army marches on its stomach. Wherever they went across the country Lennie always knew where the best places were. But then, according to Tomas, Lennie had been all over the country with the company, week in week out, always on the road, towing his caravan behind him like a snail, not just fitting but servicing and customising the company's integrated smart systems.

Truth was Jimmy didn't care how Lennie knew where the best cafes were. He was just grateful. There was a canteen over on the far side of the site, well away from the show homes, but the food was crap and a local gang of ground workers, great hairy arsed buggers with tattoos, who were doing the footings and digging out the service channels on the new sections, had made it obvious that they weren't overly welcome.

The van radio crackled with static. In one of the seats at the back, Robbie, the new dad, shook out his newspaper. 'Switch that row off, will ya? It's getting on my nerves.'

'Just give it another minute,' Jimmy said, playing with the buttons. 'There's got to be something worth listening to on here.'

Robbie snorted.

Outside the rain ran down the windows, cutting through the grime.

Jimmy shared driving the crew bus with Tomas, a Polish guy, Billy drove the truck with the tools, while Lennie drove the van with the more expensive and fragile parts and materials that they might need that were too expensive and too precious to store in the lock up storage container the main contractor supplied them with.

Richard, their boss and the guy they were subbing for, had a bloody great Nissan pick-up with a crew cab on the back. But come breakfast time everyone was crammed in the crew van. Richard included when he showed up. All of them bar Lennie, he liked to eat on his own but didn't mind doing the fetching and carrying - he was the brains, or so everyone reckoned. Apparently back in Poland he was some kind of Professor or so Tomas told anyone who would listen, but here in Denham he was the man the company had hired who joined up all the services and intelligent devices to the central computer inside every new house and ensured they all worked, sweet as a nut while everyone else fetched and carried, bolted and bent.

Lennie was a quiet man. Jimmy had stopped trying to exchange banter with him; first of all he had thought it was a language thing but had come to the conclusion that Lennie had no sense of humour, and certainly didn't see himself as one of the lads. But he was the man in charge of breakfast, because he was reliable, conscientious and always remembered who had ordered what. And Tomas would add, had all the brains.

All the brains to connect up the house and its integrated systems to make it all work at the press of a button or from an app, that magic internet of things that Jimmy kept hearing about. The smart house was a big thing in the sales pitch, houses you could control from your smart phone, houses where you could switch your lighting and heating on as you left the office, houses that told you if someone was at the door and sent you live video feed so you could check it out. Houses that could tell you what was in the fucking fridge. Clever, very clever but a bit unnerving. Jimmy didn't want his house ratting him out.

Jimmy's phone pinged to let him know he had a text. He hoped it might be Kathy. If he could just talk to her then maybe he could convince her to take him back, make up and try again. It wouldn't be the first time. Or maybe it was Mel. It had been good to see her. She'd looked hot as hell in that robe, her hair all mussed up, all warm and sleeping, still sexy even when she was angry, maybe even more sexy. Jimmy grinned. He had always liked a challenge.

The radio was still running through the stations.

He could never understand why someone like Mel had ended up as a copper, seemed like a waste of a good woman.

He tapped in the code to unlock his phone. 'Are you going to switch that bloody radio off?' said Robbie. 'It's doing my head in.'

The text was from Lennie and read, 'Five minutes.' The number written out in full, but then that was Lennie all over.

'He's on his way,' Jimmy said over his shoulder, ignoring Robbie.

There were grunts of approval from the seated men.

'Not before bloody time,' said Roland grimly.

Breakfast in their hotel was a help yourself cereal and toast arrangement, fry ups were extra and had to be booked the night before, and from what they had seen coming through the hatch for a couple of brickies, didn't look worth the money. They were all staying at the same place, except for Lennie who had a caravan somewhere, and Richard who had just rented a house for him and his missus. She went with him everywhere. He didn't like leaving her on her own.

Jimmy's phone pinged again.

Jimmy glanced at the screen again. 'We still on for

later?' it read. He grinned. Maybe his luck was changing after all.

'*And in breaking news it has been reported that a body has been found on a farm in-*' The radio had finally homed in on the best signal, the reporter's voice was sharp and clear as a bell.

'It'll be yours if you don't switch that thing off,' snapped Robbie

Jimmy glanced at the radio; he'd found Radio Norfolk. He leaned over and pressed a button so the radio scrolled on. He didn't want news, he wanted music, in the back of the van, Robbie groaned.

*

A bitter wind rolled in over the fen making the sides of the tent in the trees on Isaac's farm flap and crackle. Someone had tipped off the press and an outside broadcast van had parked itself up behind one of the police cars blocking the entrance to the farm road on the A10. A helicopter chopped through the air overhead, coming in low over the farm, so low I could feel as much as hear the distinctive sounds of the engine and the whup-whup-whup of the rotor blades. People are curious about death. I sometimes wonder if we all share some ancient sense of relief that this time we have been spared. I also wondered how the hell the press had managed to get onto it so fast.

I watched the helicopter circle and head back towards the copse. Someone would have words, but not me. I got into my car and then made my way back out the way I came, turning left at the farm gate and following a narrow B road towards the village and Gary Heath's home.

Chapter Six
Linda Heath

'We've been married nearly thirty years, me and Gary. We met at a Young Farmers' barn dance.' Linda Heath took three mugs out of the dishwasher and set them down alongside the kettle. 'I don't think Gary ever danced before or since. Is he all right?' She glanced across at the uniformed PC who had arrived with me.

I nodded. 'He's fine.'

'Gary's not good with stress. He always reckons I'm the brains of the family and he's the brawn.' She smiled. 'He worries, you know? Do you want tea or would you prefer coffee? I can make both. I've got proper coffee if you're prefer? Does he want one?'

'No, thank you,' I said. 'I'd like to talk to you about last night, and we need to collect your husband's computer and any external hard drives or storage devices he uses to store CCTV footage.'

She hesitated. 'I'm not sure about that. Does Gary know?'

I nodded. 'Yes, he does. We just need to take a look at the footage from the farm. He said he saw a vehicle driving onto the farm sometime last night. We're hoping that it will help us find whoever who did this.'

'Right, as long as he's all right about it. He can be funny about people touching his things,' she said. 'Everything is in his office. I'll show you. It's through here-'

Linda Heath was as tiny and fragile as Gary Heath was large. Their great sprawling bungalow was on the outskirts of Longbank, the village a mile or two from the farm on Isaac's Fen. The place dwarfed her and looked as if it had been built for someone else altogether. Standing barely five feet tall in her fluffy mules, Mrs Heath was still in her dressing gown and a pair of pastel pink pyjamas when we arrived, her bleached blonde hair was twisted up into an untidy top knot and held in place with a diamanté clip.

In one corner of the kitchen the tumble dryer rumbled as it turned, filling the air with the scent of fabric softener and warm fabric.

'Can you tell me about last night?'

She nodded. 'Yes, of course. Although I'm not sure how it'll help anything.'

I followed her into a cavernous hallway with corridors going off in all directions. A fat, elderly Labrador padded along behind us.

'We had it built,' Linda said, in answer to an unspoken question. 'Gary designed it himself and then got an architect to draw up proper plans. I know it might seem a bit big for the two of us, but we both like our space.'

At the end of one of the corridors she opened a door into a square, almost featureless room with magnolia walls and a straw-coloured carpet. A large mahogany coloured desk dominated the centre of the room. Off to the left of the door was a window, with its curtains still closed, on the opposite wall was a large framed aerial photograph of the farm, under which sat a row of half height filing cabinets, the same utilitarian design as those in the farm office. The smell was almost the same too although subtler - a lingering scent of onions and dogs - but this time with something floral and slightly cloying overlaying it.

My gaze moved slowly around the room – other than the picture of the farm there were no other photos, no books. The only personal touch was a glass cabinet by the door filled with trophies.

I glanced in the cabinet. 'Darts,' she said in passing. 'Gary plays for the local team.'

I nodded. 'Do you play?'

She shook her head, 'No, but it gives him some time away from the farm, a chance to relax.'

'Does anyone else live here with you besides your husband?' I asked.

'No, there's just us two. We neither of us really wanted a family. I wasn't fussed one way or the other but Gary had a sister. She wasn't,' Linda hesitated and glanced around at the PC. 'I don't know what they call it these days, but she wasn't right, right from the get go. His mum and dad were always having the doctor out to her or were up the hospital with her with one thing or another. And they couldn't leave her, even when she was older. They never had a break or went on holiday.

'We used to have to go up to theirs for Christmas because in the end she couldn't leave the house. It was really hard on Gary when they were little. I mean he was just a little boy when she was born; he wanted to do all the things kiddies do but they never could. They did think about sending him away to boarding school, which I think in some ways would have been kinder, at least that way he would have had some sort of a life, but his mum didn't want to lose him too. And they wouldn't even think of letting her go, so we decided against-' She reddened. 'Sorry, I'm running on. Anyway it's all in here. If there's anything you want just say and I'll try and find it if I can.'

On the desk was a computer, a blotter, notepad and diary and very little else. I sat down in the chair behind the desk. It swallowed me whole and was so big that my feet barely touched the carpet.

Linda Heath watched me intently

'You won't mess anything up, will you?' she said. 'Only Gary really doesn't like people touching his things. You know, his computer and stuff-'

The truth was, if we had to, we'd tear the place apart, but I didn't tell her that, instead, I said, 'This officer will take the computer. I'll make sure you have a receipt and it will be returned to you as soon as possible,' I said. The truth was that it might be weeks, possibly months, before they saw it again but other than bagging it up, we wouldn't be touching it. We needed the computer exactly as Gary Heath had left it to preserve the integrity of any evidence found on it. 'Are there any other devices, maybe an external hard drive, somewhere Gary stores all the footage?'

She frowned. 'I don't know really what he does with it all. Do you want me to log in for you? Only it's got a password.'

I shook my head. 'That's kind but no, thank you. We need it as is-'

I nodded to the PC. 'Can we get this bagged up now please?'

Her eyes narrowed. 'But we could get in there and have a look. You said Gary said it was all right. Sooner you find out what was going on the sooner you'll be gone and he gets the farm back; he'll be happy about that. I was just thinking maybe I could help.'

'Thank you, but we just need to take it.'

What I didn't tell her was that despite what you see on TV and films, where the detective casually opens up a computer and browses through the files, the truth is that a defence lawyer would make mincemeat of an officer on the stand if we did that. Gary Heath's computer was like any other piece of evidence and needed to be untouched so that any evidence found was pristine and beyond question. The last thing we wanted was some smart-arse defence team saying we – or Linda Heath – had in some way interfered with CCTV footage. Every key stroke you make on a computer is registered and leaves an impression and potentially changes the data stored on the machine – altering dates when files were last viewed or edited for example, so I wasn't going to touch it, and certainly didn't want Linda Heath touching it, that way if we found any information on Heath's machine that tied a vehicle to a suspect for example, then no one could say we tampered with the evidence.

She tipped her head to one side. 'If you're sure. I'm

happy to help.' The way Linda Heath said it made me wonder how often she came in to take a look at Gary Heath's computer. Ignoring her offer I asked Linda if Gary had any other method of backing up the footage.

She hesitated, her gaze moving across the top of his desk. For a moment I thought she was going to say something but then stopped herself and looked up at me, though not quite meeting my eye and said, 'I don't really know. You'd have to ask Gary.'

I glanced down at the desk again and pulled on a pair of gloves. All the drawers were locked. I wondered what it was he was keeping from his wife.

Images, especially film, eat space on a hard drive. I made a mental note to get an officer to check if the cameras and recording were triggered by movement or ran continuously. Realistically it would require a lot of storage to be of any use for his insurance.

Alongside the monitor was a note pad with Topham and Roper Security Services printed across the top and the same blue thunderbolt logo that had been on the sticker on the monitor in the office. It wouldn't be too big a leap to assume they had provided Heath's cameras. I made a note of the number. As I stood up, I noticed four tiny indentations on the leather top of the desk, just under the screen, that marked out the corners of a rectangle and suggested that there had been something reasonably heavy that had been standing alongside the computer until quite recently, a thought reinforced by the spare USB cable, dangling down from the back of the computer.

'Do you know what was on here?' I asked Linda, pointing to space.

Her gaze moved slowly across the desk, lingering for a fraction too long on the space below the monitor before she shook her head. 'I don't come in here that often.' The lie showed on her face. 'I look after the house, Gary looks after the business, you know, we're old fashioned like that.'

I turned to the uniformed officer. 'Best we get this

bagged up and gone. Can you get it to the techs as soon as possible?' He nodded. I turned back to Linda who was watching us like a hawk. 'I'd like a note of the spare cable there.'

She shifted her weight, watching as the officer gloved up and carefully removed the power cables and leads before bagging up the machine and heading out towards the car.

I made a note to ask Gary Heath about what was now missing from his desk, along with the name and number for the security company from the pad, then Mrs Heath and I went back to the kitchen.

'I don't know what I can tell you really,' she said.

I smiled. 'We just need to know what happened over the course of the day - yesterday. When things happened, where people were-'

Instead of sitting down she busied herself with finding milk and a tin of biscuits, making tea for us, shooing their elderly Labrador out of her way as she moved.'

'I'm in a bit of state,' she said, 'I think it's the shock. I'm better doing something. It doesn't seem possible really. Me and Gary have been together thirty years and there's never been anything like this, you know.' She shot me a look. 'Gary used to be a bit of a lad back when we were younger but he's soft as−' Her voice trailed off. 'Are you sure he is all right? He might look like a great lump on the outside but he's not. He suffers with his blood pressure and his nerves. Takes tablets. He'll be in a right state about all this.'

'One of our officers is with him,' I said, making a note about Gary Heath's health issues. 'Has he got his medication with him?'

She shook her head. 'I wouldn't have thought so. He usually takes the tablets last thing it at night.'

'I'll make sure that the officers are aware. They're just taking him to the local station to give a statement.'

'As long as they know. And he's a bit squeamish. I think to be honest that's why he wasn't all that keen on us having a family. When you're young it doesn't seem to matter but now sometimes-' she stopped. 'Sometimes I wish we'd at least tried. And that thing I said about his sister. I didn't mean anything by it. You do understand? I don't want you to get the wrong idea. His sister was a sweet thing but everyone could see that it ruined all their lives, and I think Gary didn't want to take the risk of it happening to us. I don't know what the chances were; I suppose we could have had tests or something, but Gary doesn't like hospitals and needles and all that sort of thing.

'He was worried sick that his mum and dad would die and we'd end up looking after her, but in the end she died in her sleep, really peaceful, she just slipped away - but by that time his mum and dad were exhausted, worn out. His dad used to drink; his mum was on tablets. The pair of them were old before their time and it was too late for them to do anything very much then. I think his mum was disappointed that we didn't have any children but Gary said it was too big a risk, and I never minded. Not really.'

'If we can go back to last night-' I began.

'We had our honeymoon in Italy, Lake Garda. Gary doesn't like going abroad really but I'd always wanted to go, so he made the effort. I go on holiday on my own now, with my sister and some girlfriends. Leave him to fend for himself. We went on a cruise last year. He always moans about me abandoning him but I think he quite likes having the place to himself.' She stopped. Her gaze was fixed on the flat expanse of open fields outside her kitchen window. 'I can't believe this is happening, you know? I've tried ringing Gary, but he's not picking up. He sounded really shook up on the phone first thing. I was wondering when you'd be done with him, when he can come home?'

She glanced at me. 'Do I need to run him some food up there? He's got tea and coffee but–'

'Once he's made a statement someone will bring him home,' I said calmly, attempting to stem the flow,

60

although I didn't always try too hard, often when people freewheel in conversation they tell you far more than they mean to. It was a case of sheep-dogging Linda Heath to make sure she didn't stray too far off track.

'He won't like not being there if you're poking around the place. It's like his very own little kingdom, that farm and his office. He's a very private person, Gary – quiet. He likes to know what's going on. Bit of a control freak – you know...'

I'd seen Gary Heath's face in the farm office earlier, peering anxiously out of the windows at the comings and goings, watching our every move. The sensation lingered that it might be something other than just curiosity.

'Last night?' I prompted.

'I don't know really. Nothing out of the ordinary happened here. I didn't know anything about any of it till Gary rang me this morning.'

'And what time was that?'

'Seven, maybe half past. The time'll be on the house phone. I think he'd already rung your lot by then. I'm not an early riser-'

'He didn't ring you earlier to let you know what was going on? Or what he'd seen?'

The 999 call had come in to the call handler at four a.m.

'No, but then he wouldn't have. It'd be no good him ringing in the middle of the night, I'm dead to the world, me. I take sleeping tablets – do you mind if I smoke?' she said, pulling a packet of cigarettes out of her dressing gown pocket. 'Gary doesn't like me smoking and I don't usually smoke in the house but I'm all over the place this morning.'

I nodded, anything if it helped her concentrate. She offered me the packet.

'No, thanks.'

'What was it you wanted me to tell you, again?' she asked.

'How about we start with what time Gary got in last

61

night?'

'You mean after work?'

I nodded. I wanted a timeline of Gary's Heath's movements leading up to him finding the body.

Linda hesitated. 'I was in the sitting room watching the telly.' She looked up at the ceiling as if trying to recall. 'I'd put a casserole in the oven, so that if he was a bit late it wouldn't matter; they're all the better for cooking a bit longer, aren't they?'

'Did he say he was going to be late?'

'Yes and no. It's the VAT, it worries him sick. He hates anything like that −figures and stuff, that why we've got Sandra, but he rung up about six to say that he had to find some receipts. I keep telling him he should just let her sort all that out, we pay her enough. But no, apparently he had to find them - right state he was in when he got in.'

I made a note. 'What do you mean? What sort of state would you say he was in?'

She pulled a face. 'It's hard to tell with Gary. He's not always easy to read but it had nothing to do with all this.' She waved a hand towards the window. 'Just ruffled feathers really, you know.'

'What time did he get home?'

'Half past seven maybe quarter to eight, I'd set the telly up to record my programmes because he likes us to eat together.'

'And it was dark by then?'

'Oh yes, black as your hat out here in wintertime. We've got no street lights or anything.'

'And when he got in what did you do?'

'I thought we'd have our tea together. I was starving by then, but he said he wanted a shower first; said he was cold and wanted to warm up and that I wasn't to wait for him. He said he'd get his when he was done. I dished mine up and left his in the oven.'

'Is that usual?'

'Well, no, not really. We usually eat about half past six, but farming can be like that sometimes, things need doing when they need doing.'

'And your husband ate his meal on his own?'

'In his office on a tray. I did say why don't you come in the warm in front of the fire and eat it in the living room with me, but he said there was stuff he really needed to get sorted out.'

'Did he tell you what that was?'

'No, something to do with the VAT I expect.' She hesitated. 'It's nothing out of the ordinary, Gary's just like that. He keeps himself to himself a lot of the time. Bottles things up.'

She took out a lighter from her dressing gown pocket and sparked it into life. Her nails were perfectly manicured, painted the same pastel pink as her pyjamas.

'I really don't get involved with the farm business to be honest. It suits us that way.'

'But you know about the CCTV, and that he can view the footage from here?'

'Oh yes, he's always in there looking at it. He's been paranoid since we kept getting broken into. To be honest I think the cameras make it worse not better. He's always watching them.'

I nodded. 'And do you know if he was watching them last night?'

Linda took a long draw on her cigarette. 'Not for definite but I expect he was, he's in there all hours. I watch my programmes and he's in there staring at the farm half the night. I don't know what he thinks he's going to see. Why do you want to know all this? I mean Gary only found the body.' She stared at me, her colour draining.

'Oh my God. You don't think he had anything to do with it, do you? I mean he can be a bit off hand at times, and he's not much for social graces, but he wouldn't hurt a fly, would Gary, and he hates anything messy. He's really squeamish, wouldn't even let me have a cat because he doesn't want it killing things.'

I kept my expression neutral. Gary Heath certainly

wouldn't be the first murderer who had claimed to find his victim in an attempt to divert suspicion.

'We're just trying to establish a timeline to help us work out exactly what happened when, and where people were.'

She looked relieved and then said, 'Right.'

'And Gary came in from work and had his tea in the office?'

'That's right.'

'And then at some point he went back out again. To the farm.'

'Well, yes he must have.'

'Can you tell me what time that was?'

Linda Heath shook her head. 'No, not really. Like I said I was watching my programmes, and then I went off to bed, read for a little while and after that I was out like a light.'

'Did you speak to Gary before going to bed?'

She bit her lip. 'He doesn't really like to be disturbed, so I knocked on the door and said I was going to bed and he said he'd got some war film on Sky that he wanted to watch, and said goodnight-'

'And what time was that?'

'Ten-ish, maybe ten past – not much later than that. He's a night owl-'

'So you didn't hear him going out later?'

'No. First thing I knew was when the phone went this morning, when he rang to tell me not to worry if I saw police cars, and then he told me that he'd found a body.' She took another long pull on her cigarette. 'A body. I mean, no one expects to find a body, do they? Anyway he said not to worry, that everything was all right and that he'd let me know what was happening when he knew.'

'Did he say anything else?'

'No, not really, I said, "Who is it?" and he just said it was a woman, and that he didn't know her. I thought when he said a body that maybe it was a tramp or something, you know, looking for somewhere to sleep then curled up and died in one of the barns. It happened when I lived at home when I was a teenager. My dad found him. Some bloke who had been in the army.'

She stopped and looked at me. 'What was the question again?'

'Did you hear Gary go out again?'

'Oh that's right. No, but then we have separate rooms. It's been years since we've slept in the same room. He snores like a train. I'd be sound asleep by half ten at the very latest. Like I said I take tablets-'

I made another note.

'Nothing serious,' she said hastily. 'Just something to get me off. They made him put it in, you know, the CCTV, the insurers. He didn't really want to have them. He said it was the thin end of the wedge, big brother watching us, checking up on us, keeping tabs, you know. Thing is we can't see the farm from here, but at least now there is a way to check up on things. He used to get himself in a right state, when they kept coming round to steal stuff. It made it seem like they were making a fool of him, and he hated that. He'd put in new locks, they'd cut the doors off the hinges. He'd move all the tools into another shed and they took the corrugated iron roof off. Using his new trailer to take the stuff away in was the last straw. That's when he started having trouble with his blood pressure. The stress, the doctor said. He never knew what he was going to find when he drove over there in the mornings. In that way the cameras have helped and once he's seen all the films, he deletes them.'

'Regularly?'

Linda's eyes narrowed as if she was trying to work out what my angle might be. 'Yes, end of most days, I think. Like I said he is a very private person, doesn't want people poking into his business.'

'So do you ever look at the footage?'

She bristled and then shook her head vigorously. 'Why would I want to do that?'

So not a flat-out denial. I waited.

'I suppose I might have looked at it once or twice,

but just to make sure that he was okay and had got there safe and sound, especially on snowy mornings or if it's frosty or been raining hard. That road along Longbank can be treacherous, icy, muddy – people die in them dykes. Just drive in and drown.'

'Did you happen to look at the CCTV last night?'

'No, like I said, I was asleep.'

'And your husband usually deletes the films once he's watched them.'

Linda Heath nodded. 'He says it takes up too much space on hard-' She stopped herself and her gaze caught mine, '- on his computer,' she said hastily. 'The one on his desk.'

Chapter Seven
Liar, Liar

Once it has been established we are dealing with a murder, there is not much that can be achieved by having detectives at the scene, particularly in this case, given how isolated and remote the dump site was. The truth was we'd mostly get in the way of the Crime Scene Team, and would be a lot more use talking to witnesses or working back at the station with full access to databases and records.

SOCO would continue to scour the site for any evidence left by the killer, the wider area around the farm being searched by uniformed officers.

Beau Shepherd, the Forensic Pathologist, would make the final decision about when we could move the body, and then once he'd called it, would head back to the lab to begin the process of carefully unwrapping and autopsying our victim. The wrapping would be sent for analysis, and between Beau and the rest of the forensic specialists they would recover any trace evidence, finger prints, fibres, possibly DNA and anything else that had been preserved by the plastic wrap, trying to find anything that could help us find her killer, and more than that, help us convict him.

Beau would be conducting the autopsy, with one of our investigation team in attendance, to establish cause of death and possibly what had happened to her in the hours, days or weeks before she died, and at each stage, every step would be carefully recorded to ensure the chain of evidence wasn't compromised. Meanwhile the rest of us would be looking for leads, high on the list being finding out everything we could about the victim, beginning, we hoped, with who she was.

The way the woman had been wrapped, and the evidence or rather lack of it around the pond and in the copse suggested that the young woman had been killed away from the farm, away from the trees. A high priority was to find that primary site, along with a list that basically ran: who, when, where, how, and despite it being the driving force in a TV crime drama, why she had been murdered and posed was often an optional extra. We didn't really need to know why he had done it, we just needed to catch him and stop him doing it again. Although there is no way of telling which of those pieces of information would come in first or from where, we just needed to get looking.

A team of officers was being assembled to go door to door, other local officers were going through missing persons' reports for the previous week before moving out timewise from that. Our victim was young and attractive, which tragically really helped; someone surely had to be missing her, although given the number of people who now live alone even that was no longer a certainty.

By the time I got back from speaking to Linda Heath, an incident room had been set up on the first floor of Denham Market police station by local officers, who were working alongside the team of specialist officers we'd shipped in from the Major Investigation Team. The room was an institutional grey, large, rectangular with windows overlooking the car park. One wall was dominated by a white board onto which had been tacked the first photos we had of the victim. Away from the board were clusters of desks, computer monitors and dedicated phone lines. There was a hum of quiet activity as the room's layout took shape and information began to filter in to be collated and recorded so that everyone was singing off the same hymn sheet.

As well as DI Paul Tomlin and myself we'd got

Sergeant Liz Turner, whose role is as a receiver on cases – she acts like a triage nurse, she deals with information as it comes in, collecting, assessing, collating and sharing. It's always hard to know at this stage what is significant and what isn't so everything has to be gone through and recorded, because anything- any little thing -might prove to be the key piece that we've been looking for. Liz was in charge of the information for this case. And then there was Sergeant Tom Green, who was currently sorting out desks but was more usually in charge of implementing the actions decided by DCI Paul Tomlin, our Senior Investigating Officer, or anyone else further up the food chain. We'd also got Sophie Rowe, a DC who had a gift for technology and social media, and Geraldine Sloane, a civilian staff member who was the IT geek and would be the one dealing with Gary Heath's hard drive.

I said my Hellos and went to find a desk. I was still the newbie on the team.

Liz Turner grinned. 'Home turf for you, I hear?'

Someone had added weather conditions and lighting up time to the white boards.

On another floor, in one of the interview rooms, I'd been told that Gary Heath was just finishing giving his statement and would be on his way home as soon as Tomlin gave the go ahead.

Over the course of the morning, uniform had been going house to house in the village and houses closest to the farm, and information had been released to the media before someone leaked it and potentially muddied the waters. Media liaison gave local TV and radio a brief statement and description of the victim which had been okayed by Tomlin and released on the local morning news, and would be used and possibly expanded on at lunchtime via social media and local TV and radio stations if we had anything else to give them. As I said, the fact the victim was young and beautiful helped, and we were all aware that there was a distinct possibility news of the murder would go national before the end of the day.

One of our first priorities was to try and establish the identity of the victim. A name opens a lot of doors and gives us so much information including a potential pool of suspects, neighbours, friends, work colleagues, partners, lovers, old boyfriends, old girl friends, husbands and wives.

Her fingerprints weren't on the national database. There appeared to be nothing obvious to identify her and no personal effects had been found at the scene.

Time of death is notoriously fickle but Beau Shepherd was putting it between five and ten pm on Tuesday, a time which could be revised, and didn't exclude Gary Heath from being a potential suspect.

According to Mr Heath the marks on his desk were an old hard drive that had stopped working weeks before and he had thrown in the bin. The search teams on the farm had been informed and asked to include the hard drive in their search. A quick conversation with the bookkeeper, who Heath had asked not to come in, identified that two external hard drives had been purchased at the same time as they had had the CCTV installed. Neither of the hard drives were present either at the farm office or Heath's house. He was adamant they had stopped working and he'd binned them, and as a result they became a priority, and we upped the search for them.

Given his local knowledge Mike Carlton had been seconded by Tomlin onto the investigation team and was busy with phone calls when I got back. He looked up and beckoned me over.

'I've just been talking to the security company who installed Gary Heath's CCTV system. The good news is that the footage is backed up onto their servers and held for three months, at the insurance company's insistence, the bad news is that they won't release it to us unless we have Heath's permission in writing or alternatively get a court order.'

I pulled off my coat and hung it on the chair beside

the next desk along from him. 'Or we could just ask him?'

Mike grinned. 'Now why didn't I think of that?'

The fact that Gary Heath's behaviour seemed suspicious didn't mean that he was guilty of murder – people act in odd ways under pressure and finding a body wasn't something most people did every day. But what had happened in the run up to him making the discovery and things like the CCTV footage being deleted and the missing hard drives, while not proof of anything on their own, did add up to something suspicious.

'Has he called his brief?'

Mike shook his head. 'No, but I can feel it coming.'

Tomlin and my old boss had both drummed it into their officers that it was all too easy to make assumptions and to stop looking elsewhere. We weren't there yet but I knew that it wouldn't take much of a leap for everyone to have Gary Heath firmly in the cross hairs. We needed to talk to him again, but before we did I needed to talk to Tomlin.

Every investigation has a strategy, every interview should be conducted with an aim in mind, and as SIO that aim and who conducted the interviews were Tomlin's call.

*

'I thought they said that they were going to take me home?' protested Mr Heath as I walked into the interview suite where he had given his statement. A uniformed officer who had been sitting by the door nodded to acknowledge my arrival.

'We'll get you home as soon as we can - I'd just like to ask you a couple more questions, Mr Heath, if you don't mind.'

'Do I have any choice?'

I kept my expression neutral.

'Do I need a lawyer?'

'It's entirely up to you, Mr Heath. Would you like me call the duty solicitor or would you prefer to contact your own?' I said, sliding a file onto the table.

Heath reddened. 'No, not really. Look, I didn't hurt that girl. I just found her. All right? I want to make that clear. That's all. How long before I can go home? There are things I need to do. And Linda will be worried sick. She's not strong you know, suffers dreadfully with her nerves. I need to be getting home.'

I nodded. 'Certainly. We'll arrange a lift home for you as soon as we're done here. I just have a few quick questions. First of all I'd like your permission to access the CCTV feed from the farm for last night.' I slipped a form across the desk towards him that the CCTV installation company had emailed over, keeping my tone light. Heath didn't even look at it.

'Why do you need my permission to look at it? I've already said you could take the computers. And I told you that the film's gone. Did you pick up the one from the house?'

'Yes, we did, along with the one from the office.' I glanced down at the statement he had given which I had already skimmed through in the outer office. It was lean on detail.

He pushed the slip of paper back towards me.

'Can you tell me what happened to the hard drives you had at the office and at home?' I asked conversationally, looking up from the paperwork.

'Hard drives?' From his expression I guessed that this wasn't the direction he had expected the conversation to go.

'Yes, I've got the serial numbers and dates of purchase here. 'I opened the file and slid a copy of the receipt across the table. 'Your bookkeeper emailed a copy over. Can you tell me why you disposed of them? And when?'

He looked away. 'They were total bloody rubbish, that's why, they stopped working. I think they went in the skip.'

I glanced at the note that had been made of how much they had cost – both were relatively new, both under a year old, neither were cheap. 'Didn't you think to contact your supplier. I'm assuming they would still be under warranty?'

He sighed. 'I suppose I could have done but it's such a bloody palaver trying to take something back or get something replaced, isn't it? You know what it's like – they're all excuses these people. And there's no law against dumping shoddy goods as far as I know.'

'So where did you store the images from the CCTV from the farm once the hard drives had gone?'

He said nothing.

'Or are you telling me that you watched the footage of the vehicle arriving live last night? You told me you had deleted it, so presumably you had to delete it from somewhere? Was it on the computer? I'd imagine all that footage eats up quite a lot of disk space.' I glanced down at my notes.

He stared at me. There are a moments when I wished that people would just tell the truth. I could see him fishing around trying to cook up a plausible answer.

'You can store up to twelve hours on the computer,' he said after a moment. 'That's usually enough. And I'm on the farm every day, so I run through it every morning when I get in.'

I made a note.

'And sometimes at night?' I asked, still looking down at my pad.

He grunted a reply. 'Sometimes.'

'And that was what you deleted? Just the footage that was stored on the computer? The film you said you had set up for the officers to look at?'

Heath reddened. 'Yes, that's right. I'm sorry about that. It was an accident.'

I nodded. 'So you said. And the twelve hours up until then along with it?'

He smiled by way of reply, something subtle in his expression implying that he had won. 'I must have. If it's not on the machines then it must have all gone.'

I nodded. 'Interesting, because your security company told me that your insurers require three months footage to be stored to comply with the terms of your cover.'

He swallowed hard, but said nothing. I smiled. Why the hell was he tying himself up in knots. What was he hiding?

'Right. The good news, Mr Heath, is that the security firm have all the footage on their servers, so you're still insured and your installation package includes cloud storage in case your computers were ever stolen.' I paused. Gary Heath blinked and then blinked again.

'Or in case your very expensive back-up hard drives turned out to be rubbish. We just need your permission to access the footage. Stroke of luck, wouldn't you say?' I indicated the form between us on the desk, took a pen out of my bag and set it down alongside the form.

He stared at me, his demeanour subtly altered.

'If you could just sign on the bottom line there – all the other details have been completed by the security firm.'

'But I deleted it,' he said thickly.

'No, you deleted the copy on your computer or maybe one of the hard drives. If you would care to just sign and print at the bottom. I can get this emailed over to them straight away.' I nodded towards the form.

He didn't move.

'Mr Heath, we are hunting for the person who murdered a young woman. The film footage from your farm is currently the only clue we have-'

'I didn't do it,' he said.

'If there is any information on the footage that can help us track the killer down then I'm sure that you would want us to be able to access it, wouldn't you?'

'You could only see lights in the distance, no details. I told your lot that.' His voice was rising.

'If it is digital then we may be able to enhance the image.'

Still he hesitated, at which point there was a knock at the door and Mike popped his head round. 'Can I have a quick word?' he said.

I left the form on the desk and headed out into the corridor. 'What is it?' I hadn't expected to be interrupted.

'I've just had a conversation with Norwich city police, apparently our farmer friend here was picked up for kerb crawling last year. He told the undercover officer he propositioned that it was all a big mistake and that he had arranged to pick someone up.'

'Isn't that the whole point of kerb crawling?'

Mike rolled his eyes by way of a reply. 'I think the implication was that he had been going to meet up with someone, and that it was all a big misunderstanding.'

'Bet they'd never heard that one before.'

'According to the officer I spoke to Heath was pretty credible. Heath said he had come to pick someone up from the railway station, but because of the traffic – there were road works going on at the time - he had arranged to meet her a couple of streets away so as not to get snarled up in it and he thought the undercover officer was the person he was supposed to be meeting. He said she looked like she was waiting for someone and he'd jumped to conclusions.'

'He was picking up someone he didn't know?'

'Apparently. He told them that he was on a blind date. He said he was nervous so when he saw this woman waiting by the side of the road he just presumed it was her.'

'I wonder if Mrs Heath knew. Did he say who the someone was?'

'From the notes he was pretty vague, he said it was someone that he'd met online. A woman called Natalia. He'd got a picture, and said that they'd met on a dating website and that they had spoken a few times on Skype and he was hoping that sex was on the cards,' said Mike.

I raised an eyebrow. 'We've all had dates like that.'

Mike grinned. 'They let him off with a caution and

flagged it up because they were concerned that this might be some new scam someone was working. Get a punter to site, set them up with a girl they thought they'd met online and then charge them for the pleasure or roll them for their wallets or maybe blackmail them if they were married and looking for a bit of fun. Apparently the picture of the woman he was meeting was pretty nondescript. He said she was dark haired, small build, mid-thirties, slim. They're sending us over a copy of the report.'

'And did anything come of it?'

Mike shook his head. 'By the look of it no one followed it up, from the notes no one else they spoke to during the operation came out with the same story, and as they said he sounded credible, he was nervous, and appeared to be genuinely shocked to have been picked up.'

'I bet he was. Okay, can you get a description of the victim over to them? And get some dates?'

'Already done. We're thinking this might be Heath, are we?' said Mike

I sighed. 'Are we? All seems a bit too convenient'

'He found the body and it certainly would explain why he deleted the CCTV footage.'

'But why call us. That body would have never been discovered if he hadn't called it in.'

'Who knows, guilt, panic, maybe he can't bear to have it on his conscience.'

I huffed out a long breath. 'I don't know, just doesn't sit right, although he has just declined my request to sign the consent to access the footage on the cloud.'

'He showed it to the first officers on the scene,' Mike countered.

'He only had a few seconds tee-ed up for them to watch according to their report. And from what they said it was just headlights. He could have been showing them film of himself arriving.'

Mike paused. 'What are you thinking? That he could have met up with someone and brought her back to the farm? I mean if he's driving to Norwich to meet some woman he met online chances are he didn't just do it once.'

'That's true. I'll get the techies onto it – social media, dating apps – have we got his phone?'

'No,' Mike said, 'I don't think so.'

'Okay, we need to speak with Tomlin,' I said. 'Decide on how we are going to do this. I'll ask if we can get access to his phone and phone records.'

'Right,' Mike said, and then he handed me another sheet of paper. 'Just so you know, uniform have found a roll of polythene sheeting in one of the barns. SOCO are taking it in to see if it matches the polythene our girl was gift wrapped in. I'll be back later. I'm off to the autopsy.'

I nodded. There is nothing much to say about an autopsy that can make it any better. I opened the interview room door and stepped back inside.

*

'So, Mr Heath, we've been talking to our colleagues in Norwich.' Heath's eyes narrowed. 'We know about the kerb crawling.'

He started to protest. 'That was a mistake,' he said, 'I told them. I said-'

I held up a hand. 'The truth is we don't care if you were with someone other than your wife last night. We're trying to find a murderer. If you don't sign the permission to view the CCTV footage, we'll need to get a court order and that will take time, and in the meantime whoever it was who killed the girl and dumped her on your land will be getting away. Do you understand?'

Heath sniffed.

'Or on the other hand maybe the film you showed the officers shows you driving the victim out of the yard? Maybe you're the one taking her across to the trees. You drive a Landcruiser and I believe you have a van-'

Heath's jaw dropped. 'You can't be serious?'

I kept my tone neutral, 'It would explain why you

don't want us to look at the footage.'

He stared at me.

'No, no of course it wasn't me,' he said after a moment or two. He paused and ran his fingers back through his hair, still not quite able to meet my gaze. 'It wasn't me. On the film. The thing is the times don't tally with what I told you or the policemen who turned up after I rang 999. But I said that, didn't I? That I wasn't sure of the times?'

I waited. His colour deepened. People generally find silence uncomfortable and feel obligated to fill it. I hung on. Gary Heath squirmed miserably in his seat.

'Thing is, I was in a chat room, talking to people, and watching films. I told you that.' He paused and glanced over his shoulder as if we were being watched. '*Films*. I mean really raunchy stuff. Consenting adults, mind – but you know-'His voice trailed off, and then he looked up again, expecting me to bite. I didn't.

'Not the kind of thing I'd want my Linda finding out about.'

'And were you watching the films at your house or in the office on the farm.'

His gaze dropped back to the desktop. 'Both.'

'You were watching the films in the farm office last night on your computer?'

He started to wring his hands. 'There was stuff on there I didn't want you to see, so I deleted it, after I found her – before I rung you.'

'And what time did you see the headlights?'

Gary shook his head, his voice cracking with emotion. 'I don't know. I can't remember,' he said miserably.

'Okay let's just take it one step at a time. Were you at the house when you saw the lights?'

It was like pulling teeth. 'That's just it,' he said, 'I don't remember where I was.'

I waited.

'I know it sounds daft but I'd got other things on my mind. I was talking to someone online and it was getting a bit, *heated,* you know and then, well I thought it might be better if I went over to the farm for a bit of privacy and I can't remember where exactly I was when I saw the headlights. It wasn't until afterwards that it really registered what it was I'd seen, if you know what I mean.'

I picked up my pen. 'So was this via a webcam or Skype-'

'Webcam.'

'Okay and would it be fair to say the exchange was sexual in nature?' My tone of voice didn't change nor my expression; who am I to judge what Gary Heath does while his wife is watching Emmerdale?

Gary Heath nodded. 'Yes, yes you could say that.'

'It's not me saying it, Mr Heath.'

He reddened. 'It was.'

'And who were you talking to?'

'I don't know her real name.'

There was another pause.

'She calls herself Moon Crystal, but I don't think that's her real name.'

'And do you think Ms Crystal can confirm what time you were talking to her?'

Across the table Heath was writhing with discomfort. 'I don't know. I mean she might be able to but I wouldn't have thought so.'

'So how does it work?' I asked.

'Is this completely necessary?' Heath asked grimly. 'I mean I've told you where I was and what I was doing.'

'You have indeed, but we'll still need to confirm the times.' I pushed the release form back across the table.

He glanced down at the form, hesitated for a moment and then said. 'I want a lawyer.'

I picked up the form and the file that had been on the desk and got to my feet.

He stared at me. 'Where are you going?'

'You said you wanted a lawyer. I can't talk to you again until he or she is present. If you haven't got legal representation then we have a duty solicitor available, or you can contact your own legal representative.' I headed towards the door. 'I'll arrange for you to have access to a phone.'

'And then what?' he asked, miserably.

'We'll ask you the same questions, under caution, only this time you have legal representation here to ensure you don't incriminate yourself.'

I let that sink in.

'Wait,' he said, as I got to the door. 'I just feel like I need someone here on my side.' Bluster gone, he sounded like a small boy.

I nodded. In his shoes I would most probably have felt the same. He picked up the pen.

*

'I'm not sure of the exact details but Mr Heath appears to have been signed into an online live sex webcam site when the body was dumped or at least the vehicle came onto site, obviously I'll need to corroborate that. There's a pay wall so I've got DC Rowe on his financials and we're contacting the website, I'm not sure if they charge per view in which case we may be able to get a time frame, or whether it's a monthly subscription.'

Tomlin nodded.

'He said that that is why the times are all over the place. He also admits to having gone back to the farm and to his house to get rid of the external hard drives before calling it in.

'While our murderer was getting away?'

'Possibly Sir; the duty solicitor reckons it was because Heath didn't want his wife to find out about Miss Whatever her name – apparently he's got all sorts of stuff recorded on both machines, what the solicitor referred to as *various encounters of a sexual nature between consenting adults, that have no bearing on our current investigation.*'

I glanced back at my notes. 'Mr Heath says he can't remember the names of the sites he's visited, but I'll see what the techies can come up with, and find out what he was doing and when. I'm not sure what they'll be able to recover from his browser history-'

'But he's signed the permission for the CCTV?' asked Tomlin.

'Reluctantly. I've just emailed it over to the security company. We should have the footage as soon as they've cleared it.'

'And have we got an identification on our victim yet?'

'No, Sir, we're still going through missing persons' reports.'

'So we've got nothing to hold Heath on?'

'No, Sir.'

'And what do you think?'

I hesitated. 'He's iffy, Sir, but we've got nothing to tie him to the murder, other than him discovering our victim.'

'Not yet. Let's face it, it wouldn't be the first time,' said Tomlin. 'Good old fashioned bit of show and tell.'

We're all aware of the risks of jumping to conclusions but in spite of training and an awareness of the pitfalls and unconscious bias, it can be hard not to. I wasn't sure that Heath had killed the woman but my instinct was that there was more to him. It didn't make him a criminal or a murderer but my guess was that he was hiding something, something bigger than wanking on a webcam.

'A lot of time the simplest solutions are the right ones,' said Tomlin thoughtfully.

'We'll keep digging,' I said.

Most criminals aren't evil masterminds, or complex geniuses, they're bullies, opportunists, egotists, coerced or driven into it, they are often ill-educated, with a kind of wily cunning that is about self-preservation and winning against the odds. Murder is different, but most violent crimes are not complex or carefully planned.

The current case showed some signs of planning - the dump site, the posing, the wrapping, indicated a narrative that was important to the perpetrator but it didn't make him a criminal mastermind – and it was important that that fact didn't slip out of view. There was a possibility that Gary Heath was involved in the murder of the young woman found on his land, but we had no hard evidence, and watching porn and lying about the times he was on the farm, though suspicious, didn't make him guilty. Or at least not guilty of murder.

Tomlin nodded. 'Then best we let Mr Heath get off home. But let's keep an eye on him, shall we? Advise him that we may need to speak to him again. Have the search team finished with the farm yet?'

'No Sir, they've got a lot of ground to cover. Lots of potential places to hide things and the whole area is covered in a network of dykes and culverts to handle the drainage, as well as all the buildings.'

We could have done with a dive team to search the waterways around the farm but without something more concrete to tie Heath in to the murder we couldn't justify the expense, although it didn't take a genius to work out that throwing something into a water course was a great way to hide and degrade evidence, especially if the water was muddy, deep and damned cold.

'And what about the hard drives?' Tomlin asked.

'Mr Heath said that he dumped them in the cesspit at the farm.'

Tomlin pulled a face. 'Bloody hell, well that's going to be a great job for someone.' He paused and looked at me.

'Do we authorise recovery?' I asked.

There's a financial cost to every stage of every enquiry and deciding how to use resources is always an issue. We'd secured access to the CCTV footage stored on the cloud, but we couldn't be seen to have overlooked, or in this case ignored something else that could give us information that might prove significant.

Gary Heath had gone to a lot of effort to dispose of the drives, but it might not take us any further forward with our murder case. There was a good chance that there was just a load of dodgy porn he was afraid his wife would find. The good news was that it wasn't my call.

'I don't see that we have much choice,' Tomlin said, after a few seconds. 'Get them found.'

Uniform took Gary Heath home to his wife, while out in the incident room I started to go through the online files to see if I could find any other crimes that bore a similarity to ours – the same MO – the problem is that while the database can save time, and hours of phone calls and paper pushing, it can still be a bit hit and miss.

Despite a supposed standardised method of entry, people still record details in different ways, they leave things out, give different aspects of a scene, different, and sometimes, no importance – for example wrapping a victim's body in polythene is not that unusual, nor is dumping a body in an isolated wood area, but this crime linked those two aspects in what appeared to be a deliberate manner – so finessing the search parameters was important, and in some ways is an art in itself.

You start off broad, not wanting to exclude too much and then slowly narrow or adjust your search as the hits or lack of them stack up. Also you're dependent on another officer's interpretation of what he or she saw - and a perpetrator whose methodology and the seriousness of their crime may or may not evolve over time.

I sifted, and shifted the parameters and came up with around thirty possibles, and then worked down again to around ten that bore a marked similarity to what we had found in the circle of trees, some were about location, most were about the victim profile – petite, blonde women aged between 15 and 35 and the remaining ones involved wrapping the victim in polythene and possibly posing the deceased. This stuff draws you in. It's like looking for dark unsettling jigsaw puzzle pieces without any idea of what the final picture will be. Eventually I brought the number down to ten.

I opened them up to look closer – ten was a

manageable number. A couple I dismissed at once – one was a sex worker killed and posed by her pimp to warn the rest of the girls in his stable, another a domestic - I combed the others and ended up with five that were close enough to make me think they might be related.

The most recently discovered victim that matched the search was of a young woman near Newbury. I scanned through the details. The victim profile was similar. Twenty-nine, slight build, five feet two, with blonde hair, Anya Vassali was a migrant worker, a fruit picker and waitress, who told friends that she planned to go travelling over the autumn before heading back home to Lithuania. She had been manually strangled and wrapped in polythene. Her body had been found in an isolated stretch of woodland near the village of Dogmore in Berks. I read through the details - it sounded a lot like what we'd got. The major difference was that her body hadn't been found for weeks and during that time the area had been hit by gale force winds that brought down trees, which in turn had brought down power lines.

Power company engineers had come across the body while repairing the lines. The damage caused by the trees had added to the problem of identification, although without the gale there was a possibility her body would never have been found. It made me wonder if there were more victims out there that we hadn't discovered yet. Without the involvement of Gary Heath there is a chance our woman wouldn't have been found for years. I fired an email off to the sergeant on the case so we could arrange to talk.

I accessed the crime scene photos but the tree damage made it impossible to work out exactly how she had been wrapped and if she had been posed, but the notes did indicate that they believed the killer was forensically aware and they'd been unable to recover any DNA from the assailant. The only image of her in life was a grainy black and white shot, that was too pixelated to see if she bore any resemblance to our victim.

My phone buzzed in my handbag. I glanced down; my sister Kathy's name came up on the caller display. It would be easier to ignore it but my eyes ached from trawling though the onscreen files and besides I'd only be delaying the inevitable. I picked up my phone and headed out into the corridor.

'Hi, how're you doing?' I said. 'I'm at work at the moment so I can't talk for long.' Given Jimmy's appearance at the door last night, setting the boundaries felt important.

I waited, when she spoke Kathy's voice was dead and flat. 'That's okay. I haven't got much to say really,' she said. 'Just that I've finally thrown Jimmy out. I know you'll say not before time. He's working on a contract on a job over your way – I thought I'd warn you – or maybe you already knew?' There was something accusatory in her voice now. 'Did you know?'

I tried hard not to sound defensive or worse still, guilty. 'No, at least not until last night when he pitched up drunk on my doorstep. I was going to ring but I got called in-' Said aloud it sounded like an excuse. 'How about you – are you okay? You don't sound too great.'

'I'm not. I am so *not* okay, Mel. I feel like I'm going crazy and I am so angry with everything and everyone and him, the bastard, the lying fucking bastard - so fucking angry. Did you screw him?'

I didn't reply.

'Because it seems to me everyone else did. Did you know? Did you?' Her voice was full of tears, accusation and fury. 'She showed up here the other day. On my bloody doorstep when I was going to take the boys to swimming.'

I didn't need to speak or to ask who.

'His latest fucking whore, on my doorstep. *My doorstep*. Ringing on the bell, on and on. Looking for him. She wanted to know where he was, demanding to know, yelling and shouting. She came round to *my* house, to *my* bloody home wanting to know where Jimmy was. In front of the boys. *My boys*. And then when I told her to sod off she told me that she was going to stay exactly where she was till I told her where he was, if it took all day, because she was pregnant.

And do you know what Jimmy said to me when I told him?' The floodgates had opened, and Kathy started to sob. 'He said, "You didn't tell her where I was, did you?" I mean what a bastard, what a stone cold straight up fucking bastard - and you knew all about it, didn't you? Don't tell me you didn't, because I know bloody well that you did.' She was yelling now. 'You knew that he was playing away and didn't say anything, because you couldn't face me. That's why you left, isn't it? That's why you didn't come to ours Christmas. I saw your neighbour in Tesco, and she told me. Fiona? She said-'

I took a breath and braced myself wondering what the hell was coming next and what exactly it was that my ex-neighbour Fiona had told her. I doubted that Fiona had mentioned that Jimmy had been paying her late-night courtesy calls too.

From the office doorway one of the local officers beckoned me back inside. I nodded.

'Look, Kathy, I'm at work.' I said evenly. 'I really can't talk now. I'll call you back as soon as I get home.' And with that hung up. Cowardly? Maybe, but I didn't know what to say to her and there was no way I could make any of this right. Jimmy was slime. She deserved so much better, and if she couldn't take it out on him then she was going to take it out on me. There was a big part of me that thought her finally finding out exactly what Jimmy was like was the best thing that could have happened to her. Maybe now she could get the life she deserved, get rid of Jimmy and start over. But I wasn't going to say that, at least not yet.

When I stepped back into the office, Sophie Rowe, one of our DCs on the Major Investigations Team, who was hunched over a computer monitor, looked up and waved me over.

'I think we might have found her, Sarge.'

I walked across the office and glanced over her

shoulder, as Rowe pulled up a missing persons' report and a photo. Laura Lamb. A friend reported her missing after she failed to turn up to a fitting for a wedding dress.'

I stared at DC Rowe. 'Oh God, not her wedding dress?' I said, thinking about my first impressions in amongst the trees.

'No, her best friend's. Her name is Kate Davies, apparently they had both booked time off work to go into Cambridge together for a fitting yesterday. Laura was a no show - when she didn't turn up her friend rang round but couldn't get hold of Laura, then she rang her work and she hadn't shown up there either, nor was she at her flat. Ms Davies said she wouldn't normally have worried but this is totally out of character, Laura is usually extremely reliable, it was a really special day and Laura had rung her on Monday evening to confirm that she was going to be there the next day.' Rowe glanced down at her notes. 'Laura said she was really looking forward to going to Cambridge with Ms Davies and they had a whole girlie day planned together.'

'So, Laura was supposed to be in Cambridge shopping on Tuesday?'

Rowe nodded. 'Ms Davies rang in to report it last night and again this morning. She is really anxious about her friend because it was so unlike her.'

It's a myth that you have to wait three days to make a missing persons' report, it can be done any time after a person has gone missing, although the truth is that most people turn up unharmed. Also how seriously the matter is taken has a lot to do with whoever is manning the front desk and how persuasive the person is who is doing the reporting. Most duty officers and call handlers, unless the person is vulnerable or poses a risk either to themselves or others, will try and persuade the person reporting the disappearance to wait another day or maybe longer to see if someone shows up of their own volition. Kate Davies' wedding dress story had obviously convinced someone that the disappearance was a genuine cause for concern.

I looked at the photo more closely. It was cropped from what was most likely a holiday group shot, Laura Lamb was framed by other people's sun-kissed shoulders. Her hair was sun-bleached, she was lean and tanned and wearing a pale blue and orange sundress, and her chin tipped up. She was laughing, her eyes bright and full of life, as she stared towards the camera. Behind her you could just pick out a stripe of cerulean blue sea and sun-bleached terrace, a holiday destination a lifetime away from the dark black winter fen.

I nodded. She certainly bore a strong resemblance to our victim.

'Let's get uniform round to check her flat, presumably we've got an address? And can we pull up details of any vehicles registered to her. And get someone onto tracking her phone and service provider down?'

Rowe nodded; it looked like we might have found our girl.

'CCTV is in,' said an officer at one of the other desks.

Finally it looked like we might be getting somewhere.

*

The sound of the rain drumming on the tin roof was a constant counterpoint to the TV playing in the corner of the room. The room was damp and dark and smelt of fried food, smoke, sweat and women. The volume on the TV was set high, bursts of applause and upbeat music breaking through the air like gunfire.

A couple of young women, one blonde, one with Asian features and hair scrunched up on her head in a lazy top knot, were huddled close to it, both were smoking, the blonde sipping from a can of energy drink, both had mascara and eyeliner crusted around tired overnight eyes. On screen a man in a sparkly turquoise jacket was guiding contestants around a screen of inane

88

questions and forfeits. Away from the glare of the TV there were a couple more girls sleeping, curled up on stained sofas that corralled a coffee table overflowing with ashtrays, dirty plates, mugs and magazines, hair brushes, makeup bags, and screwed up food wrappers: the detritus of communal living. Other young women were sleeping in the bunks that lined the walls. No one spoke. The eyes that were open had a slightly unfocused expression, not so much that they appeared too drugged just drowsy, ditsy, slightly out of it. It was a fine balance, a fine balance to keep them compliant and responsive and conscious.

Chapter Eight
Mike Carlton

No one ever talked about the sounds of an autopsy; Mike Carlton thought grimly watching Beau Shepherd at work in the stark confines of the new lab. It was impressive, state of the art this, top of the range that. Mike had taken the tour when it had first opened at the beginning of the year. But no amount of gleaming white surfaces or stainless steel fittings could disguise what was going on there. He swallowed hard against a little roiling wave of nausea.

Under bright, unforgiving white lights, Beau Shepherd and his assistant, Ralph, worked methodically, with a slow deliberate precision born of years of practise and working together, the squeak of the Crocs on the tiled floor, the hum of the extractor fans and air conditioning a backdrop to other more unsettling disturbing sounds.

These days attending officers watched from a separate room, situated above the autopsy suite, and from behind a pristine glass panel. The same room could be used for students to come in and observe and attend lectures and dissections. Back in the old days when Mike had first joined the force the observing officer stood a few feet away from the pathologist and whoever was occupying the table. A ringside seat for the main performance.

Attending your first post mortem back then had been a rite of passage for every young copper. Mike's first one was seared into his memory; an elderly man who had been gassed by his daughter who hadn't wanted to pay his care costs. She had blocked up all vents and a chimney and taken down the smoke and carbon monoxide alarm in his bungalow so the old boy succumbed to carbon monoxide poisoning. Mike's chief recollection was the unsettling cherry red colour of the old man's skin.

To his credit, Mike hadn't fainted or thrown up when the first cut was made, but the smell and the workmanlike approach of the pathologist, still lingered in the darker corridors of his mind. These days officers were spared the proximity, but the autopsy room still had an open microphone that relayed every sound into the viewing area.

Besides viewing the events in real-time they were being caught on camera in unforgiving HD, both to record the procedure for future reference and also because Beau taught students at the local university.

Over the years Mike had grown accustomed to what he might see – though he had never got used to it. And despite the evidence to the contrary he preferred to believe that the inside of his own body was more stainless steel and titanium than bile, blood and bone. Being the officer present was all part of the job; first of all it gave an early steer on what may have happened to their victim, which could be explained in plain language face to face with a chance to get anything he didn't understand clarified, without having to wait for the Pathologist's report, which usually took a few days, and was heavy with medical terms. More than that Mike was there to ensure continuity - part of a meticulous, well-documented trail of the body from the scene to the mortuary through to the post-mortem, which maintained the chain of evidence.

Any items found on or associated with the body would be bagged in tamper proof bags, recorded and taken into evidence. In court it could then be shown where that evidence had come from and where it was at all times.

Mike had learned to take and make all the jokes, heavy with the blackest of humour, to get a grip when he felt faint, or worse, felt sick. He accepted the offers of *Vicks* vapour rub to rub under his nostrils to help with the smell of decomposition in the riper ones – and generally steel himself for what he knew was coming - but it was the sounds of ribs being opened, the wet slither of organs as they were lifted out of the body and hefted onto a scale, the sounds of the oscillating saw, the skull key and mallet used to remove the top of the skull, those were the things that stayed with him.

And then there were the sounds of the Pathologist's voice, talking into an overhead microphone, so matter of fact and so calm, noting the details and his observations, starting with the things that were available for everyone to see– the victim's gender, ethnicity, hair colour and height, and the general appearance of the body, before he began to delve into things very few people in an ordinary lifetime ever saw except perhaps on TV, on film or in their worst nightmares. Mike wondered what Beau dreamt of at night.

Some cases were harder than others to deal with. Children were the worst but young people, people who should have had a whole life ahead of them came a close second.

Looking at the body on the table Mike couldn't help thinking about what the young woman had been doing before all this, the plans she had made, the friends and family she had, the people she loved and who loved her. He thought about his wife, and their baby daughter and swallowed hard, and set his jaw, all business, and turned his attention back to Beau's voice.

'No obvious signs of trauma...'

Her killer had used a combination of rope and tape to keep her hands in position; she was tied at the elbow with a rope that ran over her upper arms and under her breasts – keeping her arms tied close to her body and then tied again at the wrist and tied and taped so her palms were pressing against the polythene shroud as if pushing it or keeping something more sinister at bay. It had taken a lot of effort to keep them in place. There were small bones broken in the fingers and wrists. The restraints had been extensively photographed before being removed and bagged for further analysis. The tape would be a good place to look for fibres and traces from the original crime scene and the killer.

'Do you think he did that while she was alive?' Mike asked.

Beau shook his head, 'From the lividity and lack of abrasions it was done post mortem I suspect - but I will confirm that. There are ligature marks on her arms which suggest she was bound prior to death, but this hand placement appears to have been done later.'

She had been beautiful in life, in a girl next door kind of way, and now she lay on the stainless steel table, naked, vulnerable, her hair carefully brushed for any trace evidence, her body examined for fibres, her nails had been scraped for any possible residue then clipped and those clippings bagged to retain any trace that there might be of her killer or the places she had been before death.

Her eyes were closed. She had a pale, creamy white skin with a scatter of freckles, and soft blonde hair, and at first glance it looked as if she might be asleep, resting, untroubled under the ice white light of the lab. From where he was standing Mike couldn't see the lividity or the beginnings of decay marbling the skin across her chest and shoulders.

She had been photographed in situ at the crime scene and in the body bag she had been brought in, in. Her plastic wrapping had been photographed carefully before being removed and bagged up and sent to the forensic lab to be examined for fibres, finger prints, DNA and any other residue that could help identify the site where she had been killed and the identity of either the victim or her killer. She had been finger-printed and x-rayed and a rape kit done. Nothing left to chance.

The scalpel making a smooth Y shaped incision was silent, from collar bone to collar bone then down between the ribs to the pubic bone. Beau carefully lifted the skin up on the stomach when slicing it open to avoid nicking the bowel. But removing the breastbone and opening the ribs was not silent. On bad nights Mike heard those sounds in his sleep.

Beau removed and carefully examined the heart, lungs, neck structure, intestine, liver, spleen, kidneys, bladder and uterus. He talked as he worked, his voice picked up by the overhead microphone, giving a commentary in a steady even voice.

And Mike took it all in, making notes as he went. Their victim was white, in her early twenties, with blue eyes and blonde hair, she had never had children, and had been in robust good health at the time of her death. She had excellent teeth but enough fillings and a crown that - if they could track down her dental records – it would mean that they would be able to identify her definitively. She had no distinguishing marks, no moles, no tattoos, wore no jewellery or nail polish. Her ears were pierced, two piercings in the lobe of each ear, but there were no earrings present. Fluids were collected to send for analysis.

As Beau worked, his technician, Ralph, a pale man with a ponytail and slight stoop, assisted as required and systematically collected, bagged and labelled samples for testing, as well as taking notes, photographing the deceased as Beau worked. They worked together alongside each other like a well-oiled machine, stepping in time, like dancers, moving with an unsettling synchronicity.

'If you'd like to take a look at the screen, Detective Sergeant Carlton,' said Beau. Surprised to hear his name, Mike glanced up. Beau Shepherd zoomed in on an area inside the neck region, exposed and glistening under the surgical lights. 'You'll see the fracture in the hyoid bone - the U-shaped bone of the neck is fractured in one third of all homicides by strangulation, and there are contusions and bruising on the victim's neck that would indicate manual strangulation as cause of death.'

'Finger prints?' asked Mike.

Under the right circumstance it was possible to get near perfect fingerprints from bruising as well as the possibility of LCN DNA from physical contact. Low Copy Number DNA testing meant that a profile could be obtained from a tiny amount of material, from an amount far smaller than a grain of salt and amount to just a few cells of skin or sweat left from a fingerprint, or not as the case might be.

Beau shook his head. 'I'm afraid not. There is some bruising and petechial haemorrhaging present in the eyes. Obviously we'll have to wait for toxicology to see if anything else was going on-'

Mike made another note. 'When can we have the report?'

'You're always so damned eager. My initial findings by the end of play today, full report in maybe two or three days, but toxicology is going to take a while.'

Mike nodded. The labs were backed up, and there was no budget to expedite analysis unless totally necessary. 'And time of death?'

'I'm happy with my original call. Between five and ten pm on - where are we? He glanced down at the notes. 'Tuesday. We've got no obvious signs of sexual assault. I've done a rape kit but there are no signs of bruising or other trauma. We swabbed for semen. And then there are stomach contents.' He picked up a small dish that had been sitting alongside the table. 'Nothing very informative I'm afraid, other than our girl hadn't had anything substantial to eat in the hours before death. There is some bruising and contusion to the wrists other than that required to pose the hands that as I said suggests she had been bound up prior to death.

Mike nodded. He would be happier when they could give her a name. Someone had to be missing her. His phone vibrated in his jacket pocket. He pulled it out and glanced down at the screen. It appeared that his wish might have been granted.

*

95

In her kitchen, Linda Heath glanced over her shoulder towards the windows, before pulling the tangle of clothes out of the tumble drier. Without bothering to sort or fold them, she dragged everything straight into a striped plastic laundry bag, zipping it tight closed. It was heavy. Sliding it outside into the covered car port, sure that she wasn't being observed by the officer who was keeping an eye on the bungalow, she slid it alongside a pile of produce boxes and headed back inside.

Chapter Nine
Laura Lamb

'Her friend was here yesterday making a right fuss, wanting me to go upstairs and see if Laura was in her flat. I kept telling her I couldn't just go barging in like that, told her not to worry. I mean they're only young, aren't they? I said she's probably off somewhere with some man.'

'Does Miss Lamb have a boyfriend?' I asked.

The building supervisor sucked her teeth and then shook her head. She had a plastic badge on her overalls that read, *Concierge* in italic script below a company logo that I couldn't make out.

'Not that I know of. To be honest I barely ever see her. She is out before I get here in the morning and gets back after I leave. But never any trouble though, and she sent me a lovely Christmas card. When she moved in, Laura and her dad bought me chocolates for staying late to help them with a few bits and pieces. Nice girl - I've rung her dad, just in case there is anything. When your lot showed up. He would want to know if there is a problem. I think he helped her buying this place. But I'm sure there's nothing to it, aren't you?' The woman looked up at me expectantly, but if she was hoping for any kind of reassurance or any information she was out of luck.

'How long has Ms Lamb lived here?'

'About a year. She was one of the first ones to move in. Bought off plan so they could choose the fittings. Came when they were still doing the building work.'

I nodded. 'And when did you last see her?'

The woman frowned. 'Must be two or three weeks

ago now at least, maybe more, but there is CCTV here in the atrium. I've got a number for the building management company if you need to see it. I can't access it from here-' She disappeared through a doorway across the atrium and appeared a few seconds later carrying a business card.

'There we go. There's an out of hours number on there as well,' she said, handing me the card.

'Thank you. Have you noticed anything suspicious recently – anything odd or out of the ordinary?'

'Not really. I mean we're quite quiet round here. It's very select.'

'Any one unusual hanging around or giving the residents any trouble?'

The supervisor rolled her eyes. 'Round my way, yes, but here? No, nothing I can think of – bit of an argy-bargy over the parking from time to time but nothing out of the ordinary.'

'And was Miss Lamb involved?'

'Not as far as I know. She keeps to her allocated space.'

Someone was already checking the DVLA for any registered vehicle.

'Thank you. If you think of anything else or anything comes to mind-' I handed her my card. 'Just ring me.'

She nodded.

'Could you direct me to Ms Lamb's flat?'

'You do know the other policeman's already up there, don't you? Said he didn't want me going inside. I suppose you have to go through the motions. I let him in when he said he needed to check if she was okay. He told me she'd been reported missing. By that girl presumably, she was in a right-' The woman stopped mid-sentence, hand flying to her mouth. 'Oh my God. She's not in there, is she? Is she dead? Oh my dear God – is she in there? I mean you see all those things on the telly.' Her jaw worked furiously.

'No,' I said. 'We don't believe so. Which floor is the flat on?'

'First floor, Flat 1A, first door at the top of the stairs. Is she all right?'

'We're currently looking into a missing person's report.' I said.

'So she is definitely missing?' said the woman.

'That's what we're trying to find out.' I managed a smile. 'Do you live here?'

'Oh no, God, not me. I couldn't afford one of these. No, but I'm on call and I come and clean the public areas, the atrium, the stairs, most days, not at the weekends but weekdays. I do three other buildings in town for the same company.'

'Okay, thank you - and we've got your number if we need you?'

She nodded. 'Yeah, I gave it to the other copper.' She glanced over her shoulder towards the partially open door of her office. 'I'll be in there if you need me for the next couple of hours. I'm waiting in for a delivery.' She paused. 'Will you let me know how she is? She's such a nice girl, only young-'

I thanked her and went upstairs.

Laura Lamb's flat was in a prestige development on South Quay in the historic quarter of King's Lynn's old town, and had a spectacular view out over the tidal Ouse. Once upon a time it had been a bustling dock that had serviced the whaling trade and the Hanseatic league but now, other than a grain store and loading gantry at one end, for the most part the Quay served as a cultural and heritage centre with a few discreet housing developments and conversions tucked into the row of handsome Medieval and Tudor buildings.

Cobbold Apartments boasted a rectangular paved courtyard set with small trees in tubs, leading the eye towards a plate glass atrium artfully set into the red brick arch that cut through into the original building. There was a central lobby with extensive CCTV coverage, key code entry and because the whole area was subject to flooding it had six feet high floodgates, and walls around the courtyard. The dock and quay outside were all closely monitored by half a dozen different agencies in case of flooding. If Laura's killer had ever been there then we would have forty ways to Christmas to track him down.

The building supervisor watched me climb the stairs with barely contained curiosity.

Laura's apartment was amongst eight others in the building, created from what looked from the outside to be a medieval merchant's house. Her apartment was part of what was probably once the great hall. Some of the walls were rich red small handmade bricks and cream render interspersed with intricately carved masonry; the historic elements of the building's fabric were protected by discreet plate glass panels, while the rest of the apartment was painted in soft greys and creams. Modern design and subtle lighting contrasted with vaulted ceilings and arched mullioned windows set deep into the walls.

Although it was small the rooms in the apartment had been well laid out, and were stylish, and thoughtfully furnished. The flat consisted of a tiny lobby that opened up onto the sitting room with its view out over the river. There was a galley kitchen off the main living area, and then a shower room, and a double bedroom with the same impressive view. There was no sign of Laura, nothing broken, nothing out of place, certainly with no signs of a disturbance or a struggle. The whole flat was magazine photoshoot ready.

'Were the curtains open when you got here?' I asked the officer who had been the first on the scene. He was a local sergeant and he and a PC had been sent to check out the address after our call.

He nodded. 'Yes, just as we found it, we didn't touch a thing, just got the supervisor to let us in and took a quick shufty round to make sure she wasn't here. We get the odd one reported missing who's been taken poorly, in bed with flu, or the next door neighbour. You know what I'm saying. We probably wouldn't have come round to check it out if it hadn't been for you lot.'

Resources are tight, the apparent disappearance of a healthy young adult woman with no mental health issues and gone for less than twenty-four hours wouldn't have rung any alarm bells and would have been considered a low priority.

I pulled on a pair of latex gloves.

'You think she's your girl?' the sergeant asked.

'We've got nothing official yet-'

He nodded. We both knew what that meant. 'Doesn't look like anyone's been in here,' he said.

I had to agree.

In the sitting room two oatmeal coloured sofas faced each other across a vintage wooden trunk that served as a coffee table, the top was arranged with pebbles, books and a bowl of oranges, the colour of the fruit was sharp and rich in amongst a sea of neutrals. The TV was discreetly tucked away inside an alcove. A single vintage leather armchair sat in the window framed by the grey of the river and the grey gold of the sky. It would soon be dark. I'd barely thought about the light levels when the spotlights in the sitting room clicked on.

I glanced over my shoulder at the sergeant. 'Nothing to do with me,' he said holding up his hands. 'I reckon they must be on some sort of timer.'

'Might make it harder to work out when she disappeared – anyone looking in would assume she had turned the lights on.'

He nodded.

On the coffee table was a remote control, which on second glance I realised would control the blinds, lights and heating as well as the TV. She had probably got them all preset.

'Clever that,' said the sergeant admiringly.

I nodded and resumed my search.

The soft light made the flat look all the more inviting, and made me wonder how the hell anyone managed to live like this without mugs and plates on the floor or a takeaway pizza box on the coffee table. There was a desk with a laptop, and neatly labelled files tucked into the drawers, shelves with books – mostly fiction and chick lit. Nothing looked out of place, nothing jarred.

In the kitchen downlighters under the wall units picked out a single mug, bowl and spoon standing upside down on the draining board. The cupboards were full of cooking paraphernalia. There was a shelf of cookery books: Nigella and Ottolenghi. The fridge was full of healthy options, the freezer full of batch cooked suppers all carefully labelled with the contents and the date. Laura liked curry and chilli and things with unpronounceable names.

The lamps in the bedroom were on. There were throws and cushions on the king-sized bed, and a wall hung with a combination of abstract prints and black and white family photos. A handsome young couple, presumably Laura's parents, were holding Laura as a baby, there was Laura as a child in a garden with an older boy, possibly a brother, Laura on a pony, then the same family at the beach, a family gathered round a piano decked with Christmas baubles. A mother, thinner now and more drawn, sitting outside a French farmhouse, Laura as a teenager, and then graduating. Laura with her father, Laura at a family wedding, toasting the camera. The edited highlights of a young life. The memory of the girl in the plastic shroud surrounded by ivy and moss rose unbidden. There was no doubt in my mind that the body in the copse was Laura.

'We'll need to get SOCO in here but I don't think we're looking at a crime scene, do you?' I said, glancing back over my shoulder.

The sergeant shook his head. 'I wouldn't have thought so, not unless the killer is a neat freak.'

I nodded; it was possible.

'Can you make sure they take the laptop in and make it high priority?'

'Will do.'

I opened up the fitted wardrobes that lined one wall of the bedroom; the clothes inside were good quality, but well worn, a combination of smart work clothes – fitted skirts and jackets with softer cardigans and coloured blouses, and casual weekend wear, Joules, Zara and Fat Face, dresses from White Stuff and Sea Salt, good shoes and leather boots.

'Have you talked to the neighbours yet?' I asked.

'No. Most of them are at work according to the caretaker. It's mostly young professionals. Doctor next door, solicitor other side of her-'

'Can we make that a priority?'

He nodded.

The flat held no surprises, no signs of a struggle, no signs of disturbance, just a snapshot of a good, diligent, careful, young woman who kept a childhood teddy on her beside cabinet, whose shoes were newly re-heeled and who had carefully packed away her spring and summer clothes in preparation for seasons she would never see.

Don't ever tell me police officers have no heart. There are things – and it is always the small things – that move me in a way that defies explanation. The newly heeled shoes made my heart lurch, and on the dressing table by the window with its view out over the grey choppy water of the Ouse was the card and little beautifully wrapped parcel that Laura had been intending to take to give her friend Kate. On the envelope she had written in a bold rounded script: *'To the trainee Bride with much love.'*

From the bathroom cabinet I bagged up a toothbrush and a hairbrush – we would need something to compare DNA and confirm that our girl was Laura Lamb. It would be expedited, although now we had a name we would be able to track down her dental records.

As I was taking a final look I sensed rather than heard something going on outside on the landing.

'I'll go and see to that,' said the sergeant.

As the front door opened, I heard a raised male voice. 'Can you tell me what is going on. That's my daughter's flat. Where is she? What the hell is going on here?'

I heard the sergeant's voice, but not the words. His voice was lower, calmer. I guessed he would be explaining that Laura had been reported missing, that we were looking into it. He couldn't tell him that we had found his precious girl in the middle of a fen, miles from here because we hadn't had the official confirmation yet. I know that he wouldn't have said that, but there was something in his tone, something in the way he said it made the man in the lobby start to keen, a low animal moan that made the hairs on my neck lift.

I opened the front door. Laura's father was standing in the corridor, an older version of the man I had seen in the black and white photos on her wall. I could see now where Laura got her blonde hair from.

'Mr Lamb? I'm Detective Sergeant Daley-' I began.

He stared at me, unseeing. Standing beside him the sergeant's expression was in neutral. 'I explained to Mr Lamb that his daughter has been reported missing.'

I nodded.

'Something's happened to Laura, hasn't it?' her father said grimly. 'I knew it as soon as Kate called – as soon as she said Laura hadn't turned up for their day out, I knew that something was wrong, that something had happened. I knew it but Carol, my wife, said I was being over dramatic. I've rung and rung Laura, trying to convince myself it was nothing, that she is an adult, that she would ring when she has a moment, that her phone was dead-' He looked up at me, his eyes full of tears. 'Have you found her?'

I extended a hand. 'Why don't we go downstairs?' I said.

Chapter Ten
Like Hungry

He felt the sensation low down in his belly. Like hungry but different, more of an ache, more of an itch, which he was struggling to ignore. Would taking another one be too greedy? Was it too soon? He'd need to be careful, really careful. When he dragged his attention away from the itch, he knew that it wasn't sensible to rush these things or take two so close together, either in terms of time or proximity, but the ache began again, *the ache*.

The real problem was that the last one had left him hungry for another, for more. It didn't pay to be rash, but it didn't feel the same as it had when he had first started. Once upon a time he could do one and feel sated, satisfied for weeks, months even, when he had first started out. And he would hold the memory in the front of his head, so that he could savour it over and over again, keep it there on replay throughout the day and long into the night, till the memory and the sensations were worn and threadbare from constant use, but that was then, when he had just started out, and the truth was that they were beginning to all blur into one now. To coalesce into just one face, just one body, just one woman.

He paused for a moment and considered that thought, actually that was probably how it should be, wasn't it? After all when it came right down to it, it was all about one woman not many, wasn't it? And even if he tried to separate the others into individual women wasn't there just one face on all of them? One face, one look of disappointment and disdain? One bitch. He suppressed a smile. One fucking bitch.

The thing was he needed to be careful that that need, his hunger, didn't get the better of him. He didn't want to get caught, at least not before he found one more, maybe one more would be enough, maybe he would stop after that, give it up. Move on. He took a breath and smiled. Truth was there would always be one more, after all if they didn't catch him, what was there to stop him?

Sometimes he hoped that they would catch him, because he knew that until they did, he wouldn't stop. He couldn't stop – why would he when he needed to feel them, take them? The look in those eyes when he did. The thought made his mouth water and his cock start to harden.

He glanced out of the window onto the car park. The police station was busy, with cars in almost every space. He smiled. He was so hungry.

*

The first team briefing was held as soon as I got back from Laura Lamb's flat in King's Lynn. It was the first chance we had had to all get together, having hit the ground running.

Tomlin introduced the rest of our team to the local officers, brought everyone up to speed and outlined the priorities for the continued searches, information and interviews.

We had secured Laura Lamb's dental records and Beau Shepherd had given us verbal confirmation that our victim was twenty-six year old Laura Lamb, an administrator with a specialist engineering company who spent half her working week in Cambridge and the other half in King's Lynn. So now we had the name of our victim.

After Tomlin's introduction, Mike fed in what he had from the autopsy. A local uniformed sergeant gave us an update on the house to house and the search in and around Gary Heath's farm, and the pumping out of the cesspit, that had led to the recovery of two hard drives, which were being worked on by the lab with some hope that we would be able to retrieve the contents.

What we had at this stage was still very sparse, but with a name and a positive ID part of the team were already assigned to chasing down Laura's contacts, her friends, her co-workers and her social and working life. We could track through social media, phone records, the DVLA and everything in between. Things were moving now but to be honest it never feels fast enough. I glanced up at the clock in the incident room; it was after six, my day off had finished around an hour earlier.

At the round-up of the briefing Tomlin took over again. He glanced down at his notes. 'Our plans are to keep Gary Heath under surveillance and this will be ongoing but under regular review. I think we all feel there is more to Mr Heath than meets the eye, but we've got nothing other than his discovery of the body to tie him to the murder. That can obviously change. But he continues to be a person of interest. Priorities are to track down the whereabouts of Laura Lamb's vehicle and her mobile phone, as well as clothing and personal effects. DVLA records show she owns a metallic blue 2014 Citroen C1 – the details and reg' number are being sent to your phones. Uniform and traffic on that, please. I'd like to concentrate our efforts on finding Laura's vehicle and tracking down the primary site, the place where she was killed. From DS Daley's visit to her flat it would appear that it isn't the likely kill site-' He glanced at me and I nodded and took up the thread.

'It's spotless in there, with better than average CCTV on all entrances and exits, including the rear fire doors. We've got officers interviewing the other tenants and going through the footage, and I've asked SOCO to take a look, but we'll only do a full work up if we get evidence from the building's CCTV that puts any suspected killer or anyone who appears to be acting suspiciously in the building. There were no signs of a struggle, no disturbance, and so while we're not ruling it out, it looks unlikely, so there is another primary site out there that we need to find and currently – I know I don't have to tell you - it's going cold.'

Tomlin nodded. 'I'd also like us to focus on Laura's friends and the people she works with. Starting with Kate Davies who reported her missing, and we obviously need to be looking at any current partners, ex's-' He turned his gaze on the group of officers crowded into the briefing room before indicating a thick set man in the front row. 'Some of you have already met Sergeant Tom Green who is working liaison and is our actioning officer, and will be sorting out who goes where.'

Tom Green smiled and picked up the clipboard that had been on one of the desks. 'Right, ladies and gentlemen,' he began, getting to his feet. 'If I can have your attention please.'

Tomlin glanced across at me. 'I'd like you to take Kate Davies, Mel.'

I nodded. Hopefully it would be my last stop of the day before heading home.

I had told Laura's father that we would let him know if there were any developments. Once upon a time it seemed like every time there was bad news it was down to me to break it – in the good old days they thought female officers were more adept at that sort of thing, or more realistically at dealing with the aftermath. I hated it, and wouldn't say I had any more of the necessary skills than a lot of the men I'd worked with. But for this one Tomlin had said that he would break the news. He didn't say father to father but I guessed he was feeling it, thinking about the suit he had ducked out of buying on his day off and his daughter's up and coming wedding. But whatever his reasons, I was relieved.

We had Kate Davies' address from the missing persons' report. She lived in a village between Denham Market and Swaffham. I recognised the address as one of the big farming estates with a country house at its centre and parkland with deer and fancy sheep. Glancing down at the file I noted that though she called herself Kate Davies, Kate should have been hyphenated and a lady - So Kate Davies, and then home.

As I drove up the tree-lined drive to the house where she lived, tucked away on the edge of Daddy's estate, I caught sight of a tall, well-built young woman in warm outdoor clothes closing up the stables for the night. She peered out through the floodlights and pulled off a pair of gloves as I got out of the car.

'Hello,' she said. 'Can I help you?' She had the tight clipped tone of the privately educated. I made a point of tucking my working-class girl-made-good chip away out of sight.

'I hope so, I'm looking for Kate Davies?'

She nodded. 'I'm Kate, how can I help you?'

I introduced myself and showed her my warrant card.

'Major Investigation Team?' she said cautiously as she took in the details.

I nodded. 'We're looking into your friend's disappearance.'

'Have you found her yet?' she asked anxiously. 'Is she all right?'

'I've come to check on a few details, ask you some questions,' I said

Kate's face fell. I kept my expression in neutral.

'You filed a missing person's report?'

She nodded. 'That's right. I'm really glad someone is taking it seriously. I thought that they would just fob me off,' she said. 'The officer at the police station was very pleasant but you could tell that he thought I was just making a fuss over nothing. Would you like to wait inside? I just need to finish up here, it won't take more than a couple of minutes. It's a lot warmer in the cottage. Have you got any idea where she might be? I mean it is so not like her.'

I kept my expression neutral. 'I was hoping you'd be able to help us with some more information.' I said.

She nodded. 'Of course. More than happy to.'

She directed me towards a backdoor that opened up into a large hallway. It was hung with all manner of coats and blankets and had a row of boots and shoes standing on newspaper along one wall. Beyond the hallway was a farmhouse kitchen - a big square room, warm, homely, and smelling of dogs and horses. The central table was littered with books, mugs and a pile of paperwork. An elderly spaniel was sleeping, stretched full length on a threadbare rug in front of the Aga. He didn't move when I walked in. Minutes later Kate came in, pulling off coat and boots at the doorway. The dog lifted his head in greeting as she slipped on a pair of slippers and closed the outer doors.

'Sorry about that, needs must. Do take a seat. I'm so pleased that you're here. Would you like some tea?' she asked, crossing the kitchen to wash her hands in the kitchen sink.

It had been a long day.

'That would be lovely,' I said.

She slid a battered kettle over onto the hot plate. 'So what can I do to help?'

I took my phone out of my bag. 'Do you mind if I record this?'

'No, not at all.'

'You told the desk sergeant that you and Laura were meeting up to have a day out on Tuesday?'

Kate nodded. 'That's right. It was the only day we could both do. I'm getting married in the summer. Greg, my boyfriend, is away skiing at the moment, so we had planned a girls' away day.' She smiled. 'We've been planning it for ages.' She turned and looked at me earnestly. 'That's why I know that something is wrong. That's why I reported it. Laura is my very best friend in the world – we were at school together. There is no way that she wouldn't show up if she could. It is so, so totally unlike her. As far as I'm concerned it's impossible, there is no way she wouldn't be there if she could. She'd booked us afternoon tea and Prosecco afterwards to celebrate. She's my chief bridesmaid – chief whipper-in for my little nieces; they're only three and four and she is just so brilliant with kids.' Her voice cracked. 'Laura wouldn't let me down. I know she wouldn't. I know something has happened to her. You have to find her – please-'

We were sitting at her big scrub top table littered with post, and mugs, and magazines and the everyday things of living a busy country life. The spaniel barked in his sleep, legs working as he chased down imaginary rabbits. We hadn't officially announced that the body we'd found was Laura Lamb, and I couldn't say anything to Kate until I had had it confirmed officially that Tomlin had informed her father. It wasn't easy.

'I've got some photos of her if that will help,' Kate Davies was saying. 'I printed them off when I went to the police station.'

Getting up she retrieved some photos from the dresser. 'Here we are,' she said, sliding them across the table towards me.

I glanced down at the first one. It was of Laura and Kate, just head and shoulders, one dark, one fair, both looking at the camera, both in summer dresses. 'That was last summer at a barbeque for my dad's sixtieth.'

I glanced through the photos. Laura Lamb was smiling in every single one.

'So, can you tell me the last time you saw her?' I said. 'May I keep these?'

She nodded. 'I'm not sure, it's probably a couple of weeks, maybe more but we spoke on Monday evening. She was just about to leave work and rang to say that she'd see me Tuesday on the train. We'd both taken a day off. I work for a solicitor in Swaffham. She said she was really looking forward to it-'

'And do you know where she was ringing from?'

Kate shook her head. 'I assumed she was still at the office. She was on her mobile.'

'So not in her car?'

'No, I don't think so, when she's on hands free it's

always a bit echoey, but it wasn't, so I assumed she was still at work.'

'And did she say if she had any plans for Monday evening? Maybe meeting up with someone? Or going out somewhere after work?'

Kate shook her head. 'No –' she frowned.

I waited. 'What are you thinking?'

'She car shares. I'm not sure with who but I think whoever it was, was running a bit late.' She paused. 'I'm not sure what she said that made me think that, but that was the impression I was left with.'

'And do you know if Laura was in King's Lynn or Cambridge?'

'Cambridge. Definitely. She always drives to work if she's working in King's Lynn. The factory there is in an industrial estate on the other side of town from where she lives. We were only going on the train to Cambridge on Tuesday because it meant we could both have a drink. I'd booked a cab to pick me up from the station and she said she was going to walk home. Stagger she said.' Kate smiled again, glancing down at the pictures of Laura on the pile on the table. 'Neither of us are really drinkers-'

'And do you know if Laura is seeing anyone at the moment?' I made the effort to avoid the past tense.

'No, she broke up with Dawnie about three months ago, well before Christmas. I don't think it was going anywhere and the break-up was pretty much mutual.'

'Dawnie?'

'Oh yes, sorry, Lewis Dawn-Hammond. He's an estate agent and auctioneer. He works in his father's firm in Ely. She had been seeing him on and off for a few months, but he didn't want anything heavy, not big into commitment is Dawnie. I mean, she knew that when they first started dating. He's happy with the whole *friends with benefits* thing.' She mimed quotation marks.

'That's what they had?'

Kate rolled her eyes. 'Well, that's what Dawnie had.'

'And what about Laura, was she hoping for

something else?'

Kate shrugged. 'I don't know. I did wonder if she was hoping it might go somewhere. But we all knew with Dawnie that it was never going to be anything other than fun. In the end I think Laura finally cottoned on and it sort of fizzled out – actually it had been fizzling out for a while before it finished.'

'Was she upset about it?'

'No, not really, we all know what he's like. She knew what he was like. But it's a while ago now.'

I nodded. It didn't mean that there wasn't life still in it or something left over that hadn't been resolved.

'Have you got Mr Dawn-Hammond's contact details? We'll need to talk to him too.'

Kate nodded. 'In my address book. I'll get it for you. Although he's in New Zealand at the moment.'

'Do you know how long he's been out there?'

She nodded. 'Two or three weeks. We got a postcard. Let me get you that address.' She retrieved an old-fashioned leather-bound address book from the dresser and I made a note of Lewis Dawn-Hammond's details, although being in New Zealand probably queered the time frame to make him a suspect.

'And so is there anyone else that Kate has ever mentioned. Maybe someone at work or socially? Or maybe online – a dating app?'

'You mean like a new boyfriend?'

I nodded. 'Or someone's she is interested in or who is interested in her?'

'If you're suggesting she went off on some hot date with a new man then no, that is so not the kind of person Laura is. I know her, there is no way that would ever happen. She would have told me about him and put off the hot date till we'd had our day out.'

'Okay. Is there anyone you can think of that she has had problems with? A work colleague, a neighbour – anyone?'

Kate shook her head. 'I don't think so. And I'm certain that she would say something if she was having a problem with anyone. We talk about everything, and I mean everything. No, I'm sure I would know if she was dating someone new.'

I made another note. 'Okay, that's great, thank you. We're looking at everyone who knows her, exploring all sorts of possibilities at the moment.'

'If Laura had to cancel, Sergeant, she would have called, and would have rung me or texted me to let me know if she had got stuck in traffic or was running late. She wouldn't have just not shown up.'

Kate turned the mug she had been cradling in her fingers round and round. 'I'm truly worried about her. That's why I went round to her flat. That's why I rang her boss and then went to report it at the police station. I know they didn't really take it very seriously but there is no way, *no way* Laura would let me down like that. Something has to have happened to her.' Kate looked at me and held my gaze, her expression cool and determined. 'I know that she is in some sort of trouble. I just know it. Here-' she touched her chest.

I nodded and thanked her. Kate Davies' hunch wasn't wrong.

As I got back to my car my phone trilled. It was Mike Carlton. 'Just thought you'd like to know that the CCTCV footage from the foyer of Laura Lamb's apartment block shows her leaving for work on Monday morning but there was no indication she ever made it back.'

'Thanks, Mike,' I said. I knew that back in the incident room the time line would have been amended.

'I thought you'd have been on the way home by now.' I said.

Mike laughed. 'You too, although you're my last call. What did you find out at the friend's house?'

'I've got the details of an ex-boyfriend but he's on holiday in New Zealand, nothing current as far as she knows, but maybe the techies will find something on social media. Laura car shares on the days she works in Cambridge; so we need to find out who with and where her car is left while she is at work.'

'I'll pass it on,' said Mike. 'See you tomorrow. I've got to go. Apparently there is a casserole at home with my name on it. And Niamh is asleep.'

'Niamh?'

'The new baby.'

'Oh God yes, sorry, I'd totally forgotten.'

The last time we had worked together Mike's wife had been pregnant, although that felt like a lifetime ago.

He laughed. 'Don't apologise baby stuff used to bore the arse off me too till we had one of our own. We called her Niamh after some decrepit old aunt. My wife, Carol's idea, although I'm thinking it's going to cause her a lifetime of grief. No one else knows how to spell it or pronounce it. But she is amazing. I have no idea how so much noise and crap can come out of something so small and cute. You should come round some time and see her.'

'Thanks. Sounds like a blast.'

'It is, it really is, anyway I'm off home for my tea.'

My stomach rumbled appreciatively. I couldn't remember the last time I'd eaten. 'Enjoy,' I said grimly, and then thumbed through my mobile to find the number of my local takeaway. Once the security light had clicked off it was pitch dark on the driveway of Kate Davies' house, a dense stand of trees cutting out the sliver of moonlight. Despite being a country girl I wouldn't want to live so far from anywhere with just an ageing spaniel and an Aga for company most of the time.

I stopped off in town at the Chinese in the High Street to pick up the takeaway and remembered all the neatly labelled boxes in Laura Lamb's freezer. Maybe I should start batch cooking so I had something nutritious and wholesome to come home to. And then thought, who was I kidding? Even my day off had been spent in the bloody office. The smell of the food made my mouth water. In under ten minutes I'd be home, shoes off, TV on.

As I got back to my car, I noticed a group of men across the road standing outside the pub, huddled under an outside light, smoking and laughing and deep in conversation, their breath and vaping kicking out great plumes of steam in the night air. It took me seconds to realise that one of the men was Jimmy and a nanosecond more for him to turn and spot me. Inwardly I groaned. He was the last person I wanted to see or talk to.

I made up my mind to pretend not to have seen him but he was across the road in seconds.

'Well, well, well, look who it is. My favourite sister-in-law. Stalking me, are you?' he said with a grin. He was post-work, done up for a mid-week evening out with the boys. He was tall and broad shouldered, dressed in a tour tee shirt under a leather jacket over skinny jeans and boots. If you didn't know him you'd think Jimmy was good looking. His hair was still damp. He smelt of aftershave and soap.

'Want to join us?' he said, nodding towards the gaggle of men gathered like moths around the light. He leaned in a little closer. His breath smelt of beer and something sickly sweet from vaping. 'Just don't mention that you're a copper though, will you? It tends to put people off. What do you reckon?'

I held up my takeaway bag. 'Thanks but I've got a better offer. Jimmy-'

He shook his head. 'Bit sad if you ask me, you want me to come round later on and warm your bed up for you? I've still got that bottle of wine.' He grinned.

I leaned in towards him, trying to swallow the compulsion to punch that stupid grin right off his arrogant face. I hated the way he made me feel. I hated the way he treated women in general, and my sister in particular.

'So what do you say?' he purred, taking my moving closer as some sort of invitation. Across the road the men started whooping.

'Fuck off, Jimmy,' I said quietly.

I climbed into my car and stood the takeaway in the footwell as he sauntered across the road. Seeing him, talking to him reminded me that I needed to ring Kathy when I got home. The thought of ringing Kathy made the hunger fade.

Chapter Eleven
Tied

He had a plan. The truth was that he liked to have a plan, he always had a plan, and there was his methodology. He had worked it out over time, problem solving as he went. In some ways it was getting smoother and more accomplished with every one – a mixed blessing because part of the rush was the possibility of things not working out quite as he had imagined – but he was worried about the growing temptation to be reckless. He had been reckless before and look where it had got him, and of course he had to find the right one, and then he liked to find a place, the right place.

Whatever he had been in the past, he was much more careful now and had learned caution, and a degree of patience and preparedness - and then when the opportunity arose, he would be ready, except this time he wasn't sure he could wait so long. That part of him, the insistent voice, that ache wanted to take another one. Soon. And come on, he had done it so often now that he could do it with one hand tied behind his back. Reckless no. Opportunist, yes – yes, he could be that. Opportunist, that was the word – after all he had already found the place.

He closed his eyes and for an instant could feel that rush, the sensation of the pulse under his fingertips, the warmth of their skin, the struggle, and then the moment when the spark went out in their eyes, and there was that precious almost overwhelming moment of peace for both of them.

*

Linda Heath lifted the bags into the back of the truck. One, two. She made a point of not letting the strain of the lift show on her face. The police officer who they'd left watching the place smiled at her. She smiled back and went back inside.

*

Kathy had been talking for almost three quarters of an hour non-stop. I'd put the phone on loudspeaker and propped it up on the kitchen table while I unpacked the takeaway, because the truth was, I hadn't eaten all day and even if my appetite had upped and died, I was still running on fumes.

She told me all the things she had told me before, and then she told me them again, all about the pregnant woman, about her turning up on the doorstep, and how since Jimmy had started to work away from home more how she realised what a shit he was. I said nothing. I already knew what a shit he was.

'He says that the money with this new contractor is really good but me and the kids aren't seeing any of it. And every day he's away I keep wondering who the hell he is shagging now.'

I made supportive noises between mouthfuls of crispy spiced beef and special fried rice. In spite of everything it tasted fabulous. I wish I'd bought a spring roll now, or maybe some noodles. 'I didn't know that Jimmy had got a new job,' I said, conversationally. I was thinking about Laura Lamb and wondering where her car was and who she had been car-sharing with.

'He hasn't, well not really. He's been with this company on and off for a while. Most of the work used to be local but then they got this contract and now he goes all over the country. Mostly short contracts on new builds. He did it a few times when you were living here – he went with his boss on the first few. You must remember, him going away?' She managed to make it sound like an accusation, as if I should have known where Jimmy was working.' That's where he met the latest one. She's all over Facebook with him. Selfies of them all loved up. Her page is set to public, stupid bitch, he's tagged in pictures and everything,' she said and then said thoughtfully. 'Or maybe she knows what she's up to and just wants me to look.'

And then I said out loud the thing I had been thinking for the last three quarters of an hour. 'Kathy, for God's sake go and see your solicitor and get away from him, don't just keep letting it drag on and on. You know this isn't the first time and we both know it won't be the last. Jimmy's never going to change. The man's a dog. If it was me, I'd have been gone years ago.'

I blame it on the tiredness. But we both knew it was the truth. The silence was deafening. And then she said, 'It's easy for you to say - what about the kids? They idolise him.' Kathy made it sound like it was all my fault.

'Only because you make them think he's some kind of saint. He's hardly ever there, truth is he's always letting you and them down. How many times have you arranged something and he hasn't shown up? What sort of role model is it when his pregnant girlfriend pitches up on the doorstep? What does that teach them about relationships and respect? I don't know what else it is you need to know, Kathy? What else is there, what other proof that you're-' I stopped, waited.

I could hear her breathing hard. I wondered if she was going to argue, to stick up for him, defend him or would she just hang up on me, and how bad would I feel if she did?

I wondered if she was going to tell me that I didn't understand, how could I? I hadn't had a relationship that lasted more than a couple of years. And she was right.

After a few more seconds she said, 'I keep thinking that I shouldn't give up on him, Mel. On us. You know? Like somehow if I was a better wife or more patient or I don't know, maybe if I was better in bed or a better cook or the kids were quieter or something, that it would all come right. But it won't, will it?'

I wished I was there with her so I could give her a hug; we both suffered from a stubborn *I can sort this out and make it right* streak. It was too painful to admit that there were just some things that you couldn't fix, however hard you tried. I thought about Laura Lamb and her newly heeled shoes and her summer clothes in their neat zipped up storage bags.

There was a long silence. And then I said. 'This isn't about you, Kathy. It isn't your fault. None of it is your fault. It never has been. This isn't about something you did or didn't do – it's about Jimmy – pure and simple - the man is a shit.' I should shut up but I couldn't. 'You need to think about yourself, for once – you and the kids, you all deserve so much better than this, so much better than him.'

'I want to talk to him,' she said. 'I keep thinking I shouldn't give up, that I should give it one more go. Maybe if I could just talk to him, you know, really talk to him -- maybe if I could explain.'

I felt a great knot of frustration. 'Explain what?' I snapped. 'You've got nothing to explain, Kathy. He's the one who should be trying to explain things to you. He's the one-' The words dried in my mouth. He was the one I had slept with.

'Trust me,' I managed finally. 'You don't owe Jimmy any kind of explanation.'

*

He slicked back his hair and checked his reflection, once, twice in the window - It would be foolish to rush it, wouldn't it? Especially as the police were all over the place trying to find out what happened to the last one. Foolish to act too soon, although the thing that ached was gnawing at him, nagging, a constant reminder of what he wanted, what he needed. And yes, of course he had to be careful, but wouldn't it be nice to get one over on them, slip under their radar, in and out and clean away. Like a game. He grinned. He knew he was brighter. Although he didn't want to play too close to home in case this time he wasn't so lucky, of course he didn't, but he'd done it enough times to know the best ways, the cleanest ways. He was clever enough to do it and not get caught. Wasn't he?

Once upon a time he had kept lists and notes and little mementoes but they had had to go, after all he was so careful, so very, very careful with everything else that might incriminate him, a list or an earring was as good as a confession. He had burned them, and binned them and mourned their loss. Such a record should have been kept, should have been treasured, not destroyed.

Chapter Twelve
Car share

Overnight, patrol officers had found Laura Lamb's blue Citroen parked up on a piece of waste ground alongside an isolated country pub on the A10. As I drove out to see it, the news on the local radio told me that there were unconfirmed reports that a body found on Isaac's Fen was that of missing office administrator, Laura Lamb, aged twenty-six, from King's Lynn. It was the first time I'd heard the two incidents linked and wished I could have been the one to tell Kate Davies, but I knew a uniformed officer had been sent out to let her know the news. News travels fast, bad news travels fastest of all.

Mike Carlton was already at the Swan and Cygnet when I pulled into the car park and was busy talking to one of the uniformed officers. Tape cordoned off a great swathe of the grass that led down to the river's edge and the area under the road bridge. He lifted a hand in greeting as I climbed out of the car and headed over to meet me.

It was bitterly cold and foggy, a classic fenland morning where the all-pervading damp seems to seep slowly into your bones. In the good old days fen dwellers had taken laudanum – a combination of opium and alcohol - to get them through the long cold winters, and there were days when I could see why it might be a good idea.

The cold sucked my breath away as I stepped out of the car. I pulled on a warm coat and buttoned it to the neck before pulling on my gloves.

Mike looked as rough as I felt. Two hours on the phone to Kathy and a shed load of guilt that alternated with blind fury was not a great recipe for a good night's sleep however tired you are.

'Baby's teething,' Mike said, as he reached me, as if he had read my mind.

I laughed. 'I thought you said she was asleep?'

'Apparently she was just gathering strength for the next onslaught. What's your excuse?'

'I didn't know I needed one. Do I look that bad?'

He raised an eyebrow and said nothing. I let him off the hook. 'So what have we got?'

The main road crossed a tributary to the Great Ouse, and on a promontory of land between the two rivers and the road was a pub that once upon a time had serviced a ferry from one side of the Ouse to the other. Under the sheltered area created by the relatively new road bridge were a number of cars, one of which was now taped off and being watched by a local constable awaiting forensics and a low loader to show up.

I glanced around as we made our way towards the vehicle. 'How the hell did they find it so fast?'

'Laura's phone. We got the details through late last night and it triangulated to this car park. Uniform came over to take a shufty, and here we are.'

I looked up at him. 'Her phone was in her car?'

'No, it was tucked under the car on the driver's side. The car's still locked,' he said. 'We're waiting for SOCO to pitch up.'

'So did she drop it? Kate Davies said Laura called her on her mobile so she had it with her-'

Mike nodded. 'Well either Laura dropped it, or our man put it there.'

I looked at the car. 'Which would bring us straight to it?'

Mike shrugged. 'Maybe he didn't think she would be found so quickly? Or he wanted us to find it? Or he goes to grab her and she drops her phone – who knows.'

'If I were him I'd have thrown it in the river.'

'The good news is you aren't him.'

'So what is this place?'

'An impromptu park and ride,' said Mike. 'It's reasonably secure this close to the pub, although it's not their car park. People park up here and then car share, most of them according to the landlord, are travelling into Ely or Cambridge or the Science Park at Waterbeach. He reckons there are up to twenty cars parked here at any one time during the week and a few over the weekend. He can't stop them because, at least technically, this piece of land doesn't belong to him, and under the bridge here it's not much use for anything else.'

'So did Laura leave her car here regularly or do we think this is just a dump site for the vehicle?' I asked, looking around at the river and the broad landscaped driveway that led into the official parking area. There was no clear view of the make-shift car park from the road or from the pub. 'Someone would have to know this was here. Same with the trees on Isaac's farm. Are we talking local knowledge again?'

Mike's gaze followed mine. 'Maybe. No one checks on who parks vehicles here, but the landlord seems to think he'd seen her car parked here before. And he recognised her from the photo. He said he's certain that she used to come in after work and eat in the pub in the summer, with a couple of other girls, possibly a man or group of people. Not very hot on detail but he definitely thought he had seen her before, and more than once.'

My expression must have been indicating another question because Mike pointed to a sign on the side of the bridge that read, 'Early bird specials, home-cooked meals, all your favourites along with healthy options and no washing-up.'

I snorted. 'Why haven't I been here before?'

'The landlord says several of the car poolers come in early doors, straight from work, have a drink and eat here before going home. They flyer the cars with menus.'

'Shrewd move, and so Laura ate here?'

I thought about all those carefully packaged single suppers in her freezer.

Mike nodded. 'Yeah, but not recently. He reckons it was more of a summer thing. They've got a big conservatory at the back, tables on the river bank – he said she was here maybe once a week during the good weather.'

I nodded. 'Winter nights you'd want to get home. These roads are grim if it's icy.' But it made me consider her car pool driver. I'd assumed it was a man, but maybe it was another woman, and they shared the driving and had supper before heading their separate ways. 'We need to find out who she is car sharing with.'

'Agreed but it might be more than one person-' Mike pulled out his phone. 'It comes up in any search you do for the pub.'

I took it and peered at the screen. It was an app for a car-pooling website.

'You just create a profile, post where you want to go, if you're offering to drive or want a lift, whether it's regular or a one off.' Mike took the phone back and scrolled down. 'Here we go. The Swan and Cygnet.' He handed it back to me. 'It comes up straight away as an unofficial parking place with no charges: *"tucked away in a quiet location off then A10 making it ideal for the Cambridge commuter".*'

I glanced at the screen and read. '*"Well lit and central, although not officially sanctioned you have the added bonus of nipping in for a pie and pint after work."* Okay, so not so secret after all. We need to see if Laura was using the app, and also can you keep one of your officers on site to have a word with other car sharers?'

'Already on it.'

I glanced around the waste ground, which mostly comprised of well compacted soil and scrubby grass, back towards the pub. Tucked in amongst the trees it looked an inviting destination, I could smell the scent of wood smoke from the chimney, trapped by the fog.

'Landlord said he could do us a breakfast if any of the lads wanted anything.'

'Nice idea, but we need to track down the person giving Laura a lift, and find out what went on on Monday evening. Maybe she was dropped off here as usual, or maybe the driver's our guy and he never dropped her off here at all, but just disposed of the phone here, or maybe our killer dumped her car here. Any CCTV?'

Mike shook his head. 'Nothing that covers this area but he's got good coverage in the pub.'

'Okay. Do you think he'll do me a take-out bacon sandwich?'

'You can always ask. I've already arranged for the CCTV to be picked up so we can see if Laura was in here on Monday evening.'

I nodded. 'And how far does it go back?'

'He reckons he's got a week's worth. '

As we spoke the SOCO van rolled into the car park followed by a low loader.

I let my gaze follow the route in, and the position of Laura's car. You had to come off the main road, and then drive off onto the grass and then down an incline towards the river to get to the car share car park, which meant it wasn't on any sight lines from the main road, the driveway or the pub that I could see. If someone had abducted Laura from the car park, unless you were in the immediate vicinity, no one would have seen it or heard her.

'Can we assume she drove here on Monday morning and went in to work from here? She rang her friend Kate from the office on Monday evening.'

Mike nodded. 'And was waiting for her lift home at what time?'

'Kate Davies said it was about twenty past five. Laura usually leaves work at five but something she said made Kate think her lift was late. We need to know if she was dropped off back here.' I turned around taking in the details of the landscape. Behind us the SOCOs were unloading gear and talking in subdued voices.

'And does her lift drive in or just drop her up there at the top on the road where you pull in for the pub? I'm heading in to Cambridge to interview the people she works with. Maybe someone there will know who she shares with,' I said.

'So have any of you been messing with my crime scene?' said a voice from behind us.

I turned to see a tall broad shouldered man zipping up a white Tyvek suit as he crossed the grass towards us.

Mike grinned. 'As if – DS Mel Daley, this is Tommy Bell.'

I nodded. 'Pleased to meet you.' I said. I knew from the gloves and his expression that he wouldn't be shaking hands.

'Okay, so can you tell me what we've got and how many of you buggers have traipsed in and out of the area?'

Mike laughed. 'Uniform have put the cordon up and as far as I'm aware it's just the officers who found the vehicle and us.'

The man in the white suit peered over his glasses. 'And have you touched anything or approached the vehicle?'

'We wouldn't dare, although uniform have informed us that our vic's mobile phone is on the driver's side on the grass and you can imagine just how quickly we need to get our hands on that.'

Tommy Bell let out a long sigh.

I turned away, grinning. 'See you later.'

'When I've finished up here I'm off to the King's Lynn branch of the company. I'm assuming I'll have less trouble parking. Shall we see about some sandwiches?'

Ten minutes later I was making my way back to the car with a take-out bacon buttie and a carton of tea.

Never mind parking, finding KSPL Solutions office was a total bloody nightmare. En route I rang the local force as a courtesy to let them know what I was up to and then picked my way through a maze of back streets before managing to squeeze my car into the last space in the tiny courtyard behind the company's offices. I'd barely turned off the engine when an officious looking woman in a smart suit hurried out from behind plate glass doors and came over to where I was climbing out of the car.

'You can't park there,' she snapped. 'That space is for-'

I pulled out my warrant card and showed her.

'Detective Sergeant Daley,' I said.

She wasn't impressed. 'If it is about that bloody parking ticket, isn't there anything more important you could be looking into?'

I stepped in closer, expression impassive, tone even. 'I'm investigating a serious incident involving one of your colleagues,' I said in a low even voice. 'If I could have your name? I'd like to speak to whoever is in charge.'

She stared at me, her jaw dropping. 'What? Who?'

'Perhaps we could go inside?' I said.

She nodded, curiosity plain on her face, and asked me to wait while she found Mrs Kingsley.

I took a seat and checked my phone. Kathy had sent me a link to a Facebook page presumably featuring Jimmy's latest conquest. This really wasn't the time. I slipped my phone back into my bag just as a statuesque blonde strode across the foyer to meet me. From a distance she looked to be in her mid to late forties, close up I added at least ten years, possibly more. She was immaculately dressed, and perfectly preserved with beautifully capped teeth and some very expensive facial work.

'Charlotte Kingsley,' she said, extending a manicured hand. 'I'm Laura's boss. I'm-' She stopped. 'I'm assuming this is about Laura going missing?' She glanced across to the empty reception desk. 'Someone rang – a friend?'

'I'm terribly sorry to have to inform you,' I said. 'But Ms Lamb is dead.'

She stared at me. 'Laura?' she said. 'Oh my God.' Her voice dropped to something barely above a whisper and her eyes filled with tears. 'Oh no. I'm, I'm so sorry.

Forgive me but this is such a terrible shock. I don't know what to say. We're all very fond of Laura. I'm one of the senior partners here. God, that's taken my breath away.'

She took a moment, swallowed hard and then said. 'If you'd like to come into my office.' She looked at me. 'Are you sure that it's Laura? I mean, it's very hard to grasp. Are you certain?'

I nodded. 'I'm afraid so, Ms Kingsley. I'm very sorry.'

'What an awful job for you. Here-' She opened the door into her office.

'How did it happen? She always seemed so well. Was it an accident – a car accident?'

'We believe that Laura was murdered.'

I let the words settle and sink in.

Charlotte Kingsley's face paled. 'Laura? Are you sure? I can't believe- She is the nicest person. Why would anyone want to hurt Laura?'

She sat down heavily at her desk and then looked up at me. 'I'm so sorry, I don't know what to say.'

'I realise this must be upsetting for you, but I'd like to ask you a few questions, if you don't mind?' I took out my notebook.

Mrs Kingsley nodded and waved me into one of the chairs. 'Yes, of course, if I can help in any way.'

'We're trying to trace Laura's movements, where she was, who she was with.'

'I'm so sorry,' she said, opening a drawer and pulling out a tissue. 'God, this is so awful. I can't believe it.'

Charlotte Kingsley's office was comfortable, less corporate than I'd expected with a maroon shabby chic sofa along one wall and a desk and leather swivel chair opposite it. There were books filling the third wall and in the fourth were French windows opening out into an internal light-well full of plants.

'They're very beautiful,' I said, as she took a moment or two to compose herself, indicating the indoor garden.

Charlotte nodded. 'My hobby,' she said. 'Laura-' she stopped and bit her lip. 'Gosh, this is awful. She bought

130

me several things to grow out there. She said she missed having a garden. She has a flat. Nigel and I went to her house warming, a nice place, down by the river.'

'You were close?'

'Yes. We were friends with her parents. Oh my God, how is Douglas taking it? And Claire? They must be completely devastated, devastated.'

'Officers have already spoken to them,' I said. 'Am I right in thinking Claire is Laura's stepmother?'

'Yes, but she is super. A lovely woman. They got together after Laura's mother died. I was really pleased for Douglas, and for Laura and Henry, her brother, of course. The children both seem very fond of Claire.'

I made a note that I needed to talk to Laura's brother.

'How long has Laura worked for you?'

Charlotte considered the question and then said. 'She came here for work experience while she was still at school. We did it as a favour to Douglas really, but it didn't take us long to realise what a find, what a treasure, she is – I mean was. Such an eye for detail, and wonderful at problem solving, visualising, just really naturally talented, and she was always very happy to do anything she was asked. When she left school she worked for us in the holidays, and then once she had finished her degree we offered her a job, and she began working here full time. We're basically a family business, my husband, and myself, and quite a tight knit team even at the manufacturing end of things. I'm the engineer, or rather I was, and Nigel, my husband, handles the sales and marketing side of the business.'

'And Laura?'

'She works –' Charlotte stopped, took a breath, and corrected herself. 'She worked in our compliance team. She'd – she'd got this amazing eye for detail, every i dotted, every t crossed. We design and develop specialist gauges and the like, they're very highly specialised, highly engineered, most often one offs and custom orders, almost all bespoke actually these days. We work

131

with all sorts of companies, medical, biological, all manner of things, developing specialist products for different processes and climatic conditions. Something that works in sub-Saharan Africa won't necessarily be as efficient or accurate in the Antarctic. It doesn't sound very interesting, does it? But it is actually, it's totally fascinating. We sell our products all over the world – you wouldn't believe the red tape and the regulations and tolerances you have to work through and Laura was the one who, for the most part, sorted all that out. She is going to be a very hard act to follow.' Charlotte sniffed. 'God, it's so hard to take in.'

I nodded. 'And was she here on Monday?'

Charlotte nodded. 'I think so. I mean I'm almost certain she was. I lose track of days. I knew she had got a few days off booked this week, but I was in Paris for the weekend with my daughter. I remember having a conversation about her taking the whole of the week but she said she had something she needed to do. We came back on Monday so I wasn't in the office until Tuesday morning. Nigel said someone had rung on Tuesday to see if we knew where Laura was. He would probably know more. But I'm more or less certain she was here on Monday. We all sign in and out electronically so it'll be on the computer. You need a pass to open the front door. I'll get Carla to check the log.'

'And you weren't expecting her back this week?'

Charlotte frowned. 'To be entirely honest I wouldn't know without checking. I can ask Roger. He's head of our compliance team. Laura's boss. He's upstairs in the office. I deal more with the technical side of the business.'

In my bag my phone pinged to announce an incoming text. 'I'm sorry,' I said, reaching down to turn it to silent. 'Do you have an HR department?'

'Yes, it's based in our King's Lynn factory, but Laura was more likely to have arranged time off with Roger. Would you like to see Laura's office?'

'Please and I'd also like to speak to Roger if that is

possible.'

'Yes, of course. I'll take you up.'

'One more thing, Laura was part of a car sharing scheme. Do you happen to know who she car shared with? Was it someone from here?'

Charlotte frowned. 'No, I'm afraid I don't. I don't even think I knew that was what she was doing. I always assumed she came in by train.'

Which was when the door opened.

A tall distinguished looking man with dark hair greying at the temples stepped into the office. He was wearing a suit jacket over jeans and a black tee shirt. 'Carla told me the police are here.' He stopped mid-stride and stared at me.

'Nigel, this is Detective Sergeant Daley. She's here because,' her voice faltered. Nigel stared at her blankly. 'Oh my God, Carla didn't say anything to you, did she? Laura's dead Nigel, someone's killed her.'

Nigel Kingsley took a breath as if to speak and as his brain processed the information his knees buckled and he grabbed onto the desk. 'That's not possible. What do you mean killed?' he said, addressing the question to me. The intensity of the emotion in his voice took me by surprise. 'You have to have made a mistake.'

'I'm very sorry, sir, but we have reason to believe that Laura was murdered.'

Nigel stared at me. 'Oh my God,' he muttered, eyes filling with tears. 'No, that can't be right.'

'You have to forgive us,' Charlotte Kingsley said hastily. 'We've known Laura since she was born and she had been working here with us since she was fifteen – we've watched her grow up. It's so awful. In a lot of ways Laura was like a daughter to us, wasn't she, Nigel?'

I glanced at Nigel Kingsley. 'Yes, yes, yes she was,' he said, his voice thready and emotional. 'And such a lovely girl. Help anyone; she's got such a big heart.'

'Were you here on Monday, Mr Kingsley?' I asked.

He nodded. 'Yes, I was in the office all day.'

'And Laura was here too?'

133

He nodded. 'Yes, yes she was.'

'We can place her here in the office until just after five, when she spoke to a friend on the phone. We're checking her phone records to confirm the location.' I said. 'We believe that she had organised a car share with someone and she had told her friend that her lift was late. So, I wondered if either of you know who she was sharing with? Had she ever mentioned anyone to you?'

The two of them glanced at each other. 'As I said, not me,' said Charlotte. 'I can't say that she ever mentioned it. Did she say anything to you, Nigel?'

Nigel Kingsley considered for a moment and then shook his head. 'I think she might have said something-' he paused as if trying to recall. 'And yes, I was here at five. I was probably still in my office at that time.'

'And did you see her leave on Monday evening?'

'None of the senior staff offices have external windows,' he said. 'They all open up into the light well. We can't see into the courtyard.'

'Have you any idea who might know who she was car sharing with? Any friends she has in the office that might be able to help? Colleagues?'

Charlotte and Nigel exchanged another glance. 'Not really,' said Charlotte. 'Laura was quite reserved, although I would say she got on with everyone, wouldn't you, Nigel?'

He nodded.

'She sometimes went to lunch with Norma Howlett. Norma handles the import and export side of things and then there's Simon, he's our finance director – and Roger of course, he might know more,' Charlotte continued.

'Let me take you upstairs,' said Nigel. 'I'll show you Laura's work area and introduce you to Roger Falkes. He's going to be absolutely devastated. He always said that Laura would be his natural successor - a safe pair of hands.'

'He's retiring?'

Nigel shook his head. 'Hopefully not yet, but it was

his joke, our joke actually, I mean he's not going for a few years, but she would have been the natural choice – if she was still working here, obviously,' he added.

'Was Laura thinking of leaving?'

'Not that I know of, I really hoped that she would stay with us. I've always thought she was very happy here, but of course you never know, do you? Things change.'

Things change; I made a mental note. What things?

The lift doors opened and Nigel stepped aside to let me go first. I thanked him.

'Such a terrible thing,' he murmured. 'Terrible.'

I nodded. He rubbed his chin, and was blinking hard to hold back more tears. 'I might need a minute,' he said, selecting the first floor button on the panel. 'I'm so sorry. I think it might be the shock.'

I watched him, as he tidied his jacket and felt in his pocket for a handkerchief. Nigel Kingsley was classically good looking, probably in his mid to late fifties, but age had been kind, carving out a slightly more rugged weather-beaten version of his leading man good looks over high cheek bones. Laughter lines accentuated brown eyes and the grey hair at his temples looked as if it was sprayed on. He and Charlotte made a handsome couple.

We stepped out of the lift into a large well-lit open plan office that contained maybe half a dozen people, although our arrival was noted and seemed to quell any conversation. Each work station was cocooned by rounded blonde wood panels that gave the individual areas some sense of privacy and personal space. People stared at us as I made my way over to Laura's desk - like I said, bad news travels fastest of all.

Laura's pod was close to one of the windows with a view out over a public park beyond. Her desk more or less filled the space: there was a phone, a couple of small filing cabinets, an artificial fern, and other than a computer and keyboard the desk top was as spotless and tidy as her flat. On a pin board on the pod wall were a few postcards, a picture of two hairy dogs and an invitation to join Simon and Amelia for drinks after work to celebrate their engagement. Her desk drawers contained all the detritus of office life, along with two breakfast bars, a box of tissues and very little else.

Nigel Kingsley introduced me to Roger Falkes, Laura's boss, who found me a spare office to talk to the staff in. 'I can't believe it, I really can't,' Roger said over and over again as he opened the door. He was also close to tears.

'I'd like to arrange to have Laura's computer brought in, along with her personal effects-' I said to Nigel.

He nodded. 'Yes, of course.'

Roger glanced across at Nigel. 'You're happy with that?'

Nigel Kingsley hesitated, then said, 'Not a problem. Roger, can give you her login details for her machine but I'm afraid we can't give you the login for the wider company network. You'll understand that there is sensitive information regarding the business-' He paused. 'But if there is anything you need and we can help, we will.'

'That will be fine, and if we need anything else we'll contact you. I'd like to have a chat with your staff although I may have to ask for them to make a formal statement at a later date.'

Nigel Kingsley nodded. 'Yes, that's fine,' he said, and then headed back downstairs.

They found me coffee and then one by one the employees on Laura's floor filed in. I could have delegated the interviews but I still really had no feel for what Laura was like, no sense of her, and it helped if I could understand what she did, what she thought, where she was likely to go, how she was likely to react, who she mixed with, what other people thought of her and everything in between.

A couple of hours later and what I had learned was that people who came to work with the Kingsleys tended to stay. Other than Laura no one on the work force was under thirty-five and most were considerably older, even the sales team were in their late forties. Here, older people were apparently valued for their knowledge and skills and expertise. It was a niche industry.

And Laura? Three interviews in and I could have written the responses myself. Everyone said the same things. She was lovely, empathic, warm hearted, efficient, mostly kept herself to herself, wasn't a gossip, was quite shy, but would help anyone with anything, and had a head for details. *Still waters*, was about the most critical thing anyone said about her. Even the people she occasionally went to lunch with couldn't shed any real light on her. The thing that struck me most was one woman who observed that even though Laura always appeared conversational she always asked questions about the people she was talking to, but gave very little away about herself. And no one had any idea who her lift share was, although they had all been aware that that was the way she got into work on the days she worked in Cambridge. Every day? They had no idea.

Charlotte Kingsley's comment stuck with me though, which was why was it that Laura didn't come in on the train? Her flat was probably no more than ten minutes' walk from King's Lynn station and around the same once she got to Cambridge Station. Certainly quicker than driving to the park and ride and then coming in by car. Why drive at all? Why car share? Why bother when she could have taken the train?

Having drawn a blank with her colleagues I went to check if the company had CCTV, the cameras in the foyer suggested they had but you could never be sure that the cameras weren't dummies.

I knocked on Nigel Kingsley's first floor office door to ask if I could view the film of Monday evening. His office was a mirror of that of his wife's, but his resembled a gentleman's club, even down to the leather chairs and matching decanters on an oversized sideboard.

'Mr Kingsley?'

He looked up face still ashen, still looking distraught, and waved me in.

'Please call me Nigel, Detective Sergeant. I hope everyone has been helpful?'

'Yes, thank you,' I smiled noncommittally. 'I'd like to view the CCTV for Monday evening if possible.'

Nigel hesitated for a second or two and then said, 'Yes, yes of course. May I ask what you're looking for exactly?'

'We know that Laura was here until at least five-twenty pm and that she was waiting for a lift. She implied to her friend that the lift was running late. Who would have been on the front desk?'

Nigel frowned. 'Most likely no one. Carla leaves at four-thirty. There's no one on reception after that. We log ourselves in and out with passes. Anyone visiting would have to ring the intercom to be let in. The outer door opening is triggered by a pass or a manual override from behind the desk. If I'm the last out I lock up, but Roger and Charlotte have keys too.'

'And on Monday, did you lock up?'

Nigel considered for a few moments. 'No, I don't think so, I think it was most probably Roger.'

'Okay, so if there was no one around Laura would have been able to just let herself out?'

Nigel nodded. 'As long as the building hadn't been locked up for the night. Yes, she would just press the button on the reception desk.'

'Whoever it was she was meeting may have rung or text her to let her know they were going to be late, but as yet we haven't secured her phone records, so I'm hoping that whoever it is might be on your CCTV.'

'You mean you think he or she might have come into the building?'

'That's a possibility, or they may have driven in to your courtyard. At the very least we'll be able to see exactly what time Laura left. We'll be canvassing the businesses in the immediate vicinity for footage, and we've got traffic cams. I'm pretty certain that someone's CCTV will have something.'

Nigel Kingsley took a breath and then picked up a pen from the desk and started to run it through his fingers, end over end. You didn't have to be any kind of psychologist to see he was wrestling with something. I waited. The air in the office felt very still.

'There is something that you need to know. About Laura's car share,' he said.

I nodded and waited some more.

He set the pen back down on the desk and looked up at me. 'The thing is, that was me.'

*

On the A10, on the stretch that passed the first ungated roadway to Isaac's farm, a silver truck heading from Denham Market to Ely slowed and indicated to take the concrete road that led up to the farm buildings and the pumping station. When the driver spotted the police car blocking the entrance he held up a hand in apparent apology, reversed out, did a U-turn and headed back the way he came. The officer on duty made a note of the registration. A while later the same truck rolled into the gateway on the far side of the farm on the Longbank Road, slowed up and stopped at the police cordon. The police officer stepped up to the driver's side.

The driver wound down his window. 'I've come to take a look at the pump,' he said. 'I just rang Mr Heath. He knows that we're coming.'

The officer made a note of the registration and waved him through, then radioed the farm to let them know there was a vehicle on its way. Ten minutes or so later an officer up at the farmyard called back to ask if the man on the gate was pulling his leg; there had been no sign of a truck.

'Probably gone straight down to the pumping station,' said the gateman.

'Probably,' said the officer, who was up at the farm.

He was cold. It had barely seemed to have got light all day and the damp chill from the fens was soaking into his bones. 'Has anyone searched the pumping station, d'ya know?'

The first man sniffed. 'Don't know. Not my call. Plenty enough to do without that.'

The officer at the farm snorted. 'All right for some, you weren't down wind of them when they were pumping out the bloody cesspit.'

*

In Cambridge Nigel Kingsley shifted miserably in his office chair. For a moment or two I wondered if he would clam up and ask for his solicitor, instead he said, 'This is very hard for me to admit. It's a delicate situation if I'm honest, but I don't want you to waste your time looking for someone who doesn't exist, when it could more usefully be spent trying to track down whoever it was who-' he stumbled over the words, '- who killed Laura.'

I pulled out a chair and sat down. 'Okay, Mr Kingsley, let's start from the beginning.' I pulled out my phone. 'Would you mind if I recorded this?'

He hesitated for a split second and then said, 'Yes of course, please do.'

I set the phone up on the desk between us, and gave the date, my name, location and Nigel Kingsley's name then began,'So, Mr Kingsley, you were Laura's car share?'

'Yes. Yes, I was.' He peered at the little red light on my phone.

'And how did that come about? Did you always give Laura a lift?'

Nigel nodded. 'More often than not. It started about a year ago, maybe eighteen months. It's hard to remember exactly when now. We had had a few rail strikes, problems on the line, signals – you know the kind of thing, and she had a problem getting in to work, so she told me she was looking into car sharing. We'd got several important orders in train and there was a limit to what Laura could do from home. She didn't really like driving very much. Hated the Milton roundabout - anyway she started coming in with a woman she knew through friends and then this woman was moved by her company-' Nigel Kingsley stopped. 'You don't need to hear all this, do you? When Laura said she was going to register on a car share website I was concerned, I mean you have no idea who these people are, do you? So I suggested that I could give her a lift in instead. It felt safer.'

'So did you take her home?'

'No, no, I dropped her off at a pub on the A10, the Swan and Cygnet.'

I nodded. 'And where do you live, Mr Kingsley?'

'Waterbeach,' he said, reddening slightly.

'That is quite some way from where Laura leaves her car?'

His colour deepened. 'Yes, I know.'

'What, about, twenty miles or so, another half an hour?' I pressed.

He nodded. 'About that, yes. Laura didn't like driving in the dark,' he said. 'And those fen roads can be – well you know what they're like. They're not great at night. And she wasn't a very confident driver.'

'So did you and your wife both drive Laura back to her car? I mean when I mentioned the car share earlier-'

'No, no, it was only me,' he said hastily. 'Charlotte didn't know about it. *Doesn't know about it.* She usually comes in at about ten. She often takes the train home and is gone by half past three at the latest unless there is something pressing. It's a hangover from the days when our girls were small.'

'You have daughters?'

'That's right, two, Cassandra and Eleanor. Cassie just turned eighteen and Elly is fifteen.'

I nodded. 'And you say your wife didn't know about the arrangement you had with Laura?'

Nigel Kingsley let out a long breath and shook his

head miserably. 'No, no she didn't, but I suppose she will have to know now, won't she?' He looked up at me. His expression held an appeal.

'I'm afraid I can't promise that she won't find out, or that I won't have to discuss it with her,' I said.

He nodded. 'I appreciate your candour, Sergeant. I suppose I should have told her myself really.'

'Can I ask you what exactly your relationship was with Laura, Mr Kingsley?'

He looked at me, his gaze wary and guarded. I was waiting for him to jump ship and ask for his solicitor, but instead he took another deep breath and began to play with his pen again. 'I can't believe Laura is dead and obviously I would prefer it if at all possible that my wife didn't find out now, after the fact. There is no point in hurting anyone, is there? But I do take what you're saying-'

I waited and said nothing. From beyond the office door I could hear a low babble of voices.

Nigel Kingsley sighed and after a second or two more said, 'We were seeing each other,' he mumbled. 'Laura and I – we were close.'

'You were having an affair with Laura Lamb?' I said.

His eyes flared briefly, and then he nodded. 'I suppose other people might see it as that and yes, before you ask, we were lovers – but that makes it all sound so sordid, which believe me, it truly wasn't. What Laura and I had was special. Very special. I love her. Loved her,' he corrected himself, breath catching. 'God, this is awful. How the hell can she be gone? We had planned a whole life together-' His voice cracked and finally broke, and the tears he had been holding back since I broke the news about Laura ran unchecked down his face.

'I don't know what I'm going to do now. I really don't. I truly loved her. I know how that sounds, and how ridiculous, but that doesn't make it any less true.' He blew his nose, the sobs getting louder.

I waited, gradually the sobbing abated and he wiped his face. 'I'm so sorry,' he said. 'But I feel like my whole world has fallen apart.'

'Does your wife know about your relationship with Laura?'

His eyes widened. 'No, of course not. I mean we were going to tell her at some point. We would have had to eventually. I was going to leave Charlotte and start a new life with Laura. Laura and I had talked about it several times. There isn't any good time to tell someone that sort of news, but Laura said that she wanted to wait until Cassandra, my oldest daughter, had finished her exams this summer. Laura said she didn't want to add to her stress. She was so mature, so understanding. It's a tricky time for them, you know A levels and all that. My marriage with Charlotte has been pretty much dead for years. I wanted to set her free so she could find someone to love too, find her own happiness. And then I fell in love with Laura and - oh my God.' He stifled another ragged miserable sob. 'What am I going to do without her?'

'And how long have you been having a relationship with Laura?'

He hesitated. 'I –' he looked down at the desk.

'Mr Kingsley, please.'

'Since she left university and came to work for us full time. I think to be honest we had both been attracted to each other before then, but I wanted to wait until she was a little bit older. Able to make a proper decision. I mean you can see how it might look, can't you? Anyway we went away to a conference. Roger was supposed to have gone but he'd been ill so Charlotte suggested that Laura went instead. It would be good experience for her. To be honest we both thought it was fate, like it was meant to be–' he paused and looked at me imploringly. 'I loved her. I really did. You have to believe me.'

'It's not for me to pass judgement, Mr Kingsley. I'm just trying to find out what happened to her.'

'Of course, and I can't see how our relationship is relevant to any of this,' he said. 'Not really.'

I wondered if Nigel Kingsley had ever heard of the

143

concept of wilful blindness. I kept my expression neutral. 'Can you tell me about Monday evening?'

Nigel Kingsley looked relieved to be back on safer ground.

'There was nothing out of the ordinary. I was finishing off some paperwork in my office and hadn't realised the time. Laura came in and said that we ought to be going. She had things she needed to do at home and I'd got to pick my youngest daughter Eleanor up from a cello lesson in Ely. We went out to my car and I drove to the pub at Fen Creek where Laura parks her car.'

'And your car is parked here in the car park outside the office?'

He nodded. 'Yes, a Silver Mercedes at the end there by the wall. All the senior staff have their own allocated parking spaces.'

'And did anyone see you leaving?'

'I don't think so. Laura and I make a point of not leaving together. Most people leave at five. Roger sometimes stays behind but he's always in his office. I've never been one to think anything can be achieved by working all hours. I'm an early bird so most days I'm in the office by seven-thirty.'

Does that include the days when you picked Laura up?'

'Yes, I mean you're always dependent on the traffic but yes around that time.'

'So an early start for both of you?'

He nodded.

'And who else knew about your relationship with Laura?'

He looked up surprised. 'No one, I mean we were very careful, we were both very aware of how difficult it could make things if anyone found out. It was hard really being around her all day, wanting to be with her. You have to understand that she was a very, very lovely person. She felt terribly guilty about deceiving Charlotte.'

I nodded, but noticed that he hadn't added himself into the guilt.

'We were always very careful. No, nobody else knew.'

I doubted that was true. My guess was that someone knew or had their suspicions; someone always knew, and according to Nigel Kingsley they had been seeing each other since she left university – a long, long time to keep a secret - and in my experience those kind of things were almost impossible to keep hidden for long.

I wondered how the boyfriend Laura's friend Kate Davies had told me about felt about sharing her, let alone Charlotte Kingsley's feelings about her husband and their twenty-something protégée.

'How did Laura seem on Monday?' I asked. 'Was she worried about anything? Had anything happened that seemed out of the ordinary?'

Nigel Kingsley shook his head. 'No, quite the reverse; she was excited about spending the day with her friend, Kate. She was taking a few days off – she'd got quite a bit of holiday due. We'd hoped to get at least one day together, maybe two.' He sniffed back a fresh tranche of tears. 'Laura was involved in a lot of the planning for Kate's wedding. On the drive home we were talking about what sort of wedding we would have, and where we'd live. Laura was quite old fashioned about things like that but both of us wanted to get married. And have a family. She really wanted a family. We thought two – close together. We laughed about it, a boy and girl. She had even got names.' He swallowed down a sob.

I wondered, watching Nigel's expression, what Laura's father would make of one of his oldest friends marrying his only daughter.

'Did you drop her off on the road or did you drive down to where her car was parked on Monday night?'

Nigel appeared to be thinking. 'I've been trying to remember. I'm more or less certain that I pulled in off the road into the entrance of the pub driveway but no, I didn't take her down to the car.'

'Is that usual?'

'It depends, on Monday evening I was up against the clock. I needed to pick Eleanor up from her music lesson and was already a wee bit late. Sometimes Laura and I would go in and have a drink, mostly in the summer. Sometimes we'd have something to eat together-'

'When you say you were up against the clock?'

'The traffic coming out of Cambridge is always awful and as I said I'd got my daughter to pick up.'

'At what time?'

'Half past seven. Charlotte usually picks her up but she and my eldest daughter were in Paris for the weekend to celebrate Cassie's birthday, so it was down to me and I didn't want to be late. Elly can be quite the drama queen if she wants to.'

'And did you get there by seven thirty?'

Nigel pulled a face. 'I think I was a bit late, maybe ten minutes but not much more. Elly was waiting for me in the hall – rolling her eyes and complaining, you know what teenagers can be like.'

'And at the pub, did you see Laura get into her car?'

'I don't think so. You can't see the car park from the road unless you drive in, but I'm sure that I saw her going down the slope towards the car. I'm more or less certain of that.'

'But you didn't see her get into her car?'

He shook his head. 'No, as I said I was going to pick Eleanor up.'

'And can you remember what Laura was wearing?'

He thought for a moment or two and then said. 'A coat, blue – teal, I think she called it, and brown leather boots. I bought them for her birthday, black tights, and a dress, in autumn colours. Burnt orange and gold.' He glanced up at me. 'I take notice of what she wore. I can't help it.'

'And what about on Tuesday? Can you tell me where you were?'

'I was here from around seven am. You'll be able to

see that on the CCTV and I left around five. And then I went home. I cooked supper. Charlotte goes to Pilates on Tuesday evenings, Cassie was out with her boyfriend, and Elly was in her room, so I watched some TV and went to bed.'

'And you were in all evening?'

He nodded.

'You didn't go out again?'

'No.'

'Can anyone verify that?'

He stared at me and looked puzzled. 'I don't know. Elly maybe, once the girls and I had eaten Cassie went out and Elly went up to her room. I put some chilli in the fridge for Charlotte to have when she got in. She sometimes goes for a drink with a couple of girls from the class afterwards–'

'And what time did your wife get back?'

He pulled a face. 'I don't know. I must have gone to bed. We sleep in separate rooms. We have done for years. Charlotte's a night owl, I'm the early bird–' he stopped.

'And what about your other daughter? Cassandra?'

'The same. I never heard her come in. She had a few days off school, study leave, and she was supposed to be in for midnight–'

'But you didn't check?'

'No, I trust her, she's sensible.'

'And your younger daughter?'

He paused. 'You know, I can't remember now. I think her light was off when I went up, but I'm not sure. I might have called out goodnight. I'm just not sure.'

'So, no one can confirm that you were at home all evening?'

He shook his head, 'When you put it like that no, but I was.'

I wanted to talk to Charlotte Kingsley again, especially now that I knew she had a motive to murder Laura, and find out where she was on Monday evening and if we could corroborate her story about being at

Pilates on Tuesday evening.

'I'll need you to come in and make a formal statement, Mr Kingsley. And we'll need to see that CCTV.'

'Of course,' he said. 'Anything to get the bastard who did this.'

I went back in to talk to Charlotte Kingsley before leaving their offices to check on her movements. She said that she had arrived back from her weekend away late afternoon on Monday evening with her daughter. They had come home by train and she was there in time to collect Elly from cello, but rather than change plans had dropped Cassandra off at her boyfriend's house and then gone shopping as there was nothing in the house to eat. She had been back home by eight thirty. On Tuesday evening she had gone to Pilates at the village hall and then gone on to have a drink with some of the other class members. She had no idea what time she got home but when she did Nigel Kingsley had been in bed – which meant neither of them had a solid alibi for either the time Laura disappeared or when her body was disposed of in the woods. And both potentially had a motive.

I arranged for them to come in for questioning, and was planning to ask for permission to search the outbuildings at their home if we couldn't substantiate their alibis

Chapter Thirteen
Appeal

Laura Lamb's father and step-mother made an appeal on the local lunch time news for any information regarding Laura's disappearance. Laura's brother, Henry who had been working in Brussels, was heading home to be with his parents.

*

Officers called Laura's ex in New Zealand who was understandably upset, but said that he and Laura had parted amicably. 'She didn't seem that much into me if I'm honest,' said Dawnie. 'First of all I thought it was because she just wanted some fun, but it was like she was just going through the motions. I kept thinking I was a cover, I thought maybe she was seeing someone else-' No one corrected him.

*

Laura had last been seen alive on Monday evening. She had been alive at 5.30 pm when she had left the office to meet Nigel Kingsley and this, taken with the time of death, indicated she had been kept somewhere prior to her murder. Officers were searching barns and sheds in the immediate vicinity of Isaac's farm and the Swan and Cygnet. The fens are dotted with barns and sheds, without something else to go on it was like looking for a needle in a haystack.

And then there were Charlotte and Nigel Kingsley. We had an afternoon meeting arranged prior to a general briefing back at the station. I still had to type up the report of my interviews with the Kingsleys' staff in Cambridge and talk to Tomlin about how we were going to handle Charlotte and Nigel Kingsley. I headed into the meeting.

Mike Carlton was first to give us a report on the interviews he had had with the staff at KSPL Solutions R&D and manufacturing plant in King's Lynn owned by the Kingsleys. Everything he had been told had reinforced the impression of a diligent, intelligent young woman, reserved, who kept herself to herself.

'The staff there – they've got a core team of twelve - hadn't got a bad word to say about her. She was well liked, conscientious, seemed to manage to get on with more or less everyone and was happy to get involved in anything she was asked to.' Mike paused. 'What they couldn't understand was why the Kingsleys had her based in the Cambridge office basically riding a desk. Her first degree was in engineering and everyone, including the head of the design team in Lynn, said she was extremely gifted when it came to product development, and was completely wasted on admin. They had assumed that she would be working with them full time in the Lynn factory when she first graduated. Apparently, the company then funded her Masters in Business Studies, but the opinion of the manager was that it was because the Kingsleys wanted to keep an eye on her.'

Tomlin interjected. 'Did they have any idea why?'

Mike shook his head. 'When I pushed her manager, he was vague, but implication was that as neither of the Kingsley's daughters were interested in the business, he thought it was that Laura was being groomed to take it over at some point. Charlotte Kingsley had mooted the prospect of retiring. Not in the short term but within the next few years-'

Which was what they had told me about Laura's line manager – at that point I fed in what I knew about the relationship Nigel Kingsley was having with Laura.

'He and his wife are coming in tomorrow to make a statement. With a feeling that Nigel was grooming Laura to take over the company, and stealing her husband, you'd have to be blind not to see motive there where Charlotte Kingsley is concerned. Also we've only got Nigel Kingsley's word that things were all roses and sunshine between him and Laura – I wonder how he would react if she had threatened to tell his wife about them, maybe she got fed up with waiting for him or perhaps she wanted to finish it.'

There was a murmur of agreement.

'And what do we know about the wife?' asked Tomlin.

'Savvy, well preserved, fifty something, maybe older. An engineer. She was a graduate working for the original company when she first met Nigel Kingsley. They bought out the then owners and between them have taken it from strength to strength. She was in Paris all weekend with her eldest daughter. 'I gave them a resume of what I knew about Charlotte Kingsley's whereabouts during the time Laura was taken and her body dumped.

'I've got someone working on checking her alibi now, Sir. The only thing that concerns me is if she would be physically capable of abducting Laura in the first instance? If we believe Nigel Kingsley's story about dropping Laura off, Laura would have been wary of Charlotte if she had shown up at Fen Creek – and then there's keeping her somewhere and carrying Laura to the dump site in the woods. I'm not saying she couldn't do it – it's certainly not impossible - but it would be a bit of a stretch.'

'Unless she had an accomplice maybe?' suggested Mike.

'It's possible,' I said. I thought about Roger, the other candidate for early retirement and being replaced by Laura. Would he step up if Charlotte Kingsley asked him?

'We need to see what we can find out about Mrs

Kingsley,' said Tomlin.' And they are both coming in to give a statement?'

'Yes, Sir.'

In the depths of my bag I felt my phone vibrating. I ignored it.

He nodded. 'Good, now what else have we got?'

I added in the details of the outfit Laura had last been seen in – Nigel Kingsley's account being supported by the CCTV evidence from his offices, and we now had a still of her leaving the Kingsley's office which would be added to the information on the main boards when the meeting was finished.

As if reading my mind, Tomlin glanced through the office window into the incident room; we all had a clear view of the boards. Although we had some leads and now some possible suspects it was all still pretty thin. We desperately needed to fill in the gaps.

As I spoke a local uniformed sergeant stepped into the room and caught Mike Carlton's eye. Mike stepped away from the table. There was a quick exchange and then he motioned the officer to take a seat. I waited till he was settled and then continued, 'Local police officers have confirmed with the music teacher that Nigel Kingsley was in Ely just after seven-forty pm, and CCTV footage from his office confirms he left the office at five-forty pm. He was alone. Laura had left the office a few minutes earlier, and according to Kingsley they met at the end of the road – there's a loading bay there where he can pull in - so they wouldn't be seen by the office staff. We're going to see if we can find any CCTV to confirm that. This was their usual pattern and this was what he said they did on Monday evening. An ordinary day, to quote Mr Kingsley. Even given the state of traffic there would be just about enough time for him to have abducted her, taken her to another location before picking his younger daughter up. We'd need another site where he could have held her until he was ready to kill her and stage the body. The timeline is tight – we're talking about a relatively short window-'

'But she would have trusted him,' added Tomlin. We all nodded.

'From what footage we have and if we believe Gary Heath, Kingsley would need access to a van or 4x4. He would have had to have had a secure hiding place between Cambridge and the Swan and Cygnet - his youngest daughter plays cello, I'm not sure if they provide one where she has lessons or whether she has her own but it might rule out Kingsley putting Laura in the boot of his car, although given that I'm not sure how you transport a cello, we need to check the boot.'

'But he would still have to have kept Laura somewhere before transporting her to Isaac's farm,' said Mike 'Somewhere she wouldn't be heard or discovered.'

Tomlin nodded. 'Have we got anything back from toxicology yet? Do we know if she was drugged?'

I made a note to check.

'And given the time frame it would have to be somewhere en route that was easy to access,' I added.

'And do you think that likely?' said Tomlin, glancing across at me.

I paused. 'Nigel Kingsley? Realistically? It's possible, but he seemed genuinely stunned when I told him that Laura was dead. But we all know that doesn't mean he didn't do it – his reaction might have been triggered by the fact we had found her so soon, or that he hadn't expected to be caught, or that he was in shock from what he had done.' I glanced back towards the timeline and the array of photos above it in the room next door. Officers were beginning to gather. 'I think I'd be more inclined to take a look at the wife. She certainly has a strong motive and the timeline suggests she had opportunity. Manual strangulation is not something we would usually associate with female perpetrators but Charlotte Kingsley is a tall, fit, well-built woman, and Laura was quite slight – and strangling face to face like that does suggest it was personal. Also, as you just mentioned we haven't had the tox' screen back yet, Laura could have been drugged which would make her easier to handle. Mrs Kingsley said she was off to get some shopping but she could just have easily been in wait for Laura at the pub. And she certainly has a motive.'

'Charlotte Kingsley has every reason to feel aggrieved – the chances are when Nigel decided to run off with Laura, Charlotte could expect to lose half her house, maybe her business, and that's before we talk about the personal impact on her and her family. One of the things she said to me when I first got there was that they had known Laura since she was a baby, that she was like a daughter to them. They had taken her into their family business, helped her, funded her Masters' degree. Finding out that your husband is sleeping with her, that's got to sting.'

There was a murmur of agreement.

'What about the way that the body was posed?' said Mike.

'When I first saw Laura's body I thought she looked like a bride,' I said. 'Nigel Kingsley told me that he and Laura had been talking about getting married. I know it sounds a bit thin, but if Charlotte knew that then maybe the way Laura was wrapped was about that?'

I could see some scepticism on the faces in the room. 'Okay so, it's weak, let's be honest none of us know what it means, but at the moment that's the best I've got.'

There was a murmur of assent; we've all been here with theories.

'Okay - so Nigel Kingsley?' said Tomlin.

'We need to speak to him again. On Tuesday evening the CCTV confirms that he left work at half past five. He said that he went straight home to have supper with his family as his wife had been away all weekend and he wanted to catch up with them.'

'And he was there all evening?'

'That's what he said. But no one else can substantiate that and he has already told us that Charlotte Kingsley was out at Pilates. As I said, he seemed genuinely upset.'

Tomlin nodded. 'True but he wouldn't be the first married man who murdered his girlfriend when she starts pressing for a wedding ring and babies. Okay. So we need to see if we can find out about the two of them. I'd like you to talk to their two daughters too. Have we got the CCTV footage from Isaac's farm yet?' he asked.

Geraldine Sloane, a civilian, who worked on our technical team and had been sitting listening to the exchange got to her feet to add her contribution to the briefing. 'We've been through footage covering the week before Laura's body was dumped, although obviously there is more to view. I'll put it up on the screen, if someone could just kill the lights? The quality isn't that great.'

On the white board at the front of the room we could see various images from the farm, the screen split into four views of the yard, the barns and the offices. A stray cobweb fluttered across one of the lenses causing the image to slide in and out of focus. As we watched a plump rat with luminous eyes clambered out of a dyke, scurried across a wide concrete pad and disappeared into one of the barns.

'We've got a lot of wildlife,' Sloane murmured, before clicking onto a long shot that covered the largest of the barns and included a section of the roadway that led into the farmyard from the A10. It wasn't great and it wasn't much.

'Okay, this is the Tuesday evening. If you look in the extreme far left of the image you can see the headlights of a vehicle coming in on the lane from the main road.' There were distant headlights and unfocused cones of light in the footage as the vehicle moved through the sliver of the camera's vision. It was impossible to make out any detail.

'This is the vehicle Mr Heath told us about and which we are assuming was the one used to dump the body. It appears at 22.37. And here you can pick out the tail lights as it turns off into the side road taking it down to the trees where our victim was found by Mr Heath.'

I peered at the screen. It was just about possible to follow it. Gary Heath must have been much more tuned into the landscape and the roadways to have noticed it and reacted as he did. The burglaries had presumably made him more careful and more aware.

'We've been through the footage for the twenty-four hours prior to the discovery and are still working our way back to see if we can find any signs of the site being recced in the last few days prior, but currently there is nothing that can't be accounted for in the hours leading up to the body being dumped. No other vehicles turn off towards those trees, but as I said, we are still going through the footage for the days leading up to it. We've tried cleaning it up but there wasn't much to go on in the first place. Mr Heath went for the cheapest options all the way round.'

'So you're saying this is the best we've got?' asked Tomlin.

'I'm afraid so, although obviously we can now establish a definitive timeline. This footage came from the cloud, so unedited by your Mr Heath.'

'He thought that it was a large van or truck,' Tomlin said.

Geraldine Sloane nodded. 'I think that's probably based on his prior knowledge of coming onto the farm down that track. The headlights are quite high up off the ground, but as yet we haven't been able to match them to a definitive make and model. It's more to do with the quality of the footage than anything else.' She glanced down at the sheet of paper in front of her. 'The geeks have been working on the images since the footage arrived but the vehicle is too far away for a positive ID.' She clicked forward to another image. 'The tail lights from the vehicle can be seen again at 23.05.'

Barely seen, I added mentally. If I didn't know what I was looking for I would probably have missed them.

'So on site for just under half an hour. And what about Mr Heath?' asked Tomlin. 'How does he feature in the footage that he was so keen to get rid of?'

Sloane took another glance at the notes in front of her and then clicked through to another clip. 'This is later on Tuesday evening. Mr Heath arrives at the farm from the direction of Longbank Road at 23.27, driving the farm van.'

'The other vehicle had been gone less than half an hour,' said Mike.

We watched as the van pulled up and Gary Heath got out. He was moving with a sense of urgency; he had his keys in his hand long before he got to the office door. Seconds later he was inside, the office lights went on and we watched as he switched on the computer and carefully pulled down the blinds. The blue white light of images on the computer screen flickered away behind the blind.

'He was there until almost 1.50 am,' said Sloane, scrolling through the footage. She clicked again and we watched as Heath came out of the office. He left the lights on and the blinds drawn. He didn't lock the door. He was in a hurry. He was carrying a torch.

'Man on a mission,' remarked Mike.

There was a murmur of assent. Heath hurried across to the van, clambered in and drove at some speed down towards the woods.

We watched the tail lights of Heath's van as he headed out of the farmyard. The film tripped through at speed. A few moments later we could see him making his way out on the roadway, till eventually his tail lights were indistinct pin prints. My eyes ached from concentrating on the sliver of film in the far left hand corner. Geraldine Sloane said. 'We've tried isolating these images but at that distance it is almost impossible. It's not what his system was designed for.'

We kept watching as the images hurried by. Eighteen minutes after leaving Heath was back. He pulled up in front of the office and jumped out, leaving the engine running, the van lights on and the driver's side door open. Minutes passed, and then he reappeared carrying a large cardboard box and assorted bags that he loaded into the rear of the van.

'What the hell is he doing?' asked Mike.

On screen, Heath pulled the office door to, got into the van and drove off towards Longbank at speed.

'And where is he going? Is he going back home?' Tomlin asked. 'We know that the hard drive from his home office went into the cesspit.'

My phone growled again to announce an incoming message. I ignored it. Whoever it was would have to wait.

'He reappears again at 03.50,' said Sloane, nodding towards the screen as headlights reappeared. 'What we can see and how far we can see him is really limited on that side of the farmyard, so all I can say for definite is that he was heading towards Longbank when he left and then reappeared from the same direction.'

'Uniform are hoping to try and turn something up in the house to house. It's quite isolated, out that way, apparently last year there was a flurry of break-ins and petty thefts from sheds and outbuildings, so we're hoping that there is a possibility that some of the savvier occupants have put in some CCTV since then,' Mike interjected.

Tomlin nodded. 'Right. So where did he go for an hour and half after he found Laura's body?' he said. 'How long does it take to drive to his house and pick up a hard drive?'

'Ten, fifteen minutes maximum, I would have thought,' I said. 'His bungalow is probably only five minutes drive away.'

'But he still doesn't ring until four am?'

Sloane nodded, and then ran the tape through to a time after the patrol car first arrived on scene. 'I'm thinking this is when he gets rid of the second disk drive; it's the only time he is alone after the officers arrive on the scene – they would have seen the CCTV footage he had teed up at this point, the first drive was presumably already in the cesspit by then.'

We watched while on the screen officers conferred

by their patrol car in front of the farm office while Heath calmly walked out of the office and walked around the side of one of the barns.

'What did their report say?' asked Tomlin.

Mike shook his head. 'They were more concerned about the body and getting people on site to secure the scene. One of the PCs said that it was really dark and Heath offered to go and turn the main yard lights on for them.'

Geraldine Sloane nodded as if to confirm what Mike had said. As we watched the whole of the yard was suddenly flooded with a harsh yellow light.

'Great cover for getting rid of the other drive,' she said dryly.

'And we're also assuming that what he told us was true, and that what we see when he leaves for the wood, is him reacting to seeing the vehicle on the CCTV, and not him dumping her body,' said Tomlin grimly.

Mike nodded. 'You're right. He had certainly had the time – he's all over the place. Although SOCO haven't turned up anything inside the van that links him to our victim.'

'Do we know where he was during the rest of the time frame?' asked Tomlin.

I glanced across at the timeline on the white boards in the room beyond Tomlin's office. Laura had disappeared on Monday evening. Heath reported the discovery of her body in the early hours of Wednesday morning.

Beau Shepherd had put time of death between five and ten pm on Tuesday evening.

Geraldine pulled the footage back to 3.30 pm on Tuesday afternoon. The day had already started to darken and Heath had the lights on in the farm office and was clearly visible through the office windows working at his computer. At 4.30pm he got up, pulled on a jacket and headed out towards the van. He opened the back doors and then, from the office, brought out two large containers that looked like water cooler refills, loaded them into the van, closed the doors, then locked up the office doors, and drove off towards Longbank.

'His wife said he was working late on his VAT in the office and that he didn't get home until nearly seven thirty. So where's he going?' I asked.

'We can't trace him once he's out of camera range obviously. Where ever it was he went he doesn't come back until 23.27 on Tuesday evening.

'Doesn't look like he was working late on his VAT returns to me. We ascertained he's got no stock, so what's the water for?'

Tomlin glanced towards Geraldine. 'What have we got for the day Laura disappeared?' he asked.

'He was at the farm all day on Monday,' Geraldine said as she worked her way at high speed back through the footage. 'He left at around five pm and comes back around seven thirty. Bear with me-'

While she scrolled through the footage I glanced down at my phone. The text was from Kathy and read: 'Where are you?'

I tapped out a quick reply. 'At work, will ring you later.' And dropped it back into my bag.

When I glanced up again Geraldine had a new section of film on the monitor.

At just after five on Monday evening – the evening Laura had disappeared - Gary Heath came out the farm offices, locked the doors, climbed into the farm van and drove off towards the A10. Exactly as before we could track him across the visual sliver to one side of the barn, making his way off into the darkness of the late afternoon, following his lights as he made his way along the concrete road.

'He's going out to the A10,' I said, pointing towards the images. 'Not towards Longbank and home.'

There was a moment's silence as the penny dropped and then Tomlin said, 'Maybe we were barking up the wrong tree with that unknown vehicle. If Heath is heading towards the A10 turning right would take him towards Fen Creek and the Swan and Cygnet. What do we think the chances are that he was there in wait for Laura when she was dropped off by Nigel Kingsley?'

'So are we saying it was just an opportunist thing, Sir?' asked Mike 'He could drive there in about ten minutes. Was he just hanging around waiting for some woman, any woman who came in to park there? Was she in the wrong place at the wrong time? Or was Heath waiting for Laura specifically?'

'We need to bring him in and have another chat. And I want to see if their lives overlapped and if so how, how, where and when,' said Tomlin, and then paused. 'But also let's not close this down too soon. Gary Heath's behaviour is suspicious but we've got nothing concrete that connects him to Laura; we need to keep looking, the Kingsleys, ex-boyfriends, the other people she works with.'

There was a murmur of assent. 'He could drink at the Swan and Cygnet,' I said. 'It's close enough to where he lives, and Nigel Kingsley and Laura used to drink in there from time to time.

'Let's get someone out there to see if the landlord recognises Heath,' said Tomlin.

The film played through on fast forward. Gary Heath drove back into the farmyard a little after two hours later. The time stamp confirmed it was Monday evening. He arrived back from the same direction, from the most direct route to the A10, and parked up, the angle at which the van was parked almost totally obscuring the view as he got out and unlocked the office doors before going back to the van, opening the back doors and reaching inside. He stooped and picked something up, by the way his shoulders were set it suggested he was carrying something that, if not all that heavy, was bulky.

'Okay, let's get him brought in,' said Tomlin grimly. 'And bring his other vehicles in, get SOCO to go over everything with a fine-tooth comb, and see if we can track down that box and the bags he took out on the night when he says he found the body.

'If it is him then we need to find out what he did with Laura between Monday evening and dumping her body on Tuesday evening.

The film moved on, faster now until we were back where we had started in the early hours of the morning before he had told us that he had found Laura's body. Rowe stopped the film.

'The thing that pulls me up short about Heath,' said Mike. 'Is why ring us and tell us about the body in the first place? Makes no sense. He could have left her there. No one was likely to have found her.'

I stared at the frozen image of Gary Heath on screen carrying the box out towards the van. He looked furtive and uneasy.

'What was it he didn't want us to find? What is it he's doing that's worse than murder?' I said to no one in particular.

Chapter Fourteen
Kathy

'Is there anything else,' asked Tomlin, addressing the room.

The local uniformed officer who had recently joined the briefing cleared his throat. Mike nodded. 'Yes, Sir. Sergeant Holland has something.'

Holland got to his feet. 'It might be unrelated, Sir, but at eight-thirty this morning, a silver Nissan truck approaching from the A10 turned into the approach road to the farm. Soon as he spotted our patrol car, he did a U-turn. The PC on the gate said it looked like the driver had got the wrong place, anyway he made a note of the registration number given that we're on the lookout for a truck or van. Fifteen minutes later the same truck was seen approaching the trackway gate on the Longbank side of the farm. The driver of the vehicle told the officer that he had come to carry out maintenance work on the pump station which is situated behind the property on one of the large drains – and that Mr Heath was aware that he was coming. The PC radioed ahead to inform the officers at the farm to expect him, but the truck didn't reach the farmyard. The officer assumed there was an alternate route to the pumping station. Around an hour later the truck returned to the Longbank gate, turned out onto Longbank Road and headed back towards the A10.'

There was a pause and then Holland said, 'The thing is, Sir, I was one of the officers who went out there when the farm was broken into earlier in the year. As part of investigation we went to check the pump house in case the thieves had taken anything, and also there was a

163

possibility that they had stashed some of the gear they'd nicked down there. It's nicely out of the way. Anyway as far as I'm aware the only way to get down to the pumping station is either on the road in from the A10 or if you come in from the Longbank side by driving through the farmyard and turning right onto that roadway. You can't get there from the Longbank side without going through the yard. I thought it sounded a bit iffy, so I contacted the company who maintain the pumps and they said they'd got no work scheduled-' He took a breath. 'And then I had one of the lads run the truck plates and they belong to a Nissan Micra belonging to a vicar in Cirencester.'

There was a ripple of laughter.

'Okay, good work, Sergeant,' said Tomlin appreciatively. 'Did any of the officers see where the vehicle went?'

The sergeant shook his head. 'To be honest, they weren't looking, Sir. You know how it works when we're monitoring access, officers are trained to look out towards incoming traffic and pedestrians, not behind them. And those concrete roads go on for miles across the fen. People reckon it's flat but there's windbreaks of trees, farm buildings, and Isaac's farm is on a bit of a rise going up to them trees round the pond – there's no clear line of sight.' He paused. 'I'm not trying to excuse them-'

Tomlin nodded. 'No, it's fine, Sergeant, I understand. Were either of the officers able to give a description of the man driving the truck?'

The sergeant nodded. 'There were two men in the truck and the lads are pretty sure they could recognise them again. I just thought it was strange, Sir.'

'Agreed,' said Tomlin. 'Can we get a description of the vehicle and its occupants circulated?'

'Will do, Sir,' said the sergeant.

'And good work,' Tomlin repeated.

As the officer closed his notebook there was a knock on the office door. One of the civilian staff peered in. 'Excuse me. Is DS Daley in here?'

I nodded. 'Yes, sure, can I help?'

She smiled. 'Your sister is downstairs. She says it's urgent.'

I stared at her, and felt a flash of heat as I re-ran the words in my head and then looked across at Tomlin. 'Thank you,' I said to the clerk, feeling myself redden. I had always tried to keep a wall between my job and my private life.

'Okay first priority is to get Heath back in.' Tomlin glanced across the room. 'Sergeants Daley and Carlton I'd like you to talk to the Kingsleys?'

'Certainly Sir,' I said getting to my feet. 'I'm hoping to talk to one of the investigating officers working on murders with a similar MO,' I said. 'I've asked for the files to be sent over.'

Tomlin looked up. 'You think there might be others?'

'So far everyone has said that this didn't look like his first, Sir.'

'And you think you might have found another one?'

'I won't know until I've spoken to them, but I think it's a real possibility.'

'Okay, we'll see what they come up with, but let's not lose sight of what's going on *here*.'

'No, Sir.' Picking up my bag I hurried downstairs.

There was a buzz of activity in and around the police station with a small army of additional extra officers brought in to help with the Laura Lamb investigation. Tom Green, the actioning officer from our squad, was co-ordinating the searches and house to house enquiries which had to be organised and co-ordinated, while Liz, our retriever, was busy in her own office, working with the incoming information, sifting and shifting, and adding to what we knew.

Support staff had been brought in to man the phones after the TV appeal for information had gone out, and I knew that Tomlin and the media officers had been working on media strategy as we were all more or less certain that the murder investigation was likely to go into the national press.

Some officers in the outer office I recognised from the Major Investigations Team, others from a previous investigation that had brought me to Norfolk when I was stationed in Ross-on-Wye, but there were a lot I had never seen before and there in the midst of it all, stood my little sister, Kathy, a single still point in a maelstrom of activity.

She looked tiny. Her blonde hair was all mussed up and her coat half buttoned. She looked as if she hadn't slept in a week and she was clutching her handbag like a shield across her chest. She saw me and for a moment I thought she was going to burst into tears. I willed her not to as I hurried across the main office through the sea of officers. I was angry with her for coming, angry with myself for not realising how close to the edge she was.

'Carmel,' she said, her expression brightening. 'I didn't think you'd come. They told me you were in a meeting.'

I rolled my eyes. Nobody calls me Carmel. My parents were neither Irish nor Catholic. I'm named after a beach resort in California that my mum saw in a film while she was pregnant and thought was a nice name. More than once I've thanked my lucky stars that I wasn't a boy. Her top pick for a boy from the same film was Monterey.

'For Christ's sake, Kathy, don't call me that,' I said, taking her arm and guiding her into a quiet corner. 'What are you doing here?' It was a minimum of a five hour drive for her from where she lived.

Kathy reddened. 'I'm sorry, I'm just glad to see you,' she said. 'I was worried that I wouldn't be able to find you. I rang your main office and told them that it was a family emergency and that I had to see you. They told me you would be contactable here. I didn't know if you'd be working.'

I stared at her. 'Why? Which bit of this don't you get?' I said, indicating the activity behind me. 'I am working. This is what I do-'

'I meant out investigating.' The way she said it made it sound like mole catching or maybe outside catering.

'I'm in the middle of a murder investigation, Kath. I don't understand what the hell you are doing here.' The words came out more harshly than I had intended. Kathy flinched. I should have apologised but instead another thought crossed my mind. I glanced past her. 'Where are the boys? Did you drive? Are they outside in the car?'

She shook her head. 'No, Lucy, a friend of mine who works at the school said she'd have them for me till I get back. She doesn't mind. Her two get on with my two like a house on fire, and she owes me. She said-'

Something about my expression silenced her. 'Sorry, Mel, I didn't know what else to do. I just wanted to talk to Jimmy face to face. I want to see what he's going to do about this bloody woman and us.' She took a breath. It was obvious Kathy had been thinking about what to say to me, and probably to Jimmy all the way on the drive over here.

'I know what you said and what you think, but I want to talk to him. And you are right, either we find a way to work it out once and for all or this is the end. Like properly end it. I can't keep going on like this. I can't keep feeling like this. Unless he makes promises he is prepared to keep then I'm going to see a solicitor next week and that's it, the end.' She held up her hands to indicate the break. 'I just thought it would be easier to talk to him if we were away from home, somewhere neutral, you know.' Her voice faded away.

'And what does Jimmy have to say about it?' I asked, my voice still low and even.

She looked uncomfortable. 'He doesn't know that I'm here yet. I thought I'd get myself settled and then I'd text him. Arrange to meet up.'

'Where are you staying?' I asked.

She looked sheepish. I suppressed a groan because I already knew the answer.

'You should have rung me first, Kathy,'

'I did,' she protested. 'But you didn't answer.'

I couldn't argue with that. 'We're in the middle of a murder investigation, I haven't even got the spare room unpacked yet.'

'It doesn't matter. It's fine, I won't get in the way, I promise,' she said, holding up her hands. 'I'll be fine on the sofa and it'll only be for a few days, cross my heart. A few days and I'll know where I stand. You won't even know I'm there-'

I laughed. 'Right.'

It wasn't her I was worried about. It was Jimmy. I could just imagine him rocking up, rolling drunk, at my place, to continue their in depth heart to heart in my sitting room, him sprawled on the sofa filling my baby sister's head with false promises and smooth, smooth lies, the bastard. Banging on the front door in the wee small hours begging for one more chance. But what choice had I got? Kathy looked up at me. I reached into my handbag and pulled out my house keys.

'There's a spare duvet and a couple of pillows in the airing cupboard. And there's a spare front door key in the cutlery drawer with the spoons.'

She smiled; it was the first time she had looked remotely happy since I'd first spotted her. 'I promise I won't get under your feet,' she said.

'Just so's you know there isn't any milk in the fridge.'

Kathy nodded. 'Not a problem, I've already been shopping,' she said.

Chapter Fifteen
The Others

On the way back upstairs my phone growled again. I think if it had been Jimmy I'd have thrown the damned thing over the handrail, but it was a text from the leader of the team processing Laura's car wanting to speak to me urgently. His name was Phil Hurst. I'd worked with him before and we'd been out a couple of times. Nothing serious, if you discount a couple of great curries, several bottles of wine and some seriously good sex.

I found his number and pressed call.

'Hi Mel, how've you been?'

'Good, and you?'

'Same. We should –' There was a little electric pause and I laughed.

'You're right, Phil. We really should, but meanwhile what have you got for me?'

It was his turn to laugh. 'Good question. We've found something under the wheel arch of the victim's car that I think might be of interest. I've emailed the details and some photos over. It's a small metal box. One of the bar staff came over and told one of the technicians that they had seen a white van in the car park early on Wednesday morning. She said she noticed it because the man in the van was wearing a white suit and hood – to quote "like you lot are wearing." When she got closer she realised he was also wearing a mask.'

'Right, sounds peculiar. I'll see someone gets a statement – did she say anything else?'

'Other than the outfit, she said she couldn't describe him; he looked about average size, not fat or thin - but she did say he was doing something under Laura's car.

She thought maybe the car had a flat tyre and someone had come out to mend it and the suit was part of the job. Anyway we took a quick look and there was this little box under the wheel arch – around the size of a match box, about 10mm deep, stuck like buggery on a self-adhesive pad; it was a devil of a job to get it off.'

'Was there anything in it?' I asked.

'No, sadly not, and no fingerprints either. First of all I thought it might be one of those boxes for a spare key - we're still running trace and fibres, but we got the brand name. The company produce a range of tracking devices for use in vehicles, some commercial but some domestic. It's similar to the thing you get in GPS and on your phone.'

'Are you saying someone was tracking Laura?' I asked incredulously.

'Well, I can't confirm that obviously, but it is certainly a possibility. Trouble is without the actual device we can't tell you much else. Not only that but the company sell thousands of these things every year, some direct and some through third party sellers. To try and find it we would need the serial number at the very least and even then it would be a long shot.'

'How big a range do these things have?'

'Depends on the model, but pretty much national by the looks of it, the only downside is if they're not wired into a power source, even though they use minute amounts of power they have relatively limited battery life. Unless of course whoever it was could pop by and swap out the battery when he was passing.'

'So you're saying it hasn't been on the car long?'

'No, I can't say that either because there is obviously a chance that this thing has been there for years. But I'd say it was a relatively recent addition - there isn't much in the way of corrosion, or discolouration or debris trapped under the edge of the box or on the exposed adhesive areas which suggests it was put there relatively recently. We are currently working on what it is and where it came from, but I can't be any more specific than that at the moment. I just thought that you'd like to know.'

'You're right. I'll pass it on.'

'Photos and what information we've got should be with you.'

By this point I was back at my desk.

I glanced down over the list of names I'd compiled of other potential victims from my search on the national database. Anya, the housekeeper, who had been found crushed by a tree, didn't have a vehicle, but possibly some of the others had. It would only take a few phone calls to find out if a tracking device had been found on any of the vehicles they had access to.

'Thanks Phil,' I said. 'Is there anything else?'

'Only that we really should-' he said.

I grinned. 'You're right, we really should, but meanwhile I need to get this information to Tomlin for the main briefing. And thanks for the photos.'

'You're welcome,' he said. 'And how about we organise something soon. Maybe supper? I could cook?'

'You cook as well?'

He laughed. 'It has been known.'

'Sounds good,' I said and with that I hung up.

The folder of photos was already in my inbox. I opened up the image and took a long look, then went over to Tomlin who was still prepping for the full briefing. I tapped lightly on the door and he beckoned me inside.

'Your sister?' he asked, tone light but I sensed his concern.

I raised a hand dismissively. 'It's okay.' And then ploughed straight back in with what I had just found out. 'SOCO thinks there is a chance that Laura's car might have been being tracked,' I said, handing him the picture Phil had sent me on my phone. 'The techies found this under the wheel arch of her car.'

He looked at the screen. 'Right,' he said, grimly. 'That's new. Did they say anything else?

I filled him in on the story the woman from the pub

had given the technician.

'Okay, let's see what we can get from the description. And she was sure it was definitely a man?'

I nodded. 'Yes, although we have already said that Charlotte Kingsley could have had an accomplice, or it could be Nigel Kingsley - at the moment all I've got is a third hand account, but, yes, Phil said she said it was a man.'

'Okay. Tracking Laura.' he paused, 'Any thoughts?'

'I'll be talking to the officers who investigated crimes with a similar MO, I can check with them to see if anyone else found anything similar.'

'Nothing in any of the reports you've seen so far?'

I shook my head. 'Not that I've seen, but I've barely had chance to scan much beyond the bare bones, Sir. But then I might not have been looking for it or linked it with the murder. Phil Hurst said it looked at first glance like a spare key box.'

Tomlin nodded. 'Okay, but don't forget I want you in with the Kingsleys when they come in. Do we think Heath is capable of tracking Laura?'

'I think they all are,' I said. 'It's probably just another app on your phone.'

'Okay, just let me know if anything comes up with the trackers. Potentially it puts it into another league.'

*

I went back to my desk, opened up the file of the shortlist I'd created, and picked up the phone. The first call was to Sergeant Terry Braeburn who was the contact for the Anya Vassali case - the first case that had caught my eye in the trawl for other victims.

Braeburn had a soft West Country accent and was happy to talk about the work he had done on Anya Vassali's murder.

I had requested the full file once I'd identified her as having a possible connection to Laura and now clicked on the images I'd been sent along with the notes from the case. She was tiny and while there was at least a superficial resemblance to Laura, it wasn't conclusive, given part of my search parameter had been petite blondes.

'She was here for the summer,' Braeburn was saying. 'From talking to people who knew her I think she had been finding the whole fruit-picking thing hard going. Then she met some bloke in a bar where she was working in the evening - Jack Fending, he's quite a well-known architect round here, and he offered her a job, cash in hand, looking after his house. He's away a lot and wanted someone there to keep an eye on it, do a bit of light house work.'

'We went out there to take a look obviously, and I can understand why. The house is amazing, state of the art everything, but in the middle of bloody nowhere, acres of glass and marble, no curtains, minimalist apparently. We had him in the frame, older man, young girl all on her own, you know the kind of thing. It was obvious talking to him that he was hoping for more than getting his skirting boards wiped down, but anyway she worked there for a couple of months and then it seems like she just vanished.

He said that he went away for the weekend to Madrid with friends and when he got back, she had gone. She had left some of her gear there. We've got it here in evidence if you want to take a look - but he just assumed she had found a better offer or maybe that she would be back to pick it up some time. He said she was like that, very spur of the moment. Or maybe, more likely she had got bored or lonely, like I said the place was in the middle of nowhere, there's no one round there, and she didn't drive-'

Which answered my unspoken question about a tracker.

'And what about him, Fending?'

'We gave it a good go but couldn't pin it on him. The weekend he said she disappeared he had left late on the Thursday evening, and we've got him on CCTV taking the London train. He was with friends continuously from then until the Monday morning, CCTV, tickets, witnesses, the lot, he was covered. She had been seen in the village pub on the Thursday evening – she biked down there - and in the post office on Friday morning. She sent her parents some money, and that was the last time anyone saw her alive. Anya told the shop assistant she had to get back because someone was coming round to the house and she had to be there.'

'And she didn't say who it was?'

'No. But the woman said it sounded like something official, not personal. She didn't sound excited, more matter of fact, bored or annoyed more than pleased, and she wasn't buying wine or cake or anything special, that's how she put it.'

'Any CCTV?'

'Nothing. There is CCTV in the house but it is only activated when the alarms are set – you can do it from some app on your phone if you want to, but anyway Anya apparently hadn't, and despite her boss insisting she should, she didn't often set it because she found it hard to remember the code.

Jack Fending didn't think to report her missing because he didn't think that she was, and eventually he just boxed up the things she'd left there and stuck them in his garage. We only managed to track her down because she had had a dental implant in Lithuania, and her parents had reported her missing.

She had always called home at least once a week and sent them money regularly. Anyhow, finding out who she was took some doing, but then we put out a local TV appeal and a couple of people remembered her. She was quite striking, small, blonde hair, curvy. She was the kind of woman who made an impression. We went over Fending's house and car and life with a fine-tooth comb, and came up with empty-'

I told him about the tracker and the position of our victim's hands.

'I can't help you with the hands. By the time we

found her she had had a run in with several tons of falling tree, but I'll get someone to look through the evidence boxes we've got here.'

'Did she have access to a car at Fending's?'

'No, not to my knowledge, apparently she cycled everywhere.'

'Did Fending know who was coming to the house on the Friday morning while he was away?'

'No, he told us he hadn't got anything arranged. His view was that she had probably met someone at the pub.'

'What about phone calls?'

'We traced everything we could; the only calls we couldn't trace were two from an unregistered mobile, one came in late on Thursday evening and the other first thing Friday.'

'Anya's mystery appointment?'

'Possibly – It pinged a tower in Newbury, and that's all we've got, we checked all the casual workers that she had met on the fruit farm, the farm owner, people in the pub and came up empty. Do you think your girl is linked to our case?'

'Truthfully? I don't know, other than the polythene and the forensic awareness I haven't got much to connect them. I'm not sure if it's anything more than a hunch. There is a physical similarity between the victims, young, slightly built women in their twenties, blonde, but I'm not sure if that is enough.'

'You got a suspect?'

'A couple, but it's too early to say how that is going to pan out.'

'Well if I can help,' he left the offer open.

'Thanks. I might take you up on that.'

As I hung up one of the local constable's came over to my desk, 'Scuse me Sergeant, but DCI Tomlin told me to say that we're ready for the main briefing.'

I nodded and closed down my computer.

The team crowded into the incident room and listened as Tomlin laid out our plan, with contributions from me and Mike, as well as updates from uniform,

SOCO and the IT team. SOCO should bring in Gary Heath's vehicles and escalate the search for any signs of the box he had been carrying. We also arranged to bring the Kingsleys in to Denham to be questioned separately that evening. I would interview Charlotte Kingsley; Mike would interview Nigel. At eighteen, Cassandra, their eldest daughter could have been left alone with their younger daughter, Eleanor, but Mrs Kingsley insisted that she arranged for the girls to stay with friends.

*

Back at my desk I resumed my calls to other forces. Two of the officers who were listed as contacts were off duty so I left messages for them to call me back, and the third said they hadn't checked the victim's car as it had been in the garage having repairs at the time of her murder, but promised to check up. The DS was based in York. I gave him the scant details we had regarding Laura and he told me about his victim, Carly Brand. Twenty-six years old, a blonde, manual strangulation, wrapped in polythene. I opened the file up. The photo showed a slim young woman with a mop of wavy blonde hair and elfin features, she was dressed in tee-shirt and shorts. I expanded the image. She looked a lot like Laura Lamb.

'Did you go to the crime scene?' I asked.

'Yes. I'll send the files over if you think it'll help. She was found in a derelict building that was due for demolition the following week. We were lucky we found her at all really. They had plans to blow the walls and then bulldoze the whole site. Two teenagers looking for somewhere private found her.' He laughed grimly. 'Reckon it'll put the poor little sods off sex for life.'

'Did you notice anything odd about her hands?'

He paused. 'In what way?'

I hesitated. I thought if anyone had seen Laura's hands, they would have noticed the odd positioning, maybe this was a new development for our killer or maybe the man who killed Carly Brand was totally unrelated to our murderer.

'I wondered if they were posed. Did the body look staged?'

He took a long breath. 'Yes, well she was in this shallow pit, the base of what had been an old hopper, so in the middle of a circle if you like. You'll see on the photos. We thought he'd chosen it because it was probably the cleanest bit of the whole place, out of the way, but clean because the guys who had bought the hoppers for scrap had had to put in boards to get the machinery in and out because the floors were so uneven.

'The boarding was still in situ when the killer dumped the body. Unfortunately there were footprints everywhere from the guys stripping out the wiring and piping, rough sleepers, junkies, the whole nine yards. They had all been cleared out because the place was going to be demolished and was likely to collapse, but it was pretty much impossible to work out whose prints were whose.' He stopped.

'But she looked, well almost peaceful - and there were all these things laid on top of her – some of it was dead plants from around the building, there was some string and some bent wires and a spring that had been screwed into the concrete – it was like he had decorated her. Might sound a bit far-fetched, I know – I mean they could have as easily fallen on her while she was lying there but it didn't seem likely and it didn't look like that.'

'And her hands?'

Another file dropped into my inbox. I clicked it open and selected images.

'There was some damage from scavengers but she had been restrained before he killed her. Why, what have you got there?'

I explained about the way Laura's hands had been bound.

On my screen the crime screen photos for Carly Brand opened up. I stared at the first picture, which had been taken from the doorway before anything had been disturbed. The images were of a chaotic derelict building, with graffiti tags and obscenities scrawled on every wall. The floor was littered with rubble, rubbish and the debris of decay. In the centre of the space was something white that almost glistened and looked totally out of place in amongst the chaos.

'No, we'd not got anything like that,' the officer was saying. 'We'd got ligature marks and the polythene over her face was just the one layer, cut back at an angle so's you could see her, but no, her hands weren't tied up like that,' the officer said.

I zoomed in closer. The polythene appeared opaque, obscured here and there with condensation and strange swirls of colour, green and yellow, clusters of flies in the creases where they had managed to find a way in. I could almost smell it.

'But like your man, it was obvious that ours knew what he was doing. I don't think any of us thought it had been his first time. It was too tidy. We didn't find any fibres, no fingerprints. It was a total bust forensically, although given the dump site it was like looking for a needle in a haystack anyway.

The girl was carefully wrapped and he was right, the springs and weeds and wire that was laid across the plastic shroud looked as if they had been carefully placed. I let the thought develop – this looked like it was him.

'And how long between her disappearing and being found?' I asked.

'Three weeks. And as I said we were lucky we found her at all. The site was being cleared for new housing. It was going up all round where she was found but only four houses were occupied at the time, so not a lot of chance anyone had seen anything.'

'And leads?' I asked clicking onto the next image.

'Nothing. Went cold pretty quick.'

She had been set down in the centre of the circle left by the rusted corroded ghost of an old hopper. Beneath the polythene her features were discoloured and horribly bloated from the hothouse created by the polythene but looking at the way she had been left I was almost certain that whoever killed Carly had killed Laura.

'We looked at all the obvious, bit of a dodgy ex-boyfriend but he was working in Ibiza when she was killed. We've tried everything but so far we've got nada that hangs together.'

'What did she do?'

I clicked away from the screen but the images came with me.

'Bit of a high flyer. She worked for an international bank. She was fluent in Mandarin and Cantonese, and worked nights, started at two am to catch the Pacific markets. She mostly worked from home, but the night she disappeared there had been some sort of a technical issue – a power failure in her block, so she was on her way to a small satellite office that her company has access to. It's on an industrial estate. She had ordered a taxi to run her to the offices but when the driver turned up, she was a no show.'

'Any CCTV?'

'Not at her building. The power outage took everything with it, cameras, lifts, the lot. We looked at the cab driver but he came up clean, and has a dash cam that substantiated his story. People at work liked her, and as I said she worked from home a lot of the time. We toyed with the idea there might be a Chinese connection given her work, but that didn't turn up anything either, and she wasn't working on anything controversial or particularly sensitive. If you can link this to yours and you can nail this bastard-' he left the words hanging in mid-air.

I wondered if Gary Heath had ever been to York.

'I promise I'll let you know,' I said, and thanked him, and then asked him to check if there was any trace of a tracker on her car. And then I went in to see Tomlin. He was seated at his desk working through a pile of paper work.

'I might have found at least one other victim,

possibly two.' I said. 'I think our man has a definite type.'

He waved me inside. After a brief recap he nodded. 'Okay. We need dates and places, and I'd like to be up to speed on whatever you've found, but meanwhile I want you to prepare for the interview with Charlotte Kingsley. Don't muddy the waters with the others at the moment. They're not going anywhere.'

'Yes, Sir.' I said and went back to my desk.

Chapter Sixteen

The Kingsleys

It was early evening when the Kingsleys finally arrived at Denham.

'To be honest I don't understand,' said Charlotte Kingsley testily, pulling her expensive overcoat tight around her like a suit of armour. 'We said that we would come in and make statements, why can't we do this tomorrow? We could go into the police station in Cambridge. And why on earth should you think that we needed to be brought in separately. Can you tell me what is going on? The girls were really upset.'

'I'm very sorry, Mrs Kingsley, hopefully this won't take too long.' I said, showing her into the interview room. 'If you'd like to sit down. I'd like to ask you a few more questions.'

'I gathered that. Look –' she began.

'Please, Mrs Kingsley, I'm sorry for the inconvenience but you do understand that this is a murder enquiry.'

She stared at me. 'Of course I do and I appreciate that, and if I can help in any way, I will, but bringing us to the police station, I can't see how that will-' and then she stopped. 'You can't possibly think either of us had anything to do with Laura's death, can you?'

I indicated the chair. She sat down. 'Seriously?' she said.

I took out my notes. 'We have to look at all possibilities.'

'Do I need a lawyer?'

'If you feel you need one. We can allocate one from

the on duty roster or if you prefer you can call your own.' I sat back a little from the table. 'It is entirely up to you.'

She sighed. 'I've not done anything illegal and I certainly had nothing to do with Laura's death.'

'The decision is yours, Mrs Kingsley.'

She nodded. 'In that case let's make a start, shall we? I want to get this over with and get home.'

I glanced down at my notes. 'You said that you were away the weekend before Laura went missing?'

She nodded. 'Yes, that's right. Cassie and I went to Paris on the Eurostar. It was wonderful, we went to the Louvre, the Eiffel tower, Versailles.' She paused. 'You don't want to know all this do you? It was exhausting but we had a wonderful time.'

'And you came back on Monday?'

'Yes, Eurostar into St Pancras, then King's Cross and home.'

'And what time did you arrive home?'

'About quarter to five I suppose. The train gets into Waterbeach just before half past four. And then we drove home from the station.'

'And then your daughter Cassandra went to her boyfriend's?'

'Yes, that's right. I dropped her off on the way back from the station.'

'We may need to speak to her.'

Charlotte stared at me, but before she could say anything, I continued, 'And then what did you do?'

She took a breath. 'I think I told you all this before. I went shopping, there was nothing in the house. So I drove into Ely-'

'Did you go straight to the shops after dropping your daughter off?'

'No, I unpacked the car, put our dirty washing on, looked in the fridge.' I could sense her growing frustration.

'And how long do you think that took?'

'I don't know, I wasn't clock watching. Perhaps half an hour.'

'And where did you shop?'

'As I said, Ely. There is a supermarket by the railway station.'

'And what time did you get home?'

She hesitated. 'I'm not sure. To be honest I really didn't expect it to matter.'

I glanced down at my notes. 'You said earlier it was approximately half past eight?'

She nodded. 'Yes, about that. Yes, half past eight, give or take-'

I waited. She bit her lip.

'So Eleanor and your husband were already home by the time you got back.'

'Yes. Yes, they were.'

'And what did you buy?'

She frowned. 'What do you mean?'

'At the supermarket? In Ely.'

Charlotte Kingsley stared across the table at me. 'I don't see what this has got to do with anything,' she snapped.

'Please Mrs Kingsley-'

'I'm not sure I remember exactly. Milk, a quiche, some baking potatoes.' I could see her struggling to recall.

'And did you go anywhere else besides the supermarket?'

She said nothing.

'We can ask for the security footage for the store on Monday evening,' I said evenly.

*

In the room next door Nigel Kingsley was on the verge of tears and struggling to keep it together. 'I don't understand why you had to bring Charlotte in as well. The girls are really worried about what's going on. Eleanor was in tears. You know that none of this has anything to do with her, with Charlotte, don't you? We would have happily gone into the station in Cambridge.'

He paused and looked at Mike Carlton.

'Does she have to know about Laura? I was thinking I ought to say something to her after your colleague came to see us today, but it seems so pointless now that Laura's gone. So destructive. I couldn't see any reason to upset Charlotte any more than she already is. Charlotte loved Laura. We all did.'

Mike Carlton looked down at his notes. 'Let's go through where you were on Monday evening, Mr Kingsley. You were the last person to see her alive.'

Nigel held up a finger. 'No, not the last person, the last person would be the person who killed her.'

Mike waited.

'You don't think that I killed her, do you? I loved her and she loved me,' he said. 'She really did.'

*

'You were gone a long time in Ely, Mrs Kingsley.' I said, glancing up from her statement. 'At the supermarket. Especially if you only needed milk, a quiche and baking potatoes.'

'I got coleslaw and salad as well.'

And then a silence opened up like a door.

'Did you wait for her?' I said, gently. In the corner of the room the single red eye above the video camera watched us without emotion.

'What?' Her colour drained.

'For Laura. Did you wait for her?'

Her eyes widened.

'Did you go to where she parks her car and wait for her? Grab her? Tie her up, put her in the boot? You drive a Range Rover. There would be plenty of room for her. She was only tiny.'

Charlotte stiffened. 'What possible reason would I have to do that?' She was wound tight as a spring. A muscle in her jaw worked overtime.

'You would have easily been able to make it to Fen Creek in the time. You arrived home before five, you said the things you did would have taken around half an hour, and then you drove to Ely. What's that? Twenty minutes tops? And came back at half past eight. So, what, two hours in Ely? You could have easily picked Laura up.'

'But I didn't,' snapped Charlotte, her eyes flaring. 'I didn't, okay. I was-' she stopped.

'You were what? Do you know who Laura's car share was?' I asked, on a hunch.

Her eyes widened and for a moment I thought she was going to deny it and then her shoulders dropped.

'Yes, of course I bloody well knew,' she said, sounding exhausted. 'It was ridiculous, totally and utterly ridiculous.' She looked up at me. 'Nigel is ridiculous. He is old enough to be her father for God's sake. I'd known about it for months. But let's be clear about this, Sergeant, that wasn't any reason to kill her. I felt sorry for her. Laura isn't the first by a long way; Nigel gets fixated, obsessed, and then eventually when it all peters out, I'm the one left to pick up the pieces. I did try to warn her.' Her expression sharpened. 'You don't believe me, do you? She wouldn't have it, she told me that he loved her. For God's sake. And she believed him. He tells them all he loves them you know.'

I waited.

'They do say it is the quiet ones you have to watch, don't they? She never said anything just pressed on with her little plans and schemes. The thing is I was genuinely fond of Laura, I couldn't believe it when I found out. She had let it slip a few times that she was seeing someone, and I was pleased for her. She was such a quiet little thing, I thought it might bring her out of her shell. She was too young to be so damned serious, and she didn't seem to have many friends or do very much with her life. It was like she was living on the surface of it all the time. She could have been a great engineer you know, but then Nigel persuaded her into bloody business studies.' She stopped, took a breath.

'It all seemed such a waste of a life. Anyway, then I

185

found a bottle of perfume in a little gift bag in Nigel's bathroom when I was looking for the toothpaste I'd asked him to pick up. Bloody toothpaste, for God's sake. I saw the bag on the vanity unit and thought it might be for one of the girls. It was the kind of thing they wear – floral, fluffy, you know the kind of thing. And then a few days later Laura had the bag on her desk. She said it was from her boyfriend, a little surprise present. It even had a splash of soap on it from where he had had it by his bloody sink.' Charlotte shook her head.

'We were at a trade show a couple of weeks later and I talked to her about it. I told her that I didn't blame her, but that she wasn't the first, she wouldn't be the last, and that she deserved so much better from life than Nigel. It was all so bloody English, so polite, so repressed. She was so bloody patronising, no, not patronising, she tried to sound sympathetic, that's how it came across. She said that she understood that we were only staying together for the sake of the girls, and how much she admired me for it – *admired me* - and that they were going to get married. She reached across the table and squeezed my hand. Dear God. She said she didn't mind waiting until the girls were older. She didn't want them to think of her as the woman who had broken their parents' marriage up. Married,' Charlotte snorted. 'Laura said she wanted me to be free to find true happiness. I laughed, stupid, stupid, bloody girl. She'd got her whole life ahead of her, and there she was planning throw it away waiting for Nigel.' Charlotte backhanded tears away. 'Poor Laura.'

'When was this?'

'Last year. In the summer, June I think.'

'It must have been hard for you working in the same office?'

'Not really, I work more or less part time now and when we were both in together I did my best to avoid her. But the truth is that actually it wasn't Laura I had a problem with. It was Nigel.'

She paused, making a show of composing herself. 'If

you want the truth, Laura was the last straw. I know she was a grown woman but the fault was all his. He made a play for her and she was too naïve to realise what he is. He didn't want her at the Lynn factory where she could have used her skills, oh no, he wanted her in Cambridge under his wing, under my nose. It might have taken him longer than usual but I could see the signs. He likes them young.'

'Your husband said they had been together since she left university.'

She threw back her head and laughed. 'Did he? Did he really? Did he mention Sarah or Lily or Rebecca, maybe he had forgotten them or got them mixed up, who knows. I don't know how long he had been seeing Laura— what a pathetic phrase that is – Nigel wasn't *seeing Laura* he was having sex with her. And he was lying to her. She is the only daughter of one of his oldest and best friends. It's obscene.'

'If he was serious, how would it affect your business? The girls?'

Charlotte Kingsley sighed. 'The last time it happened it was the au pair of one of my best friends, she was eighteen. He begged me to have him back, to be forgiven, totally contrite, all that, *"I'll never ever do it again, Charlotte, please you have to believe me,"* nonsense. At that point we put the business in trust for the girls so that if we did split up, he wouldn't get a bean. He also signed over the house to me, and if it came to the crunch, we agreed we would carry on working and both draw a salary.

'My having him back last time was conditional on Nigel agreeing those conditions.' She paused and looked me straight in the eye. 'I didn't kill Laura, Detective Sergeant Daley, I felt sorry for her. Nigel would have got tired of her once the novelty wore off and then what would have happened? I mean she could hardly keep on working for us, and it would have been such a waste. Such a terrible waste. She was a very talented and very clever young woman, to be honest in terms of business and reliability I would rather Nigel left and Laura stayed.'

'So where were you on Monday evening, Mrs Kingsley?'

She sat back a little and let her hands drop into her lap. 'I'm leaving Nigel. He doesn't know it yet. I don't think he's ever considered it was a possibility, or how I might feel about any of this, it's always been about him. Always.'

'So where were you?'

'I don't suppose it matters now, but I was with someone else. I've been seeing him for the last few months. We met online. He knows I'm married. He's divorced. It's nothing serious, it's not going anywhere but we have a very nice time together. I'll give you his contact details. He likes me and thinks I'm good company. Nigel might be with the girls and me in a day to day sense, but never in any real sense – can you understand that?'

'And what about Tuesday?'

She coloured a little. 'The same man, same place. He has a flat close to the river in Ely. I think I've been able to see things a lot more clearly since I've met him. Nigel is never going to change and the girls will soon be going off to university. I'm not getting any younger. I can't spend the rest of my life waiting at home for Nigel to come wailing to me with some new confession about his latest conquest and expecting me to help him nurse another broken heart.' Charlotte paused. 'I've been to see a solicitor, and a counsellor. She helped me to see that I've been enabling him. The last few months I've lost weight, cut my hair, joined the gym, really started to feel better about myself, not that Nigel has noticed.'

I nodded.

*

In the interview room next door Nigel Kingsley dabbed at his eyes with a large paisley handkerchief.

'Laura was everything to me,' he said, his voice tight with emotion. 'I don't know what I'm going to do without her.' He paused and looked up at Mike Carlton. 'Is there any way we can keep this from Charlotte? Please, she is going to be absolutely devastated if she ever finds out that I was leaving her for Laura. I know I said that our marriage was over, but family has always been very important to her. It will kill her. She might look strong but I was worried what was going to happen to her once I finally left. She'd never be able to manage on her own.'

Mike Carlton nodded.

*

Mike met me in the back office once Charlotte and Nigel Kingsley had made their statements.

'Tea?' he said holding up a mug.

I nodded. 'Yes, please. I've arranged for them to be taken home. We need to get Gary Heath back in. I think I might have found another one.'

'Really?'

'I can't be sure but it looks really similar. I'm waiting for the full file to be sent over and I've got a couple of others to check out.'

'Tomorrow?' he said.

I looked up at the clock.

'Yes, I suppose so. All the sane people are home already.'

Mike leaned back against the counter. 'Nigel Kingsley's got an alibi for the time Laura's body was being dumped at Isaac's farm. He rang up for a takeaway from his home number at just before ten, and it was delivered at ten-thirty. He's got a receipt, said he answered the door himself, said the driver will probably remember him because he checked the order while the guy was there and they'd forgotten his sag bhaji and the papadums. *Again.*'

My stomach rumbled in protest.

'We'll obviously need to confirm that but assuming it's right, it takes him out of the frame.' The kettle clicked off. 'He was more worried about his wife finding out about Laura. He said it would kill her if he left her-'

I rolled my eyes and dropped a bag into the mug.

'I really need to go home,' I said. 'I need to eat, sleep and-' a thought struck me. Kathy would be there. I wasn't up for entertaining or listening to her telling me about Jimmy. Maybe I'd drink my tea, stay in the office a bit longer and send out for a takeaway. Maybe by the time I got home she would be asleep.

Chapter Seventeen
Going Out

Kathy took a long breath, straightened her shoulders and pasted on a confident smile to disguise her nervousness. Driving to Denham to talk to Jimmy had seemed such a big, brave idea when Kathy had been talking about it with her friend, Lucy, after she had dropped the boys off at school.

There was something empowering, heroic and madly romantic about driving halfway across the country to try and save her marriage. While Kathy had been talking about Jimmy, Lucy had said all the right things, especially when Kathy had been weighing up the pros and cons of whether to go or not. Now she was actually in Denham she wasn't so sure.

'If anyone can work this out it's you and Jimmy, Kathy,' Lucy had said. 'Men can be so bloody weak at times. I bet she threw herself at him. And think about the boys, they love their dad – and he adores you, you know that, he's always saying so. Look, I'll have them for a couple of days and you just go and see if you can sort it out, and if you can't then you'll have nothing to blame yourself for - at least you know that you've tried. And don't worry about the boys, just have a weekend away together. Just you and him. The two of you.' Lucy had paused then and hugged Kathy. 'Go on, go home and pack,' she'd said. 'There is nothing spoiling here, is there?'

Lucy's husband had left her for a younger woman. Five years on and Lucy still blamed herself. Maybe on reflection, thought Kathy, Lucy hadn't been the right person to talk to.

'It's so easy to lose each other when it's all about the kids and school runs and work.' Lucy had said, making coffee and handing Kathy a mug, and she would know. Her whole life had been blown apart by her husband's betrayal. So, it had all seemed like a good idea when she was sitting on Lucy's sofa torn between fury and fear and hurt.

But now? Kathy took another long breath, trying to breathe away the tension in her shoulders, and pressed her lips together to fix her lipstick. She had spent what felt like forever in Mel's bathroom getting ready. Even as she had been walking down into town it had felt okay. A couple of blokes who had passed her on the street had looked her up and down admiringly. But, now she wasn't so sure.

The old coaching inn with its low beams and wooden panelling was right in the centre of Denham, just off the market square. They'd got some kind of a do on and the place was heaving. It was busy and loud, even the tables and benches outside in the courtyard were full of drinkers and smokers despite the miserable weather.

Kathy took another deep breath to calm her nerves, unbuttoned her coat and stepped into the bar, peering across the room, trying to spot Jimmy in the crowded bar room. It wasn't so easy in the crush.

'Excuse me, can I just get through, please?' she said, easing herself sideways, shoulder first between the people. 'Excuse me.' She wormed her way slowly forwards.

Outside it was cold and misty, and the smell of the damp and cigarette smoke crept in with her. She could barely see anything between the press of bodies. There were times when being small could be a total pain in the arse. She was armpit high to most of the men in the room.

'Excuse me, excuse me,' she said, threading her way between the knots and groups of people gathered around tables. 'I'm just trying to find someone. Can I get through, thank you, thank you.'

'We need to talk,' she'd texted.

Jimmy had replied straight away.

'Okay to ring you?' he'd asked.

Asking permission. She really liked that. 'Sure,' she'd said. 'Where are you?'

There had been a pause in the conversation then, but she could have guessed his reply: 'Just having a drink with some of the lads from work. I'll find somewhere quiet and give you a bell. I love you.' It read.

Kathy thought that in his own way Jimmy did love her, but his way wasn't her way, and the truth was that his way wasn't anywhere near enough, not now, not after what had happened. She wanted more and wondered if it was possible. If he really wanted her back he had to step up and make the effort.

If she closed her eyes, she could still see the young woman on their doorstep shouting at her, see that tangle of bleached blonde, see that long lean skinny body and those eyes like a startled deer. She had looked a lot like Kathy had when she was that age, except her blonde hair hadn't been dyed and she wouldn't have kicked off like that, or used that kind of language in front of someone's children.

At one point Kathy had thought about ringing the police, but how would that look? Someone was bound to let Mel know, and there was a part of her that was ashamed of Jimmy and what he was, and didn't want her dirty linen washed and aired all over the local police station.

She pushed past a group of elderly men deep in conversation by one of the tables, all the while scanning the faces and the bodies.

There was a log fire in the pub, away from the door the room hot and airless, and there was a smell of wood smoke mingled with beer and bodies.

'Don't bother finding a quiet spot,' she had tapped into the keypad. 'I'll come and find you.'

'What? Where are you?' texted Jimmy.

'Where are you?'

193

'Denham.'

'Funny that. Me too. Which pub?'

'The King's Arms, it's the one in the market place. You can't miss it. I could meet you outside.'

'Be there in ten,' she had typed, and then after that she had texted Mel. 'Key under brick by front door, have taken spare. Won't be late.' Then she had switched her phone off and headed into town.

He hadn't been waiting outside. But then again, she had been more than ten minutes. Maybe he thought it was a joke. A bad, cruel joke. It didn't help her state of mind. Would he be angry? Annoyed? Maybe she should turn her phone back on? Maybe she would, if she couldn't find him. Her heart was beating a tattoo in her chest. God, this was crazy. A man stepped backwards onto her foot. She winced.

Mel's house was close enough to town to walk, and as Kathy was planning on having a drink, she'd left her car behind. Maybe the high heels had been a mistake, her feet were killing her before she had gone two hundred yards, but she knew how much Jimmy liked her in heels. What Jimmy liked best was – she caught the thought. Was that what it had come to, what Jimmy liked?

Kathy had already decided before texting that if Jimmy said yes to meeting up that she didn't want to meet him somewhere quiet and intense with the pressure on the two of them. She had visions of him in some tacky restaurant grabbing her hand, talking in that low intense voice of his. He could be persuasive and in his own way he was a bully, controlling. She knew all these things, and yet there was a part of her that loved him, that wanted him in spite of everything, in spite of the fact that she knew he was bad for her. Stupid really.

So, she had decided even before she got to Denham that it would be easier, better for her, for them to meet somewhere public, where he couldn't get heavy and emotional, better to meet somewhere lively and relaxed. They could talk somewhere quieter later, but for now she wanted just to see him, to look at him, to see if, when it came right down to it, it was worth one more try. It was hard trying to control the flutter of anxiety, but at least the adrenaline meant she forgot just how much her feet hurt.

The cheerful noisy buzz of the pub in some ways made it feel like she had stepped back in time, back to the time before the kids had arrived when she and Jimmy first got together, when things were simpler. She eased her way closer to the bar, pushing her way past one body at a time. She felt a little frisson at the appreciative glances she was getting but she still couldn't see Jimmy anywhere.

It had been a while since she had made this much effort. It had felt good to put on something smart and sexy – even nicer when Kathy had realised she could still get into the little black dress that had been hanging in the back of the wardrobe since some Christmas do in the dim and distant past. Maybe she hadn't put on quite as much weight as she thought. She had done her hair, put on some makeup, added earrings and perfume and was struck by how much better she felt for it, feeling more like her real self than she had in years. Was this all it took? It had made her wonder if part of the problem was her after all.

Jimmy had said more than once that since they had had the kids that she barely had time for him, but then she barely had time for herself, and he was always making little digs about her weight and her clothes, and it hurt. Surely, he should be able to see that she was trying to keep the family going, haring around after the boys and him, making the money go round, cooking, cleaning, washing, helping him with his books, trying to keep it all going for all of them? The thoughts trickled down her spine like iced water.

He'd never been one to help much around the house or look after the boys, or get up for night feeds, and when she suggested going back to work when things were a bit tight he'd been annoyed because it would have meant him having to take the boys to nursery, and then school, so in the end she hadn't, and they had managed – or rather she had managed.

She looked at the men – the majority of people there were men – in the pub, laughing, chatting, a lot of them already half cut.

It was always her who picked up the slack, picked up the pieces, made the peace, backed down, went without, bit her tongue when he went away or went out for a night with the lads when they had had barely enough money to pay the mortgage. Something was shifting, something dark and angry.

Kathy still couldn't see Jimmy. She bit her lip, wrestling with the inner voices – thinking like this wasn't doing anyone any good at all. So Jimmy wasn't perfect, but who was? People could change if they wanted to. He could change, he would have to. It was that simple. If he wanted their marriage to survive then he would have to change.

Over in one corner of the main bar there was a group of men and women in team colours playing darts and dominoes, which explained the crush. It was a nightmare getting between the people, maybe she should put her phone back on after all and get Jimmy to come and find her. A yell went up as one of the darts players won their game.

She took advantage of the ruckus to shoulder her way between a group of supporters. 'Scuse me,' she said, as they moved aside and looked down.

'Sorry, love,' said one man. 'Want to get to the bar, do you?'

'No, I'm looking for my husband,' she said.

'What's he look like?' asked the first man. 'Is he one of the away team?'

Kathy shook her head. 'Tall, dark brown hair-' she stopped and shook her head. 'Like half the blokes in here, but it's all right, don't worry. I'll know him when I see him.'

'Well, if you can't find him you come back here and

we'll buy you a drink, love,' the man laughed, and let her by, which was when she finally spotted Jimmy. He was with a small group of men on the far side of the bar. He was wearing the blue shirt that matched his eyes. It had a button or two undone at the neck to show a sliver of hairy chest, his hair was still damp from the shower. He hadn't shaved, and was wearing a battered leather jacket that emphasised his broad shoulders. He was cradling a pint in those large capable hands, and was looking around, presumably trying to spot her, but she couldn't help notice the way his eyes lingered on the woman on the next table and then the young woman behind the bar and the tall dark-haired girl she was talking to. He looked like he was hunting, a predator on the prowl. He grinned as the tall woman turned to look at him, said something in a low voice and she grinned right back at him.

Kathy stared at Jimmy, taking it all in, and froze. It felt like someone had reached into her chest and grabbed hold of her heart. She was seeing Jimmy for the first time in years, *really* seeing him. She could see exactly what it was that made women want him, had made her want him. There was something about him that was slightly dangerous, edgy, a bad boy with those big blue eyes and strong rugged features, that easy grin, those eyes. She felt an abstract flurry of desire low down in her belly. *Bloody hell, where had that been hiding for the last few years?* she thought wryly.

She remembered what it had felt like when they first got together when she felt flattered and excited that he wanted to be with her, when they couldn't keep their hands off each other, when he had wanted her as much as she had wanted him. Before they got married, before the kids, before the bills and the cooking and cleaning and drudgery of the every day, when everything had been new and exciting.

She felt her pulse quicken, and then she knew. She took a breath, feeling the shift deep inside her. The trouble was, she knew for certain in that instant, all these years later, he hadn't changed. He was still looking for the exciting and the new. She had grown up, but Jimmy? He was exactly the same. There were maybe a few more wrinkles around his eyes but that was about it, but her. Before the thought could unravel any more, he turned and spotted her, raising a hand in recognition.

'Kathy –' he said, and as soon as she heard him say her name and their eyes met, she knew that finally the spell was broken. Any hope, and wishing was all gone in that instant. There was something in his voice. He wasn't a bad boy he was a bastard.

He grinned.

Kathy felt the breath catch in her throat.

He thought that he'd won. She could see it in his eyes. Jimmy thought she had come to make everything all right again and to let him off the hook. He was expecting to be forgiven, for her to say how sorry she was that she had over reacted, had thrown him out of his own home, had let herself go, so sorry that she had practically driven him into the arms of another woman. It was all there in his face.

She didn't move.

By coming to Denham, by getting herself all dolled up she had let him know that she thought he was worth the effort, worth begging for. She felt a great white hot flash of fury and frustration. How could she have been so bloody stupid? This had been such a mistake. What the hell had she been thinking of coming all this way? Kathy stared right back at him. His grin widened.

She noticed the group of men Jimmy was with were all looking in her direction. Presumably they were the men he was working with and she wondered what it was he had told them about her.

He pushed his way through the press of bodies.

'Well, hello, will you just look at you,' Jimmy purred. He leaned in closer. 'God, you smell good. And that dress, bit of a change from tracksuit bottoms and that ratty old blue jumper.' He looked her up and down. 'I love that dress. Let's get out of here and find somewhere we can talk. I want to explain. I want us to get back to how we were, Kathy. How it used to be. I love you. You know that, don't you-'

She stared up at him, wondering why it was he hadn't asked where the boys were, or how the drive was, or if she was okay or say how sorry he was, and it occurred to her then that what Jimmy meant was that he wanted them to go back to the time when she was taken in by all this crap, that low husky voice, those cheap lines and lies that he had spun her over the years.

She pulled away, resisting his guiding hand.

'Come on,' he said. 'Let's get out of here.'

'No, you're all right,' Kathy said. 'I'd rather stay in here in the warm. It seems like a nice place.' She looked across the bar at the group of men he had been standing with. 'Why don't you introduce me to your friends?'

He carried on smiling but she noticed the look in his eyes had subtly changed and she felt his fingers tighten on her arm.

'You don't want to meet them. They're just blokes I work with, not what you'd call great company. Let's get out of here and go for a drink somewhere else, or get something to eat – somewhere where we can hear ourselves think. Somewhere we can be alone.' As if on cue someone at the dartboard yelled *one hundred and eighty*, and a huge roar went up from the crowds around the darts players.

Kathy pulled away from him.

Jimmy's expression hardened. 'What the hell's the matter with you? I thought you wanted to talk?'

Kathy looked up into his face and smiled. 'So did I, Jimmy, but you know what? I was wrong. I really don't think there is anything left to say, do you?' And with that she turned and pushed her way back into the crowd.

Jimmy called after her and tried to follow but the jubilant away team closed in around him.

'Kathy?' he shouted over their heads, but she didn't look back.

'For fuck's sake,' he muttered under his breath.

What the hell was the matter with her? He watched her vanish into the sea of people. She'd be back, he thought, after all where else was there for her to go? He felt his phone vibrate in his pocket and grinned. There we are, he thought, that was quick.

'Off at 9,' the text read, followed by a little horny devil emoji.

Jimmy snorted. It was from one of the hotel receptionists that he had been chatting up. He started to reply and then hesitated, finally he tapped. 'Sorry, something has come up. Maybe tomorrow?' And before he had time to change his mind pressed send.

As he was about to push his way through the crowd Lennie and Tomas appeared at his elbow carrying empty glasses.

'Another drink?' Lennie said, lifting a glass. 'Tomas is getting another round in.'

Jimmy glanced back at the rest of the gang and then took another look over the heads of the crowd to where he had last seen Kathy. She was nowhere in sight. 'I'd better not,' he said, considering whether to go after her.

Tomas waved the barmaid over. 'Please yourself.'

Jimmy hesitated. Maybe he should stay, let her cool off. 'Okay, maybe just a half then,' he said.

'Who was that?' asked Lennie, following Jimmy's gaze.

Jimmy shook his head. 'Her? Oh she's no one,' he said, turning away. There was no way he was going to tell any of them that his wife had followed him to Denham and that rather than talk had just walked out on him. 'Just some random woman.'

Lennie smiled and then nodded. 'You want to help with drinks?' he said, nodding towards Tomas who had managed by some miracle to squeeze himself up the bar. 'I have to go to the gents.'

Jimmy considered his options. 'Okay.'

He turned towards the bar. He knew Kathy. She'd be back. She'd be on the phone, texting him, ringing, wanting him to take her back. He knew what Kathy was like. And not just Kathy, in his pocket the phone vibrated.

Chapter Eighteen
Night – Mel

It was well after ten by the time I got home. There weren't any lights on in the house, and outside it was dark and cold and mist hung in a corona around the street lights. There was a car parked in front of my garage that I was really hoping was Kathy's but which left me with nowhere to park. There was no on-street parking left so I had to cruise round for ten minutes till I found an unnumbered space in front of one of the blocks of maisonettes five minutes' walk away, which really didn't help my mood.

There was a big part of me hoping that Kathy had cooked a *thank you for putting me up* supper, that was probably currently drying up in the oven, which was really an unfair expectation given the circumstances, or maybe she was having an early night after the long drive, but if I'm honest I knew full well that she had gone off to find Jimmy.

I retrieved the key from under the brick and let myself in.

The house was in darkness barring the hall light, but you could already see where Kathy had been. The house smelt different. The bin was empty, the dishwasher was flashing a cheery message to say that it had finished a wash cycle, the clothes on the airer had been folded and the ones I'd slung on top of the machine had presumably been put away, and in the sitting room the coffee table had been cleared and a bed made up on the sofa.

I went from room to room. She couldn't have been there more than a couple of hours but had managed to tidy up, vacuum, dust, clean the bath and it looked suspiciously like the sheets on her makeshift bed had been ironed.

I'd obviously missed out on the domestic gene. In the fridge was fresh milk, along with yoghurts, assorted berries, a quiche, vegetables, chicken portions – hummus, for Christ's sake. I took out a couple of yoghurts, then cut a hunk of bread off the cob loaf that had magically replaced the mouldy crusts in the bread bin, along with a bag of crisps, took a slice of quiche, a dollop of hummus and some tomatoes back into the sitting room and switched on the TV.

Laura Lamb's murder was the top story on almost every news channel. It always helps if they are young and beautiful or old and fragile. The newsreader played a short video clip of Laura at a friend's wedding and then a still of her on holiday with friends, the same one we had seen on Facebook. They cut away from the photo to the earlier press conference and appeal with Tomlin and Laura's father and her stepmother, asking for information about Laura's movements, pleading for help to find Laura's killer and to ask if anyone had seen anything suspicious.

The camera and the bright lights weren't kind. Laura's father looked like a man barely holding it together, while her stepmother, a sharp, beautiful, well preserved woman with unnatural eyebrows and slash of peach coloured lipstick on an otherwise ashen face, turned a handkerchief over and over in her fingers. It made me wonder what it was that made you remember to apply lipstick when someone told you your stepdaughter had been murdered.

I flicked through to the Discovery Channel and watched unseeing, wondering when would be a reasonable time to go to bed or if I was obliged to wait up for Kathy to find out how it had gone with Jimmy, or maybe she would go back to his hotel with him. I groaned, of course she would. I glanced up at the clock. Another half hour maybe and then whether she was home or not I really would need to sleep.

I was finishing off a second yoghurt when my phone rang. I wondered if it was Kathy wanting a lift or maybe crowing about make-up sex. I really hoped not. It was Mike.

'Hi, what's up?' I said, turning the TV to mute.

'We've lost Gary Heath,' he said grimly.

'What?'

'Yes, exactly. We'd got a patrol car at the bungalow keeping an eye. He left there about half seven and went into Hilgay and then on to Denham to the King's Arms. He parked up on the public car park next to the Town Hall and walked across the road to the pub.

'Okay, I know exactly where that is,' I said. It was no more than ten minutes' walk from my house.

'Right, okay well the officer in the first car called up a second patrol to cover the rear of the pub and sat outside while we got authorisation for two officers to go in, in plain clothes. Trouble is when they went inside there was no sign of Heath. The place was rammed to the gunnels.'

'Bugger.'

'Second car got diverted to assist in an RTA. We're working on the assumption that Heath went in, and then went out to the back car park and had someone else drive him away.'

'Any idea when that would be?'

'Not a bloody clue,' said Mike, the frustration obvious in his voice. 'The second patrol car didn't arrive until half an hour after the call came in and didn't have a clear line of sight to the back door of the pub. I've already made my views very, very clear-'

'Okay, these things happen. Let's regroup. We need to keep eyes on his car and make sure there are officers back at the bungalow, presumably there is still a team up at the farm?'

'Yes.'

'Okay. And you've alerted patrols? I knew I was stating the blindingly obvious but even the obvious can sometimes be overlooked.

'And then some.'

'Have you let Tomlin know yet?'

I heard Mike take a breath.

'So that would be a no then, would it?' I said. 'I'll call him; meanwhile make sure everyone has eyes out for Heath. I know you will and I'm telling you what you already know-' I glanced up at the clock above the TV. It was after eleven. More than three and a half hours since Heath had arrived at the King's Arms.

'Trouble is he could be anywhere by now,' I said aloud. I wondered if I ought to go back in to the station although realistically if I did, there was nothing I could do that couldn't be done from here.

'And what do you want us to do if anyone finds him?' asked Mike

'I'll call Tomlin and let you know what he says. Thing is we've got nothing on him. But meanwhile if anyone spots him keep him in sight. You at home?'

'Yep, long enough to have microwaved lasagne and half an hour in front of the telly with the Missus. You?'

'Hummus,' I said, 'And something about dolphins on Sky.'

He laughed. 'I didn't have you down as a nature lover.'

I snorted. 'I'll ring Tomlin.'

Sometimes it didn't pay to dwell too long on what had gone wrong only on what we could do to put it right. Heath might be ringing all kinds of alarm bells but we had got nothing to connect him to the murder of Laura Lamb. Tomlin's view was simple enough, we needed to find Heath fast, find out where he was and what he was doing, which would be the time to decide on a course of action, but in the meanwhile the instruction was – unless he offered any threat – to continue with observation only.

'And if he's done a runner, Sir?' I asked

'We'll cross that bridge when we come to it, but we'll alert ports and airports to be on the safe side.'

'Do you want me to come in, Gov?'

'No, Daley get some sleep. By the way how was your sister?'

'Out trying to patch up her marriage.'

Tomlin sighed. 'Well best of luck with that. I'll deal with the Heath situation and ring Carlton. See you in the morning.'

'Yes, Sir, goodnight Sir. Thank you.'

I didn't need telling twice. I left the hall light on for Kathy, pulled the sitting room door to and went upstairs to bed, dropped my clothes onto the floor, turned off the light, pulled the duvet up over my shoulders and was asleep in seconds.

I didn't hear Kathy come in.

*

The next thing I remember was the alarm going off. I pulled on a dressing gown and headed downstairs. The hall light was still on. I went into the kitchen, switched on the kettle, got two mugs out of the dishwasher and then went back out into the hall and very carefully pushed open the sitting room door to see if Kathy was awake. She was a light sleeper. I couldn't imagine she had missed my alarm or the sound of my feet on the stairs - when we were little me and Mum had called her bat ears. There was no sound from the sitting-room. Nothing.

If Kathy didn't stir, I decided I'd leave her, God only knows what time she had got in. She had looked exhausted when I'd seen her at the police station, there couldn't be many mornings she got a lie in with the boys. It crossed my mind that Jimmy might be in there with her.

I don't know – given those thoughts – what made me do it, but I pushed the door open a little wider. A wedge of light from the hall cut across the room. The sofa was exactly as it had been the night before, sheets tightly tucked, pillows plumped. Obviously the making up had gone better than anticipated. I turned on the light and picked up my empty plate and mug from the coffee table and padded back into the kitchen. So much for a lie in.

There was a part of me that was disappointed that Kathy had stayed overnight with Jimmy. There was a bigger part of me that had hoped she would blow him out, have a final showdown and tell him where to get off. But if I'm honest I wasn't surprised, that man could charm the bloody birds out of the trees when he wanted something.

So I drew the curtains, made tea and toast, had a shower and got ready for work, all the time with one ear out for the sound of the key in the lock. Kathy and I might have our issues but I wanted her to be all right, to be happy, to have got it sorted and get on with her life and I wasn't sure that any of those things involved Jimmy. She deserved so much better. But then again who was I to talk about making wise choices when it came to men?

By the time I left for work Kathy still hadn't put in an appearance, so I texted her: 'Hope you are okay. Let me know how it went - nothing too graphic, please – oh and I've eaten half the yoghurts and most of the bread.'

It was a miserable morning. Fog hung in the air like a damp grey blanket and there was a frost. All the lights were on at the station when I drove into the car park. The back office was already humming with activity. The national TV coverage on Laura's murder had generated a lot of calls. Call handlers were sorting through everything that was coming in.

A murder investigation generates a lot of paper and a lot of information, someone has to go through it all and decide on its importance. No one wants to be the one who misses something vital.

I made my way upstairs to the incident room. Tomlin was ahead of me and on his way to his office. I wondered if he had had any sleep. I passed Mike, already at his desk, who lifted a hand and came over to join me.

We followed Tomlin, who waved us inside.

'Morning Daley, Carlton,' he said pulling off his coat. 'So I hear we've found Heath? Let's have a quick update shall we before the next briefing.'

I glanced at Mike. I had hoped someone might have called me to let me know if we picked him up.

'Yes,' said Mike.'11.20 last night he walks out of the King's Arms, bold as brass, walks across the road, climbs into his car and heads off home. He's been at the bungalow ever since, although the officers in the patrol car said he's just left and is now on his way to the farm.'

I stared at him. 'Are you saying that Heath was in the pub all the time?'

Mike shook his head. 'No, or at least very unlikely. We had plainclothes in there checking the bar room and the restaurant and they are certain he wasn't on the premises.'

'Didn't we have cars at the entrances?' ask Tomlin.

Mike nodded. 'You'd like to think so but apparently there's a third way in − some sort of mews with pedestrian access only that goes from the pub through an alleyway and opens up onto the High Street? One of the civilian staff lives in a flat there-'

I nodded. I had walked past it more than once on the way into town. 'It's a newish development,' I said. 'Small, maybe ten houses set either side of a wide passageway. I think they're refurbished stables and outbuildings or something. Really pretty-'

Tomlin looked at me and raised an eyebrow.

'It runs between the High Street and the back of the pub yard,' said Mike. 'It's gated with a security coded keypad on the outside of each gate, and it should be locked as a default, but the residents apparently often leave it open if they are expecting deliveries or are coming back late as, and I quote,' Mike opened his notebook, *'"It's a bugger to find the right numbers on the keypad in the dark because the light is busted, especially if you've had a drink."* So I think it is highly likely that our Mr Heath walked out of the pub, possibly through the car park before our lot pitched up, and was picked up or alternatively walked in and out through the mews straight onto the High Street-'

'And went where?' I asked, knowing full well we didn't have an answer.

'That's what we're trying to find out now. I'd like to get Rowe tracking his phone.'

'I'm not sure we've got just cause,' said Tomlin grimly.

'There's got to be some CCTV along there though?' I said. 'Especially on the High Street?'

Mike nodded. 'I've got uniform on it. There's no local council or traffic cams on either the rear of the pub or the High Street, best we've got is some grainy footage of the market square from a privately installed camera they put up to stop the kids vandalising the tree at Christmas, but we're hoping the shops might have something, they aren't open yet but as soon as they are-'

'So there's no official CCTV covering the streets in Denham?' asked Tomlin.

Mike shook his head. 'Apparently not.'

'So, he could have just gone off to another pub by the shortest route? Gone anywhere?' I said. 'Are we still bringing Heath in this morning, Sir?' I asked, looking across at Tomlin, who nodded.

'Ten o'clock apparently, along with his solicitor. If we consider that Mr Heath was driven away from the King's Arms, we also have to consider that he had help. Do we know where his wife was last night?' asked Tomlin.

Mike looked uncomfortable. 'The officers had instructions to watch the farm and Mr Heath. They were keeping eyes on Heath not his wife.'

'But not very well,' said Tomlin, with mild reproach in his voice.

'We don't know what he was doing while he was away from the King's Arms,' Mike said. 'He could have been getting a kebab.'

'Indeed he could, I suggest that when he gets here,

we ask him. The trouble is what we've got is all pretty thin – we've got no other leads, no real suspects - other than him discovering the body, nothing links Heath to Laura Lamb's murder. No evidence, no forensics, no discernible motive nothing. How are we doing with the farm van and the hard drives?'

As we spoke there was a tap on the door. DC Rowe was standing outside. Tomlin beckoned her in. 'Excuse me, Sir, but I've just got the information from Heath's phone for last night.'

We waited.

'How the hell did you manage that?' asked Tomlin.

She grinned. 'Friends in high places, Sir.'

'And?' prompted Tomlin.

'It shows him going into Denham and then about an hour later we've got pings off the mast on Hilgay Church and then one from a mast at Longbank. It looks like he either went back home or onto the farm, or somewhere close by. I've accessed the cloud storage from the CCTV cameras at the farmyard but I can't see any vehicles arriving in that time frame.'

There was a moments silence.

'Like the pickup the other day,' I said. 'It went onto the farm but didn't arrive at the farm buildings.'

'There's something else on the farm that we haven't found yet,' murmured Tomlin.

Mike looked at me. 'Somewhere Heath could have kept Laura Lamb?'

'It's a large area to search,' said Tomlin.

'There's a huge aerial photo of the farm on Heath's office wall,' I said. 'His wife said he had had it taken this year. Maybe there's something on there?'

Tomlin nodded. 'Okay, send out someone to pick it up and also I'll authorise a drone search. Let's see what else we can find.' He looked across the table.

'How are you getting on with the other possible victims?'

'Working through them.'

'And?'

'I think I've got at least one other, looks too similar to be a coincidence.'

'Okay let's get everyone up to speed and then I'll see what you've got.' Outside in the main office the rest of the team were already gathering.

*

Once the briefing was over, I walked Tomlin through the Carly Brand case and the other names I had on the list. Tomlin wanted me to keep looking, but our main focus was to remain Laura Lamb. I spent the next hour or so chasing up SOCO and IT geeks to see if we had anything that would link Heath to Laura, and then writing up the notes on the interview with the Kingsleys, all the while keeping an eye on the clock. Heath and his solicitor were coming in at ten. Local officers had been pulled in to take statements from the Kingsleys' staff at both locations, and track down CCTV to corroborate their stories.

Mike came over to let me know the request for a drone search had been authorised but it was a no go until the weather cleared.

I kept an eye on my phone, expecting Kathy to ring me, or at least text me, even if it was only to complain about the yoghurts.

Heath arrived late. He had his solicitor in tow and was shown into one of the interview rooms. Tomlin was going to lead in the interview. I followed him in and set up the recording. Tomlin explained we intended to question Heath under caution, I cautioned him and we made a start.

The interview was painfully slow. We had nothing on him. We had no real leverage and didn't want to show our hand by letting him know we knew that he had gone back to Longbank when he left the pub, at least not until we had had a chance to try and work out where he had gone. There is no law against leaving a pub, or driving home. He had done nothing, was charged with nothing.

We needed him to tell us what was going on, but between him and his solicitor it wasn't happening. We really needed something else. I was hoping we'd find something on the aerial photo.

I felt my phone vibrate in my jacket pocket.

We went over and over the events leading up to Laura's disappearance and the subsequent discovery of her body in amongst the trees, we pressed him about potential accomplices and about the items we had seen him remove from the office on the CCTV. I teed up the film to show him his own odd actions after coming back from when he said he had found Laura. The bags, the boxes.

'What I don't understand is why you didn't ring the discovery of Laura's body in straight away,' said Tomlin.

Heath took a moment to consider his answer. 'I was flustered.' He was sweating.

'I'd like to remind you my client is on medication for high blood pressure, and while it might not be ideal the delay in making the 999 call was not illegal,' chipped in his solicitor.

'And does your medication impair your judgement?' asked Tomlin, his tone flat.

'No, but I do get myself in a bit of a state about things, I needed a little while to get myself together. All right?'

'And what was in the box?' I asked. He stared at me as if he had no idea what I was talking about.

'If you take a look at the footage Mr Heath,' I noted the time stamp for the tape. 'Can you tell us what you were carrying out to your van?'

Heath looked up at me with those little piggy eyes. 'Vegetables,' he said after a moment or two. 'That's one of our vegetable boxes, see-' He indicated the logo on the side. 'We've got hundreds of them round the farm.'

'So you had just found Laura's body and you decided to move a box of vegetables,' said Tomlin.

'No, well not exactly. I thought I'd go home and check on my wife, make sure she was all right. And I'd been meaning to take the vegetables home, so that's what I did.'

'And the bags?'

'Clothes,' he said. 'I always have a change of clothes up at the farm. They were dirty. I thought I'd take them back at the same time.'

Tomlin looked at him. 'And was there any reason to believe that your wife wouldn't be all right?'

Heath was sweating.

'Did you change your clothes after you found the body?' He pressed.

'No, no, you took those clothes. I'd been clearing out one of the long drains during the day, most I did with the excavator but some I had to dig out by hand, everything was filthy, covered in mud. Boots too-'

Heath ran a hand back through his hair. 'I wasn't really thinking straight. It was the shock, I reckon. And they were in the way.'

'In the way?'

He nodded. 'Bags and boxes, anyone could have tripped over them.'

'So where are they now? The vegetables?'

'At home,' he said. 'In the garage.'

I made a note to have someone check.

'And Linda will have washed the clothes,' he added.

'We'd like those clothes as well, Mr Heath,' Tomlin added and glanced at Heath's solicitor who nodded.

'You'll need to speak to Linda about that,' Heath said.

'We will.'

'Why didn't you ring us straight away?'

'Like I said I wasn't thinking straight-'

'So you went home with a box of vegetables and a bag of dirty clothes? And checked up on your wife?'

He nodded. 'That's right.'

'And took the hard drive for the CCTV cameras from the house?'

He nodded.

'Exactly why did you do that, Mr Heath?'

213

He gnawed at the inside of his cheek and shot a glance at his solicitor.

'I believe my client has already explained that there was material on there of an adult and sensitive nature.'

'Pornography,' said Tomlin dryly.

Heath sniffed.

'Adult content,' said his solicitor. 'And nothing that could be considered illegal.'

We moved on. Heath's excuse for dumping the drives was weak but it was plausible – just about. But there was something at the back of all this, something not right. You didn't have to be psychic to pick up on it. Gary Heath was hiding something.

'And where did you go on Monday afternoon?'

This time Heath didn't hesitate. 'Food shopping,' he said. 'Ely Tesco down by the railway station.'

'And can you tell us about the water cooler bottles?'

Heath pulled a face. 'What about them?'

'You don't have a water cooler in your office.'

'It's a lot cheaper than buying water in them little bottles. There's a man gets them for me, trade. Water out of the taps is full of additives, where we are you can taste the bleach in it.'

'I don't remember seeing a water cooler in your kitchen,' I said.

'That's because we haven't got one. We keep them in the garage, stacked up, and I pour the water out and bring it in when we need it.

He had an answer for everything we asked, including giving our officers the slip the night before.

Yes, Heath, who had been supporting his darts team at the King's Arms, had nipped across to the Dabbling Duck for a pint at some point in the evening. But just the one, and then soft drinks because he didn't drink and drive. No, he couldn't remember when exactly. Yes, he had gone on his own. Yes, he had cut through the mews because that was the most direct route. It had been really busy in the King's Arms. He wasn't sure if anyone had seen him or if anyone would be able to remember

him. No, he hadn't gone anywhere else. Absolutely not—
He stuck to it even when we pressed, even though we
knew we had him in a lie. And so what had he done when
he left the King's Arms? Well, then he had gone home.
No, his wife couldn't confirm that because she had been
in bed.

I understood now why his wife had told me Gary was
hard to read. When I had caught him on the day he
discovered the body he had been flustered and wrong
footed, today he had come prepared and although he
was answering our questions, the shutters were down.

No, he had never met Laura Lamb when she was
alive. No, he didn't know how she had come to be left on
his land. It was only when we asked him about the silver
pick-up truck that I saw the slightest reaction in his face.
There were apparently a lot of them in the area and he
couldn't say for certain that he didn't know anyone who
drove one.

He gave the photofit pictures of the driver and his
companion a cursory glance, and said he had no idea
who they were. His solicitor pointed out that his client
was very distressed by this intrusion into his life, that he
had been nothing but helpful and that if we didn't have
anything to hold him on and we had no plans to charge
him then he would suggest we let him go home. Mr
Heath was a busy man.

Tomlin nodded.

The trouble was that he was right. We had nothing
to hold him and no evidence to connect him to Laura's
murder, so we had no choice but to let him go. And the
worst thing was that I think we all knew that Heath was
hiding something. The only thing was, did it relate to
Laura Lamb?

Tomlin had kept the information about Heath's trip
back to the area around the farm to himself. The plan
was to intensify and expand the search of his property to
see if we could find out where he had been and why, and
see if that led anywhere.

'Get onto Geraldine Sloane and see if she's found

anything else on those hard drives. There's got to be something we're missing,' said Tomlin, as we got back to his office. 'And see if the aerial photo has arrived yet.' As he spoke he glanced out of the window that overlooked the car park. We both waited for a few moments, watching Heath leave.

'What the hell is he up to? And where did he go back to last night if it wasn't the farm? And if he was going home why didn't he go in his own car?' he asked in a low voice.

'He knew he was being watched. Maybe he's seeing someone else. We already know he was looking elsewhere, so maybe it was another woman?' I suggested. 'Maybe she picked him up, maybe he was off somewhere for a quickie.'

Tomlin snorted. 'That's as plausible as anything else we've got. And I'm worried that we are wasting resources on Heath that might be better used elsewhere. Do you think he's our murderer, Daley?'

'Honestly Sir? I don't know, he doesn't seem right for it - but he is hiding something.'

Tomlin let out a long sigh. 'I think you're right.'

I rang Geraldine Sloane who was working on retrieving the data from Heath's hard drives. Pleasantries exchanged, she said, 'When Mr Heath got rid of the drives he did his level best to erase a lot of the material on there, but short of taking a hammer to the disks the information for the most part remains. It's just a case of trying to sort out what's what. We've obviously got a lot of duplicated material from the cloud – there are a few areas that are unreadable but nothing that appears suspicious or significant, but what we have got is a significant amount of porn, lots and lots and lots of porn. Your Mr Heath must have been spending a fortune on what appears to be pay to view, which he was recording from a live feed.'

'I haven't been able to identify where it is coming from yet, they've got very high levels of encryption - but

I'm hopeful. Anyway, your Mr Heath was recording and rerunning highlights. Most of it appears to be young adult women although obviously you can never be sure. I've sent you a couple of snippets over on the secure server and I'll carry on working on the rest of it to see what else we've got. There could be something more incriminating on here but if there is, so far I've not found it.'

I thanked her and hung up. So was Gary Heath telling the truth about what he was hiding? His porn stash? I opened the attachment Geraldine sent me and clicked play. The film flickered into life. On screen a slim naked young Asian woman and a tall blonde girl with hooded eyes were kissing. The blonde girl was wearing a red bra and knickers and held a cigarette between her fingers. They both looked stoned. The underwear looked scratchy. A male voice somewhere out of shot was calling instructions. A couple of seconds later and the girls really got down to it. I sniffed and turned the sound down before plugging in the headphones. Bloody hell. Perfect mid-morning viewing, not. I wondered if there was any relevance in what I was watching.

The room was dark and as the action heated up the girls moved to a sofa. The camera angle momentarily widened, catching the chaos and squalor beyond the more carefully managed film set; the wider angle, slightly out of focus, caught the glimmer of a TV screen, a coffee table covered in cups and ash trays and piles of boxes stacked against the wall.

I clicked the pause button, sent the machine to sleep. Just what I needed, Gary Heath's grimy internet porn. I pushed back my chair and stretched. I needed coffee and to let Tomlin know what Geraldine had found so far on the disk, and then start looking at what else we had. If Heath was paying for his porn then there had to be a record of it, because one thing I was pretty certain of was that he wasn't paying for it in cash.

My call was going to be to Jackie Neil, one of the civilian workers who worked with us, who was small and portly but was a genius with figures, and who had been taking a look at Heath's financials. Another one of the team was doing the same for the Kingsleys.

It is easy to find yourself being pulled off track with this kind of enquiry, while at the same time it was often hard to decide at any point what was important and what was just background noise. Truth was that despite everyone's best efforts we had nothing concrete so far to connect the Kingsleys or Heath to Laura's murder, so while other people traced movements and phone calls, fishing around in their private life was currently the best use of my time.

Information from uniform came in during the course of the morning to say that the box we had seen Heath carrying to his van from the office was in the garage, along with at least a dozen others and yes, there were water cooler bottles there too. There was no sign of the large carrier bags and Linda Heath had said that the overalls and sweatshirts that had been inside had been washed and the officer was bringing them in. The van had also been taken in but was going to take time to process. Both Nigel and Charlotte Kingsley had voluntarily surrendered their vehicles for a search. Charlotte Kingsley's alibi – the new man in Ely – had also checked out, backed up by CCTV footage from the man's building.

A patrol officer on a follow up call let us know that Gary Heath had played darts at the Swan and Cygnet on Fen Creek on more than one occasion. So was that the link we were looking for? A chance encounter in a pub? Simple bad luck? A phone call ascertained that there had been no darts match in the pub the night Laura had been taken and as far as anyone could say they hadn't seen Gary Heath that evening either.

I went back to my desk and looked at the names of the other potential victims I'd jotted down on a pad. It concerned me that we were concentrating so much of our efforts on Heath.

Mike, who had been on the phone, hung up and said, 'The drone has just got clearance to take off.'

'Let's hope they find something,' I said.

I headed off to find Jackie who had set up in a back office off the incident room. I peered in through the door. She was totally engrossed in whatever was on the screen. We'd barely started and Jackie had already brought in a plant, a fancy chair and her own coffee machine. I often wondered if she had them packed in her car just in case.

'Comfy?' I said as I opened the door.

She smiled. 'So, so. Come in. Help yourself to coffee.'

She was going through all Heath's personal finances and those relating to the farm, line by line, entry by entry and would flag up anything that looked odd.

'So,' she said, turning to give me her full attention, 'Finally it all comes down to money.'

'You've got something?'

'I'm not sure yet, and I can't connect it to your girl but there is something odd going on here.'

I pulled up a chair alongside her. 'What have we got?'

'Okay, so first of all at the moment I can't find anything going out to feed his online porn habit. Obviously there might be a debit or credit card we don't know anything about. We've also got an awful lot being spent on food. There are multiple bills in excess of two sometimes almost three hundred pounds a time at local supermarkets. Given there are only two of them it seems excessive. Unless of course he is drawing down cash with each transaction and paying off another card, which is obviously possible. If the card isn't in his name or he is paying someone else to pay it, obviously that's far harder to trace. And then there are some payments to mail order clothing companies.'

I glanced across at her. 'Gary doesn't strike me as a man who enjoys shopping, or maybe his wife uses his debit card?'

Jackie pulled a face and then clicked through onto a website. 'Maybe. This is one of them,' she said. 'I doubt they've got anything much in his size.'

On screen were half a dozen girls in various stages of undress, all corsets, pouty lips and doe eyes. I looked down at the price list. 'Christ, you don't get a lot for your money, do you?' I stared at the faces, none of the girls resembled Laura Lamb.

Jackie Neil snorted. 'Last month he spent nearly four hundred quid on this site alone and it isn't the only one. Although this is high end, the others carry cheaper stock.'

"Maybe it was Mrs Heath's birthday?'

Jackie Neil looked sceptical. 'If my old man bought me something like that I'd wonder what had got into him.'

'Maybe it's for a girlfriend? We know he's been online looking for female company.'

'Maybe. His order history certainly suggests he is buying more than one size.'

'So more than one woman?'

Jackie grinned. 'If so the man's got more energy than I have. The other thing I can't account for is this.' She clicked back to another page on the screen which showed a spread sheet. I peered at the figures.

'Okay, what am I looking at?'

She highlighted a name in one of the columns. 'Here. There are some payments coming in from a company called ESJHoldings. The money is coming in via the farm account but as yet I haven't been able to find out who they are. They haven't got a website and the address is some industrial unit in the West Midlands. The phone number is a bust and the email I just sent them says the domain name is no longer in use.'

'How much are we talking?'

'Initially a few hundred and then a couple of thousand a month, and then five thousand plus, the amount has been gradually rising every month for the last six months or so. It's not a huge amount of money but I can't tie it in to anything.'

I stared at the screen trying to work out what it meant. 'We need to ask him about it.'

In my jacket pocket my phone vibrated again. It was probably Kathy, having finally crawled in. I pulled it out and took a look. There were two messages, both of them were from Jimmy.

The first read, 'Is Kathy with you? I've tried ringing but she's not picking up.'

The second sounded more anxious. 'Have you seen Kathy? If she's at yours can you tell her that I want to talk? Please tell her to ring me. I don't know what I did but please tell her whatever it is I'm sorry.'

Trust Jimmy to want me to do his dirty work for him. I wondered what it was he had done or said, and then blotted the thought out. Hopefully whatever it was Kathy had decided enough was enough.

I started to type in a reply and then hesitated. If Kathy was ignoring him then maybe I should.

'Sorry, Jackie, what were you saying.' I said, turning my attention back to the screen.

She clicked through to another document. 'The thing is I found something similar for last year. Same sort of nondescript name, this time the payments were in the high hundreds. At a first pass I can account for more or less everything else in the financials but not this.'

'Can you send me details over and I'll pass it on to Tomlin. You thinking he's money laundering?'

'Who knows. Anything is possible. I can't see what it links to. I mean the income must be coming in for something, the bad news is that I'm not finding anything that intersects with our victim.'

I stared at the girls on the home page of the lingerie site. None of them had an even passing resemblance to Laura. It wasn't connected. The likelihood was that we would have to pass over what we had found to another team, so we could focus on Laura's murder. As I stared at Jackie's computer screen letting my mind turn the thought over, my phone rang.

It was Jimmy. I excused myself to Jackie and took the call.

'Look Jimmy, I'm at work,' I snapped. 'Can you please stop texting me. If Kathy doesn't want to talk to you then I can't help.'

'She's not at your house,' he said. 'I've just been round and she's not there.'

'So maybe she's gone shopping. Maybe she saw you coming and decided not to answer the door. Maybe she's gone home.'

'I found her phone,' he said.

The words stopped me in my tracks. 'Where?'

Chapter Nineteen
Lost

'I found her phone in the pub car park just now,' Jimmy said, words staccato and tight. 'I didn't go in to work today. I was hoping that me and Kathy could meet up and have a chat. Just the two of us, me and her. I don't know what I did last night but she – cut a long story short she took one look at me, turned tail and walked out – just walked into the pub, said half a dozen words and left me standing there.'

I said nothing.

'Anyway, after I'd been round to yours, I texted her to say why didn't we meet up there for coffee, maybe have lunch. No strings, no pressure. Just to talk. I'd said I'd be waiting for her at the pub.'

'So she didn't stay with you last night?' I asked, the words dry as sawdust in my mouth.

'No, like I said she barely spoke half a dozen words to me and then she walked out.'

I felt an icy trickle down my spine. 'Which pub?'

'The King's Arms, you know – the one off the market square, the one through the archway?'

'I know it,' I said.

Jackie Neil detected something in my voice and looked up concerned.

'Tell me about the phone,' I said, taking out my notebook.

'After I walked up to your place I went back to the pub, just in case she'd gone there. I was walking through the car park and thought I'd give her one last call, and that's when I heard her phone ringing. I thought that was a good sign. Like, you know, she was already there waiting for me. Anyway I couldn't see her so I rang again and then I saw it – it was up against a bin near the wall, the screen's cracked and the messages look like they hadn't been read.'

'Where are you now, Jimmy?'

'I'm still at the pub. I didn't know what to do. I didn't know who else to ring.' He sounded anxious.

'You did the right thing,' I said.

My sister is five feet two inches tall with soft blonde hair and probably weighs seven and a half stone wet. From where I was standing by Jackie's desk I could see across to the white boards where Laura Lamb's photo was pinned. Her picture dominated the incident room and I knew who Laura Lamb had reminded me of on the morning we had found her. And I knew who Anya looked like and Carly – I was right, he had a type – and they all looked like my sister.

I felt bile rising up in the back of my throat, I couldn't understand why I hadn't seen it before. Was it because I thought these things happened to other people, that nothing like that would happen to someone I knew, to people like me?

'Stay exactly where you are,' I said. 'Don't touch anything. Just stay there. I'm on my way-' I hurried across the incident room and grabbed my coat from the back of my chair. As I pulled it on the movement was enough to wake my computer up. On screen were the two women in the porn film caught in a single frozen frame. Their eyes looked heavy and dead. I glanced at them as I grabbed my keys and bag.

'What's the matter?' said Mike.

'I think Heath's got Kathy,' I said.

'What?'

'I think he's got Kathy. She didn't come back last night. I have to talk to Tomlin.'

Mike was on his feet and coming with me. 'We don't know it's Heath,' he said.

'Who else is there?' I snapped.

Tomlin looked up as I got to the door of his office

and was on his feet when he saw my expression. 'Are you all right?'

'I think there is a chance that Heath has taken my sister,' I said. The words came out in a hurry, while a part of me felt like I was speaking inside a dream or maybe a film. I'd got no proof it was him. I'd got no proof, a voice screamed in my head. Kathy was off somewhere, she had picked someone up, a revenge thing to show Jimmy that two could play at that game. She wasn't a victim; Heath hadn't got her.

'What makes you think that?'

I gave him the briefest of explanations. The briefest of descriptions, leading him back to the theory that there was more than one victim.

'She looks like Laura. She didn't come home last night. I need to get down to the King's Arms, Jimmy's found her phone. That's what he was doing when he went missing. He's got Kathy. He's taken Kathy. If it wasn't him on his own then it was the guys in the silver pickup.' I stopped talking aware of how crazy I sounded. She could have dropped her phone, lost it, gone off for a one-night stand but I knew that wasn't true. I knew.

I could see Tomlin wasn't certain. We'd just sent Heath home because we couldn't link him to Laura, and I'd barely had a chance to scratch the surface with the other possible victims.

'Okay, but let's take this one step at a time, Mel. Let's check out your house first, and we'll get someone down to the King's Arms. Your sister could be anywhere — there are other explanations, other reasons-' he began, his voice calm and reasonable. I knew that. I knew that, and it is exactly what I would have said if it had been someone else. I knew it, but that wasn't what I felt.

I pulled out my phone and swiped through the photos to a family album. Kathy and I haven't got much in the way of family so it didn't take me long to find it. The last picture I had of Kathy was maybe two years old, before I had messed up by climbing into bed with Jimmy, before I had moved back to Denham Market to get away from him, and her.

The photo was Kathy and me at a barbeque, a rare moment of sisterly solidarity, a selfie with the both of us sitting at a bench with a bottle of wine between us. I favour my dad, five feet eight, dark hair, skinny, and beside me Kathy, built like our mum, five two, a natural blonde, with her hair down for once, curvy – a pocket Venus, both of us laughing at the camera.

Tomlin looked at the image and I saw his expression change. Laura Lamb and Kathy could easily pass for sisters. He nodded. 'Let's go,' he said. 'Do you want to check your house first?'

'I want to see Jimmy and check the phone.'

'Go home, check to see if she's there or maybe left a note,' Tomlin said. 'We'll go to the pub.'

I was about to protest and then stopped. Tomlin was right. Maybe this was all a mistake, maybe she would be sleeping it off on the sofa having spent a crazy wild night with a guy she picked up in the pub, one mad fling. Maybe she had walked the streets all night, maybe she was home now. Maybe. Please God let her be home.

'Mike, I want you to drive Mel home,' Tomlin said, following me out of the office. 'And, Mel, ring your brother-in-law to let him know we're on the way and not to touch anything.'

I climbed into the car beside Mike.

'Don't worry,' he said, turning the key in the ignition. 'She'll be fine.' Before we drew away he turned to look at me and said in a low gentle voice. 'It's too short a time – it won't be him. That's not how these guys work. If you think he's done it before there is always a gap. It isn't him.'

'You don't know that.'

He sighed. 'Even if he's got her, Mel, he kept Laura for a while, remember that. We'll find her, even if he's got her. I've asked the drone team to ring me the minute they find anything.'

'If there is anything to find,' I said. 'If we've rattled him, he might do something desperate.'

'He's being watched,' said Mike.

'Heath knows he is being watched and he managed to give us the slip last night. What's to stop him doing it again?'

Mike said nothing, put on the blues and twos and we tore through Denham, the traffic pulling out of our way as we drove.

'You know you're going to feel such a twat if she's sleeping it off on the sofa,' he said, as we swung into the courtyard in front of my house. Kathy's car was still parked outside my garage.

I was out of the car before it had stopped. 'It's a risk I'm happy to take,' I said, running across the yard.

I unlocked the front door and stepped into the hall calling her name, willing her to answer. I willed her to come rolling out of my bedroom, half cut, leaving some long lean barman she'd picked up waiting for her under my duvet. But the house was silent. I went from room to room. She wasn't there. I had known from the instant I had opened the door that the house was empty.

Mike followed me in. 'Anything?'

I shook my head. 'No, and I don't think she's been back. She wouldn't be able to resist doing the washing up. Come on let's get down to the pub.'

By the time we got there they were already cordoning the area off and a marked car was blocking the entrance. As I got out of the car Tomlin came towards me. I read a lot of things on his face.

'What?' I said, forgetting rank, forgetting respect, forgetting he was my boss.

'We've found a handbag and a shoe. Your brother-in-law has confirmed they belong to your sister.'

I stared at him. Up until that moment I thought that maybe Jimmy had been wrong, maybe lying, maybe Jimmy had made a mistake, maybe Kathy really was off shopping.

'He's taken her,' I said.

Tomlin rested a hand on my arm. 'We're going house to house to see if anyone saw anything. The mews over there is close enough, there might be CCTV.'

'If there was we would have been able to find out where Heath went last night,' I said.

'Someone will have seen something,' said Mike. They were platitudes, I know that because they are the kind of things I might have said if the situation was reversed.

'If they had seen anything someone would surely have done something or called it in? If you saw a woman being grabbed, wouldn't you stop them?'

Mike shrugged. 'It depends what they saw. They might have thought she was drunk. He might have drugged her.'

Across the car park beyond the tape I could see Jimmy. He was ashen. He caught sight of me or maybe he heard my voice but whichever it was he looked up and started to sob.

'Where the fuck is she?' he yelled, backhanding tears away. 'Where is she?'

I didn't know what to do. There was no part of me felt any pity for Jimmy, no pity, no empathy, how wicked was that? I stared at him, if it hadn't been for him Kathy would never have been there. She would have been at home with the boys, waiting for him to come back. It was such a stupid irrational thought, but I wanted to know too. Where the fuck was she?

I made as if to cross the tape, but as I did Tomlin gently tightened his grip on my arm. 'You know you can't be involved in this, don't you?' he said. 'We need to get your brother-in-law back to the station, take a statement, find out what he knows. What's his name?'

'Jimmy, James Grenard. I could question him, please,' I said. 'He would tell me things that he might not tell you.'

Tomlin shook his head, 'You can't do this, Mel. You can observe but you can't be involved. I'll get Mike to take his statement.'

*

Kathy's shoe was under a car that had been left parked overnight by one of the guests staying in the pub. I didn't recognise it but apparently Jimmy did. A midnight blue high heel, a tiny size 4 with a diamanté trim. I wondered fleetingly what the hell was she doing walking into town in those, her feet must have been killing her.

'We've got SOCO on the way, Sir,' said one of the uniformed officers who had been helping to set up a perimeter.

'Did Mr Grenard empty the handbag?' Tomlin asked, nodding towards Jimmy.

'He says not, Sir,' said the officer. 'He said he found it like that with the phone alongside it.'

'Let's get him down to the station,' said Tomlin. He looked at me. 'And you.'

I knew Tomlin was right. I had to stand back, step away in case my involvement compromised any future prosecution, and the truth was that for all the things Jimmy might tell me there might be a dozen more that he wouldn't, things that might be vital. But I couldn't just leave him there on his own, couldn't ignore him. Tomlin nodded. Jimmy was sitting at an outdoor bench in the smoking area. I made my way around the police tape.

As I stepped forward I saw Kathy's bag, on one side, the contents tipped out, spilled across the tarmac, its position partially obscured by a couple of commercial wheelie bins. The last time I had seen it she was holding it tight across her chest like a shield. Holding on tight. The sight of it pressed the breath out of my chest. I would find her, and then I would kill whoever had taken her. The thought surged up inside me like a white hot fist. *I would kill him.*

Jimmy stood up as I got to him and made as if to embrace me. 'Don't,' I snapped. The police officer who had been waiting with Jimmy asked if we wanted to go inside.

I shook my head. 'No, thank you. We'll need to take

a statement. Can you arrange for Mr Grenard to be taken to the station?' The officer nodded and stepped aside to make a radio call.

'Have you found her?' Jimmy said.

I shook my head. 'No, no we haven't, but we will.'

'And what about the boys? Do you know where they are? Are they with you?'

'No, they're with one of Kathy's friends, Lisa? Lucy?'

'Lucy. I'll give her a ring. I don't suppose you've got her number?'

I shook my head. 'I'll have someone see if we can get it off Kathy's phone for you.'

He nodded. 'Where do you think she is, Mel?'

'I don't know, but everyone will be looking for her. Can you tell me what happened last night?'

'I don't really know. Nothing. I was amazed when Kathy texted me and said she was in Denham. I couldn't believe it.'

'You've still got all the texts?'

He nodded.

'Good, we'll need those to help establish the timeline.'

He stared at me. 'What do you mean? What do you think's happened to her?'

'We don't know yet, but it helps if we know where she was and when. So, you were saying, she texted you?'

'Yes, the pub was heaving. I hadn't realised how busy it was going to be, so I thought once Kathy got there, we could find somewhere quieter and talk.'

'Were you there on your own?'

He shook his head. 'No, I was out with the blokes I work with. I mean I wasn't expecting Kathy to show up, was I?' He sounded defensive.

'So, then what happened?'

'I saw her and she came over and I said hello, and I can't remember exactly what she said, but I said maybe we could find somewhere to talk and-' he stopped, reddening. 'She walked out on me.'

'Just like that?'

He nodded. 'Yes. It was weird, I don't know what I'd done or said. But she just turned tail and went back out.'

'Didn't you go after her?'

'No.'

'You can't think what it was you said?'

He shook his head. 'No, I've been wracking my brains ever since. Look, Mel, I'd do anything to get her back safe. You know how much I love her.'

'So, you didn't think it might be an idea to see what had upset her, follow her outside?' I said, tone cool.

'No,' he said miserably. 'No, I didn't. I thought she'd be back; she'd come all that way to see me. You know what Kathy's like. She can go up like a rocket when she wants too. I thought I'd leave her to cool off a bit and that she would maybe ring me or text me. Or maybe just come back in, and then we could have a chance to talk.'

'So you thought Kathy should make the next move?' I snapped.

'Christ, Mel, I didn't know what to do. She'd driven across the bloody country to see me and then we'd barely said hello and she kicks off and refuses to talk to me? I didn't know what was going on, I didn't know whether to text, to ring, to go after her. I just wanted us to talk and I was afraid that whatever it was I did I'd only make it worse, so I waited. Okay? I waited.'

'And then what did you do?' I said.

Jimmy stared at me. 'What do you mean?'

'You said you waited. For how long? Your wife drives for five maybe six hours to try and patch up your shit heap of a marriage, Jimmy, and you say half a dozen words to her and she walks off. And you just stand there? What the fuck is that about? What did you do after she left the pub?'

'I don't know, I didn't do anything-' he protested, wiping his hand across his mouth. 'I was assuming she'd ring me or come back or something.'

It took me all my time not to punch him.

'So you stayed in the pub with your mates from work until when? Closing time?'

'Yes,' he said, but there was something else in his voice.

'Yes?' I repeated.

'I might have slipped out for a little while. I mean not long – maybe half an hour or so.'

'And what did you do while you were out?'

He couldn't meet my eye.

'Jimmy, where the fuck were you?'

He coloured.

'I need to know-' I started. As I spoke I heard a commotion behind me and turned to see Mike hurrying over.

'Come on, Mel. We've got a call from the drone pilot; he's spotted two thirty foot shipping containers in trees on Heath's farm.'

I turned to the officer with Jimmy. 'Get him to the station and get a statement,' I said. 'And Jimmy, give the officer your phone.'

Jimmy was about to protest but I stopped him. 'You told me you'd do anything to get Kathy back, Jimmy. Just give him your phone and the passcode.' Before he could reply I made my way across the car park.

Mike was getting me up to speed as we hurried back to his car. 'They're in trees, looks like they're hidden by farm machinery and crates from the ground. You can't see them from the road and the only way down to them is by driving along the headland and what looks like some sort of disused trackway. You can get there either from the A10 road or Longbank. It's not a proper roadway but the pilot says by the way it's rutted it looks like it's been in regular use.'

Tomlin was on the phone, but as we got there, he said, 'Have they got thermal imagining?'

Mike shook his head. 'Not as far as I know. I'm assuming if they had then they'd have let me know what was going on inside.'

Tomlin turned his attention back to the phone and continued to talk into the handset. 'I don't think we can wait that long. There appears not to be any imaging. The problem is we don't know what we're walking into. No, not armed as far as we know, but according to our records there are three shotguns registered to that address - okay.'

He looked at me. 'Did you see a shotgun or gun safe in Heath's office?'

'No, Sir.'

Tomlin went back to his phone conversation and then said, 'Okay, Sir.' He looked at me and put his hand over the microphone, 'I have the go ahead to go in to the containers as long as Heath is secured beforehand.' He took his hand away and continued, 'I've called in a firearms support team and tactical-' Obviously something was being said because Tomlin's attention went back to the caller. 'Yes, Sir, they'll get us in but we'll have to wait for them.'

Minutes later he turned to me. 'You heard that? We're going in but we have to wait for tactical support. I can't send Foreman's bobbies in, we have no idea what we'll be dealing with.'

I stared at him.

'I know what you're thinking Mel, but we can't go in unprepared. They're bringing up their own drone and we'll meet them on site.' He glanced across at Mike. 'Have you got the co-ordinates?'

Mike nodded.

'I need to be there,' I said.

Tomlin shook his head.

'He kept Laura Lamb alive,' I protested. 'I need to be there.'

'We are assuming, given the two men in the truck that he is working with other people. God knows what we're going to find.'

'Sir,' I said, the plea in my voice obvious. 'I need to be there.' Tomlin took a breath as if to say something and then relented and waved me into the car with Mike.

'I don't want you going in until it's been cleared,' he said. 'Do you understand me, Mel – you have to stay out of the way. We can't afford to compromise any prosecution?'

I nodded.

Minutes later we left the King's Arms on blues and twos, heading out through town, onto the bypass and then out onto the A10, other vehicles moving aside in front of us as if we were parting the sea. We would need to drop the sirens as we got closer so as not to alert anyone in the shipping containers, and would have to wait to liaise with the tactical team that had been mobilised by Tomlin. The idea of delaying made me even more anxious.

As we headed out past Hilgay word came through that Heath was on the farm and officers had been sent to detain him so he didn't have a chance to either abscond or phone ahead to warn anyone in the shipping containers of our arrival on site. He was saying nothing.

As first to the scene Mike and I went in along the Longbank Road, the other team would be routed in via the A10 - the more direct route - when they arrived. Seniors officers off site would now be calling the shots.

Waiting truly is the worst part of any operation and this one was a thousand times worse. I kept thinking of where Kathy was and what was happening to her. Laura Lamb's face flashed through my mind. Had something gone wrong? Was Heath afraid of someone and thought by calling Laura's body in that he would be able to escape from something worse. What the hell was going on? I tried to push the thoughts down but my brain was racing.

I felt cold and shivery.

When we got to the Longbank we drove into the farm entrance Mike stopped, got out of the car and pulled out two protective vests from the boot, we put them on and sat waiting for word that the others were in position. It seemed to be taking forever. My heart was beating so fast for so long that I wondered if Mike could hear it.

'Are you okay?' he asked. 'How are you doing?'

I glanced across at him. 'How do you think?'

He lifted his hands by way of reply. 'Sorry.'

'Don't be. There's nothing you can say that will be right. I'll be better when we're moving,' I said.

He nodded.

I don't know what we talked about, we must have said something but I can't remember what it was now. It took time to get the tactical team on site, time that passed at a glacially slow pace. I tried hard not to think about what we might find, I tried hard not to let fear catch hold of me.

Finally a message came in to say that the new drone had gone up.

'What if –' I began.

Mike glanced across at me. 'Don't,' he said.

Over the radio I heard Tomlin saying that they had Heath in custody but he was refusing to say anything, and the tactical team were in position and we could begin our approach. We had no information on what the drone was picking up. A route was sent through that would allow us to drive to an area where we would have visual contact with the containers but be out of harm's way. We'd have to go the rest of the way on foot across the final stretch of headland if they deemed it safe.

I took a breath. This was it. This was it.

The route we had been assigned took us towards the farmyard then down alongside a huge open barn. Here and there ahead of us were the wrecks of old machinery and crumbled outbuildings. It struck me that Kathy could be in any of them.

Ahead the ground looked pretty compacted, and the chill of the morning had brought with it a sharp ground frost that thankfully had frozen the top soil, so despite the ruts the surface was quite stable although the uneven ground definitely slowed our progress.

'We could have done with a 4x4,' said Mike grimly as we worked our way slowly past the barns.

But it wasn't the ruts that held my attention. It was the wall of boxes in the open barn. I stared at them as we drove past, trying to work out why they had caught my eye and why they were significant. Ahead of us across the far side of the field I could see a police Land Rover and a minibus as well as officers making their way to the containers on foot. The radio crackled with call signs and codes that meant nothing to me. We turned off over a piece of rough scrubby concrete and down onto the headland around the edge of a field of rough rutted grass and crack willow.

We were coming in mob handed. I just hoped that we weren't too late.

Mike's expression was fixed.

'Hang on,' he said, as we started to accelerate over the rough ground and then finally, after what seemed like an age, the car bumped down onto another narrow concrete track that appeared to lead nowhere. The firmer surface meant that we could go faster, although the road appeared to have been abandoned for some time, with grasses and weeds sprouting up down the centre of concrete.

'Over there,' Mike said, pointing toward a dense clump of trees, boarded on all sides by abandoned machinery and piles of empty wooden tonne crates. I followed his finger with my gaze.

In the distance I could see there was a silver pick-up truck tucked into the gap between the crates and a rusting tank, a ragged tarpaulin was strung above it. I had no idea how it had got there, I could only assume the driver had found another way in that wouldn't take him past the farm. We were closing in fast now. Ahead of us the tactical officers, dressed all in black, were almost at the trees.

Mike brought the car to a halt and we both jumped out to join Tomlin who was waiting a distance away with a uniformed officer and a thick set man in black combats who was likely to be the Tactical Liaison Officer. From where we were it was just possible to catch a glimpse of the doors to the containers but little else. Ahead of us the tactical team were about to go in. The first officers had reached the doors. They were calling a warning. Two officers carrying a door ram stepped forward and drove it into the door, which buckled with a horrible clanging sound, they hit it again and then whatever was holding it gave and the door burst inwards to the sounds of shouting and screaming. There was more shouting, more instructions, more warnings.

A dark-haired thick set man in a tee-shirt and jeans burst screaming through the knot of officers and made a break for it, running across the scrub towards us. He had barely gone twenty metres before two officers had brought him down and were slapping handcuffs on him. They were in, and we were edging forwards.

From inside the building came the roar of more male voices, banging and shouting and a woman screaming and I willed it to be Kathy, but I knew it wasn't. Even as I was heading across the scrub, lungs bursting, I knew instinctively that there was something not right.

As we got to Tomlin's group a radio crackled into life.

'We've got nine,' said a voice on the radio, 'Repeat nine.'

Some part of my brain already had all the answers and the realisation came into sharp unflinching relief as I heard the voice repeat the message again. 'We've got nine.'

'She's not in there,' I said aloud.

Mike and Tomlin turned to look at me. 'What?' said Mike.

'She's not here,' I said. 'I know what this is,' I said. 'This isn't where he kills them.'

Tomlin turned to stare at me and then we were stepping into the rancid, damp, into the fetid over-heated space created inside the containers. They had been crudely joined along the longer sides. Inside it was poorly lit and reeked of cigarette smoke, sweat, women and worse. One wall was lined with narrow makeshift bunks. In one corner was a television, two sofas and a couple of arm chairs surrounding a low coffee table strewn with cups and paper plates and where the girls were all huddled together, all sobbing, some screaming, corralled by the tactical officers. I recognised one – a tall blonde one with doe eyes. None of them spoke English, all of them looked terrified.

Tomlin was on the radio calling up for support.

On the far wall was a stack of boxes with the Isaac's farm logo stamped on them and alongside, three water cooler bottles. This was where Heath had been coming the night he found the body, not to check on his wife, not just to secure the hard drive but to stock up the girls with food and water while the police were on the farm.

Two officers were holding down a tall thin man who fitted the description of the man in the photofit who had been driving the pick-up. Another man, dressed only in his boxer shorts, was kneeling on the filthy floor, being cuffed by a police officer.

A curtain hung across the container dividing off a space. I knew what I'd find when I pulled the curtain aside. It was the film set I had seen on the footage from Heath's hard drive earlier that morning.

For a moment I stood there, taking it in and then turned and walked back outside glad to be breathing in the cold air.

'Kathy isn't here,' I said flatly to Tomlin as I reached the door. 'I noticed the boxes in the film that Heath had on his hard drive this morning. I should have put it together. This is where the films are being made. He wasn't subscribing to a porn channel he was running one. That was what he was watching the night Laura's body was dumped. This is what he's been hiding.'

I felt my head begin to swim and thought I was going to be sick.

By the door were two large striped laundry bags. Pulling on gloves I unzipped the first one, the smell of fabric softener and detergent seemed incongruous amongst all this squalor. 'He brings them fresh clothes. It was on the CCTV. He had those big bags. Food and clothes and water. His wife said she washed them for him. She said it was his overalls.'

It made sense of everything, of the increased food bills, and the water bottles and the lingerie and the unexplained payments into Heath's account. This was it, the thing he was hiding, the thing he thought was worth lying for. He was farming women.

Tomlin called up the officers still up at the farmyard.

'Bring Heath in, we've got him on suspicion of trafficking,' he said. He glanced back towards the open laundry bag. 'And bring his wife in as well. There's no way she didn't have known what was going on, and make sure they're both cautioned.'

*

Along with a canine unit they went through both containers and all the surrounding tumbled down sheds and barns, they searched the pick-up, Heath's house and garage but though there was plenty of evidence to support the trafficking charges there was no sign of Kathy.

A specialist team arrived with transport and an ambulance arrived to start processing and examining the girls. Once they were on site Tomlin could officially hand the scene over to them. Officers took Linda Heath into custody.

I had peeled off the tactical vest and was sitting in Mike's car, staring at my phone willing Kathy to ring.

'We've got nothing,' I said, drained now, the adrenaline all gone, leaving exhaustion and a grim realisation in its wake. 'Nothing. It isn't Heath, is it? It never was him. This was his big secret, wasn't it? The nights he sloped off he was bringing them food and water, and doing God knows what down here.'

'And we've got him for it. He won't be doing it again,' said Mike.

It was no comfort.

'We need to go back through what we've got on Laura Lamb with a fine tooth comb.'

239

'We've got bugger all,' I snapped. 'That's the problem. No suspects. Nothing, and no idea where Kathy is, no idea. If it's not Heath or the bloody Kingsleys then we've got nothing.'

'It might not be him,' said Mike.

'It is him. You're just trying to make it better. He has a type. Kathy is his type. It's too much of a coincidence.'

Tomlin came over, his face full of concern. 'I'm so sorry, Mel,' he said. 'It was our best shot-'

'I should have worked it out sooner,' I said, making the effort to keep it together.

He looked back towards the containers, now surrounded by officers. 'They'll be a while processing this.' He moved in closer. 'We've got officers combing the pub and the area around it. The Kingsleys are out of the picture, both accounted for last night and today. I've got a team going house to house, interviewing the bar staff and pub regulars. We're doing everything we can to find her, Mel. Everything. We've got this, I promise you.'

I nodded, blinking back tears that had threatened since Jimmy had first called me.

'I'll get Mike to drop you off at home,' Tomlin said gently. 'We can get your car brought later.'

'I don't want to go home, Sir. What good can I do there? I need to come back to the station.'

'I understand, Mel, I'd be the same.' He looked at me and then as if coming to a decision said, 'Okay, I want you to keep working the Laura Lamb case, go back through the files, see if there is anything that we've missed.' He paused. 'You understand that you can't be directly involved with investigating your sister's disappearance, don't you?'

I nodded. The trouble was I was already directly involved, and my every instinct told me this was the same man who had taken Laura.

Chapter Twenty
Searching for Kathy

In the incident room officers were also working through the files, some looked at me as I walked in, some studiously avoided looking in my direction or catching my gaze. On the board along with Laura Lamb's photograph was a print off of my sister's picture cropped from the one on my phone. There was a question mark next to it.

I made my way into one of the smaller service rooms. It was barely bigger than a cupboard and had a video link through into the interview rooms. DC Rowe was sitting at the control desk and beckoned me to join her.

'I'm so sorry about your sister,' she said.

I nodded. 'Me too.'

'They'll find her, they're good. You know that,' she said, and then looked at the screen, as if afraid of what my reply might be. I said nothing, I felt every possibility creeping like fire over my skin, so many possibilities that in the end I just felt numb.

The screen showed my brother-in-law, James Alexander Grenard sitting at the table in one of the side rooms at the police station that we had set aside for informal interviews. He was ashen, unshaven and cradling a mug of tea between his fingers. He didn't appear to know that we could see him.

I was surprised when Tomlin stepped into the room. I had thought that perhaps Mike or another member of our team would take the interview. Jimmy was on his feet the minute he heard the door begin to open.

'Have you found her yet?' Jimmy said, the anxiety in

his voice was palpable.

'I'm afraid not, Mr Grenard, but please rest assured we're doing everything in our power to find your wife.'

'Where's Mel?' he said, looking past Tomlin towards the door.

'She's busy working,' said Tomlin gently, pulling out a chair and sitting down at the table. 'You've had a chance to talk to the friend who is looking after your children?'

Jimmy nodded and started to pace. 'Yes, I've told her not to tell the boys anything. Not till we know something definite. She said they're fine there for the time being.'

Tomlin nodded. 'Good. And is there anything else that you need?'

'I'd like my phone back. Just in case Kathy tries to ring me, you know? I don't want to miss it – if she rings, if she can borrow a phone or something.' His voice tailed off and dropped away.

'I'll see what I can do. Why don't you sit down so we can talk? And don't worry. If your wife rings or texts we'll make sure you know.' He picked up a sheaf of documents. 'I've had a look through your statement. There are one or two things that I'd like to clarify if you don't mind, Mr Grenard – may I call you Jimmy?'

Jimmy looked confused. 'Yes, but shouldn't you be out looking for Kathy?'

'We are, I can assure you,' Tomlin said, indicating the seat. Reluctantly Jimmy sat down. Tomlin asked him to go through the events of the night before and of the morning, making notes as he went. He listened carefully. I could see Jimmy beginning to relax a little. And then Tomlin said, 'You say in your statement that you and your wife have been going through...' Tomlin looked down and read from the sheet of paper in the file. 'A *bit of a rough patch.*'

Jimmy took a long breath and nodded. 'That's right, we have, but nothing we can't sort out,' he said. 'That's why she had driven over here. So we could talk.'

'Did you know she was coming to see you?'

'No. No, I didn't.'

'So quite a surprise then?'

Jimmy nodded. 'Yes, you could say that.'

'And was there anything particular you were going to talk about?' Tomlin steepled his fingers and leaned forward.

Jimmy peered at him. I saw him tense. 'What has Mel said?'

Tomlin shook his head. 'Nothing.'

Jimmy bristled. 'Kathy hasn't run off if that's what you're getting at,' he snapped. 'She wouldn't. She wouldn't leave the kids, and she wouldn't have left her phone and her bag if she was buggering off, would she? It's got all her bank cards in it and her purse – and then there's her car. That's at Mel's. Kathy's not someone who would try and frighten me or do something for effect if that's what you're getting at. Something's happened to her and you sitting in here talking to me isn't doing any good at all, all right.'

Tomlin nodded. 'Please bear with me, Jimmy, you understand that we have to look at all possibilities? Would you say that your wife is under any strain? How is she coping with your marital problems? Would you say she was depressed?'

I took a breath, I wanted to go into the interview room and shake him. I hadn't considered the direction in which Tomlin was taking the questioning. I suppose it ought to have done but it hadn't occurred to me for one moment, not one moment that Kathy might have killed herself or run away. I wanted to go in there and tell Tomlin, but didn't – this might be my sister but it wasn't my interview. And I knew too, realistically that he had to exclude the possibilities.

I could see Jimmy considering the idea for a few moments and then he nodded and his expression subtly changed from angry to anxiety, maybe, his face said, *he* was the victim here. 'Yes, I mean she might be,' he said, an almost theatrical catch in his voice. 'The boys are still small and I'm away a lot of the time. It's not easy for her, or me come to that. Tough on us both. I'm missing out on so much of them growing up, all the milestones, you know.'

I wanted to scream.

'How old are they?' Tomlin was asking.

'Four and six, I mean they can be a handful, but they're basically really good lads. And every couple has its ups and downs, don't they?'

'And what do you do, Jimmy? What sort of work?'

'I'm a builder. General builder, really, but I'm working on the second fix at the moment on a new estate. We're working with the technology boys – they're all singing and all dancing these new houses, but I can turn my hand to most things.' There was a little swagger in the way he said it. 'I've been all over the country with this company on new builds. Reading, just outside Harrogate, Southampton – we go all over, and the money is good.'

Tomlin nodded. 'And it gets you away from your wife,' he said.

It was a comment so far out of left field that even I was taken aback. Jimmy stared at him, his eyes alight with indignation. 'What the hell is that supposed to mean?'

Tomlin's voice was calm and even. 'We've been through the cell phone you left with the officer this morning and recovered the deleted texts.' He slid Jimmy's phone across the table sealed in an evidence bag.

Jimmy's face flushed scarlet. 'What the fuck-' he said.

But Tomlin was now focused and reading from the sheet in front of him.

'"Will see you soon, baby, can't wait to be with you." And, "We still on for later?" Those are anonymous, and not from your wife's phone. There are several here from someone called Milly who wants to tell you that you're going to be a father and she can't wait to spend the rest of her life with you.'

Tomlin looked up at him.

Jimmy was ashen.

'And this one, "Will be in Denham next week, when can I see you?" Those are just a small selection of what we've managed to find over the last month or so. I've got someone now tracing who those calls are from, Jimmy.'

I could see the muscle working in Jimmy's jaw. He said nothing.

Tomlin waited, and then said. 'Would it be fair to say that your wife showing up in Denham was not only a surprise to you, but also cramped your style?'

Jimmy looked down at the desk and then said in a low even voice. 'I would never hurt Kathy.'

'But after Kathy walked out, you didn't go after her?'

'No, I thought she would calm down and come back or call me or something.'

'So you stayed in the pub for the rest of the evening?'

'Yes,' said Jimmy.

'So you were there all evening until closing time.'

Jimmy nodded.

'And can anyone verify that? You said you were with the men you work with, presumably they can corroborate your account.'

I saw Jimmy turn slightly, saw something pass over his face, and then he said. 'I might have slipped out for a bit.'

Tomlin nodded. 'After your wife left the pub?'

Jimmy nodded.

'How long after?'

'I don't know.'

'Ten minutes, half an hour?'

'Maybe ten minutes.'

'And did you see Kathy when you went out? Try to find her maybe?'

'No, no I didn't.'

Tomlin made a note. 'And how long were you gone for?'

And there was that little movement again in

245

Jimmy's face, uncomfortable at being put on the spot, unsure how to answer without revealing something he would prefer to keep hidden.

'I don't know,' he said. 'Maybe half an hour. Maybe a bit longer.'

'And where did you go?'

This time he knew the answer. 'I went to get something to eat. A pizza. Meat feast with extra pepperoni.'

'Do you know the name of the café? I presume it was a cafe?'

'It's a takeaway place, but you can eat in little booths - I don't know the name but I can tell you where it was.'

Tomlin wrote down the directions.

'And your wife didn't try to contact you again after she left the pub? None of your colleagues told you that she had come back?'

'No, and she didn't phone.' Jimmy gestured across the table. 'You've got my phone – you know she didn't.'

'I wondered if you maybe saw her in the car park? Or maybe spotted her in town somewhere? Did you suggest maybe going back to the pub, walk her in through the back of the car park, away from the crowd so you could have that chance to talk.'

Jimmy shook his head. 'No, look I don't know what you're doing here, but I would never ever hurt Kathy, and while you're wasting time with me, she's still out there somewhere.'

'Did you ever hit your wife, Jimmy – you know in the heat of an argument?'

'Christ no, no of course not. What are you trying to say? I love Kathy–'

'What time did Kathy arrive at the pub?'

Jimmy considered his reply and then said, 'It was about half past eight, maybe a bit later when I saw her.'

Tomlin made another note. I knew that we couldn't assume that Kathy had been taken or had left then. It was possible that she had gone somewhere else, another pub, gone somewhere to eat and then gone back to the pub car park possibly to talk to Jimmy or meet someone else, but the time she had been in the pub with Jimmy allowed us to begin to frame the event.

On screen Tomlin was wrapping up the interview. A few minutes later they were taking Jimmy back to the hotel where he was staying, along with a police liaison officer, with instructions not to go anywhere. We'd need more but not yet. Officers added Jimmy's photo to the ones being shown house to house and around the pubs, cafes and restaurants.

And I went back to my desk to reassess the work we had done on Laura Lamb and go through my notes. It was hard to concentrate but I was certain that somewhere in Laura's case was the key to finding Kathy, although it was close to impossible to keep that in my mind on the screen or the page.

One of the local detective constables came in, eyes roaming the desks till he found me. 'We've just had the tox screen in on Laura Lamb.'

'And?' I said taking the file he was holding.

'Standard prescription sleeping tablets, Temazepam. A big enough dose to make her drowsy and compliant.'

I nodded, 'Thank you. I took the file from him.'

So our killer drugged Laura, kept her somewhere for around twelve hours, and then strangled her before wrapping and staging her. There was a glimmer of hope that if our man had taken Kathy, and followed the same pattern, then she was still alive. I stared down at the report, my mind making no sense of what I was seeing on the page. Laura Lamb's murder was supposed to be my main focus. If I couldn't work it then Tomlin would be justified in sending me home.

I struggled to concentrate. If we didn't think it was related, then Kathy's disappearance would be handed off to another team. Was there enough to suggest they were linked? Mike was right, it seemed too soon after the last one. Kathy bore a strong resemblance to Laura Lamb and Anya, but was that enough?

247

I pulled up what I had and went right back to the beginning, trying hard to concentrate, trying hard to focus on what we knew, what was missing. I read and reread. Officers had been on site and interviewed all of the Kingsleys' staff and had found nothing inconsistent that raised any flags and all of them, including Roger, her immediate boss, had solid alibis for the time of Laura's disappearance and the time her body was dumped.

I had asked DC Rowe to go through missing persons' reports for the last five years to check for women matching Laura Lamb, and now Kathy's description, while I had checked off points relating to the killer's MO and it was this list I went back to, trying to drown out the panic that threatened to overwhelm me.

I looked at the names, Anya Vassali, who had been found by a line repair crew under fallen trees near woodland in Dogmore in Berkshire, Carly Brand found on an old industrial site outside York. I looked at the other two names, Lisa Rhodes from Southampton, who had been found in the New Forest and Kylie Roberts, living in Maidstone, who had been found in a derelict shed on an isolated stretch of coastline overlooking the Isle of Sheppey. I looked at the dates. Five women over three years if you included Laura.

Laura had been taken in February, Anya had last been seen in early September, Carly in November, Lisa in December and Kylie in May - I pulled up a map and dropped pins into their towns of origin and the dump sites to see if I could see any sort of a pattern. If there was, it wasn't obvious. They were geographically diverse, the only thing they really had in common was isolation and a strong possibility that it would be a long time before their bodies would be discovered, but this was by no means unique.

The thing that linked them was the appearance of all five women was very similar, around the same age, build and colouring. Were we really looking at something bigger than just the murder of Laura Lamb or was I seeing something that wasn't there?

I printed off the pictures I now had of Anya and Carly, both women bore a strong resemblance to Laura Lamb. I hadn't heard from the two other officers I had left messages for so picked up the phone and called the first, anything if I thought it might help me find Kathy.

As the phone rang at the far end of the line I glanced up at the clock. It was almost three o'clock. According to Jimmy, Kathy had left the pub around half past eight. Another wave of panic rolled through me. Time was moving too fast. We had to find her soon.

I called Sergeant Robert Lees, the listed contact for the Lisa Rhodes murder investigation. Walkers in the New Forest had found her body. Lisa was slightly older than the other victims, in her early thirties, but a similar build. Certainly close enough for me to see a similarity between Anya, Carly and Laura. Lee's first remark echoed that of the other two officers that I'd talked to.

'We were lucky to have found her at all. She was in a small culvert off the beaten track. One of the ramblers was looking for a quiet spot to answer a call of nature, and that's when they found her.

'Lisa was thirty-two. She'd dropped out of college, got a caution for possession of cannabis in her twenties, got picked up at an illegal rave, dealt Molly from time to time – a bit of a wild one but nothing too serious, and she seemed well liked. She had been working a series of casual jobs, living with a boyfriend in a bedsit, although it wasn't going well and he wanted her out. We liked him for it. They had had a pretty fiery relationship and every indication was that she had overstayed her welcome, but we couldn't pin it on him. When she disappeared she was on the dole, doing a few hours here and there cash in hand, and working as a volunteer for a housing charity. Indications were she was getting herself sorted out. The charity was looking to fund her training as a social worker. To be honest we turned up a lot of possible suspects from that connection, but you know how it goes, one by one we ruled them out; we worked the case for months but nothing panned out.'

'You said in the report that she was posed?'

'It appeared that way, although she'd been there awhile so it's impossible to be completely certain. The culvert is in a pleat of land, steep sides, only one way in, anyway she was in a ring of tree stumps that looked like they'd been dragged there, although actually at least half of them had been growing there at one time or another, and there was greenery and branches arranged round her, not to conceal the body, just placed over her and the polythene was cut away so that you could see her face. There were ligature marks on her hands and feet that suggested she had been restrained prior to death. The timeline we'd got was her leaving to go and view an empty housing association property in the late afternoon. It was part of a new development, there were three self-contained one-bedroom flats in a big warehouse conversion that had been set aside for social housing. The rest of the flats were all for sale, really nice places - and at that stage there were probably only two or three residents moved in, so nobody saw anything - and the residents' alibis all checked out.'

'Given the trouble she had been having with her boyfriend, her boss had been pulling strings to ensure she got one, nice they were, shame the poor little sod never got the chance to move in.'

I thanked Lees, and asked him to send me the names of their possible suspects and photos. 'Did she have a car?'

'I got your message about the tracker, but no, she didn't have so much as a bike let alone a car, neither did the boyfriend.' He promised to send me over anything that he thought might help.

'Can I just ask,' he said as I was about to hang up. 'Have you got another one?' he said.

I felt a flutter of anxiety, talking to him had momentarily made me forget about Kathy. The thought made me feel guilty.

'Possibly,' I said.

'You're ringing round because you think there's more, don't you? I always felt the same, it didn't feel like his first, more like we'd just uncovered the tip of an iceberg. Have you called Rachel Purvis yet?'

It was the next name on my list, the officer listed as the contact for Kylie Robert's murder. 'No, not yet, why?'

'She thought we'd got a serial killer and that he was maybe a travelling salesman or a lorry driver, spent God knows how much time on it; we spoke several times, but she just couldn't pin down the link. How long have you gone back?'

'Five years.'

'She thinks he might have been operating for closer to ten – you need to talk to her. Last time we spoke she had a file on this guy a mile thick but she couldn't find the common denominator.'

'I will, thank you.'

'And remember me to her.'

'I will.'

I took a breath; there was a part of me wanted to talk to him about Kathy but I wasn't sure I could, so I thanked him and hung up.

I looked back at the dates of the disappearances spread over the previous three years.

I kept to what we knew, trying to quell the thoughts that Kathy might join this list. So, Laura Lamb would be his latest victim, in February 2018, and although Anya's was the most recent body found, Carly was most likely to have been his previous victim, found in November 2017 in York, prior to that there was Kylie in May 2017 and Lisa in December 2016 then Anya in September of that year. So we had dates to help pin down any suspect we found, and it looked like he was taking two a year, possibly. I needed to get this in front of Tomlin but first I wanted to talk to Rachel Purvis.

I picked up the phone. The number I had on file turned out to be unavailable so I called the station switchboard at Maidstone where she was stationed. The operator put me through to the duty sergeant who told me that DS Purvis was currently unavailable and on sick leave, but would put me through to someone who could perhaps help. Telephone tag.

The woman who eventually answered the phone was another DS, Carol Hardy.

'I'm afraid she's not here, she's off on sick leave at the moment,' she said, telling me what I already knew. 'Is there anything I can help you with?'

I explained what I was looking for, told her about Laura Lamb, the similar MO, the things kicked up by the database, the polythene, the possible posing, and the similarity of appearance between the victims. I didn't mention Kathy.

Carol Hardy took a breath. 'I'm not sure how much Robert Lees told you, but Rachel was absolutely convinced that Kylie's murder was the work of a serial killer.' She paused. 'When I say convinced, to be honest she was obsessed. She just wouldn't let it go.' I could hear the concern in her voice. 'We all have one, don't we,' she said grimly. 'Something that eats away at you, and that you just can't let go, or maybe it won't let go of you? Anyway, she is off on extended sick leave - so I'm happy to help if I can-'

'Can you tell me about Kylie's murder?'

'Yes, sure can you just give me a minute to pull up the files?'

'Did you work the case?'

'Yes. Everyone was working it. But if you mean did I go to the dump site, then yes, I went with Rachel. We were the first detectives on the scene. Kylie had been missing for about two, nearly three weeks by that time.'

I pulled up the photo of Kylie on my desk top. The image was pixelated as if it had come from a newspaper. She looked to have darker hair than the others although the description had her down as a blonde.

I could hear Carol tapping away at her keyboard as she retrieved the file. 'Here we go. Twenty-seven, living with a female partner; she worked for a local estate agent doing clerical, accounts and some reception work. She was last seen leaving their offices at five pm the Thursday after the May Bank holiday. She told the woman she worked with that she had got to drop something off. Her colleague had no idea what the something was or whether it was work related or personal.

'Her partner, a teacher, reported her missing the following morning after she failed to turn up at home. We asked the estate agent to do an inventory of keys after the fact to see if any were missing – that was Rachel's idea. She thought maybe Kylie was going to meet someone at one of the properties they had on their books after work, but nothing came up.'

'Easy enough to have another one cut?' I suggested.

'True, but we hadn't got anything to prove that was the case. We interviewed everyone including the local key-cutting shop and locksmiths, and realised pretty quickly that the estate agents often held duplicates of keys for houses, and on more than one occasion Kylie had been sent out to get extras cut. No record by the key-cutters of which keys she was having cut or to which properties they related. And the estate agent's system wasn't exactly watertight.

'So Rachel could have been right?'

'That's true, but we also discovered she had been having an affair with a male co-worker. We spent a lot of time on him, and the girlfriend, oh and there was a co-worker that Kylie had caught with her hand in the petty cash, but they all came up empty. Rachel became more and more convinced that we were dealing with someone from outside the area who had done this before. And started to trawl for cases with a similar MO-'

'It says she was blonde but in the photo I have she looks like a brunette. I was thinking maybe this guy has a type?'

'Uhuh, I see what you mean.' There was the sound of more keystrokes. 'Yes, hang on, there is a better picture here. I'll send it over.' She was murmuring something. I assumed she was skimming the information she had on file. 'Bottle blonde,' she said after a moment or two.

The photo that dropped into my inbox was of a group of young professionals in a promotional shot, all dressed in the universal uniform of the estate agent – a good suit, perfect hair, nice teeth. In the front row smiling for the camera was a young woman who could have passed for Laura Lamb in a line up, with jaw length bobbed blonde hair tucked behind her ears. I wasn't imagining it. He had a type.

'Okay,' I said trying to keep the tremor out of my voice. 'What about the dump site?'

'Tucked out of the way, it had been a fishing shack at one time or another but had been abandoned and was partially collapsed, not hard to get to if you knew where it was, but bloody nigh on impossible to find if you didn't. It looked like the placing of the body was very deliberate – she was inside the remains of an old rowing boat; it was really unnerving when you went in. The sunlight came through the holes in the roof picking her out in the dark – really shook me up.

'And were there fewer polythene layers over the face?'

'What was left of it, yes.' I heard something of the shock of it still in her voice. 'It had been really warm. Students were out doing some sort of ecological survey. The bloke who was in charge of them was ex-forces, recognised the signs when he saw all the flies and then the smell, kept them back and called it in.

'And was the body decorated– flowers or leaves or–'

'I don't know, certainly nothing conclusive. It could have been but it was hard to tell. She had been there a while by the time we found her. There were some plants in there but I couldn't say if they were put there deliberately or had blown in. It was hot. She'd steamed inside the polythene. It stank in there and what I remember most is the light on what was left of her face from the sunshine and the smell rolling out to meet you.'

Carol paused. 'It's why Rachel is off sick. She was sure he had to have killed others. When she started to look, she ended up convinced that there were at least eight she'd been looking at that she was certain were linked, and there might be more, once you dragged the net a bit wider.' She paused.

I had found five including Laura. I wondered who else she had found. I'd like to talk to her or at the very least see her notes.

'And what do you think?' I asked.

'Really? I don't know. You know what it's like - you go looking for bogeymen in this job and they're certainly there, but whether they are the bogeyman you're looking for is another matter entirely. Rachel saw all sorts of links in all sorts of places that she couldn't prove, and in the end, she had a breakdown. I understand, she just wants to stop him.'

'When do you think she'll be back?'

Carol sighed. 'Honestly? I don't think she will be coming back.'

I asked the last of the questions, asked her if she would mind sending me the files and Rachel's list, thanked her and hung up.

Tomlin came over. 'I wanted you to know that we've got everyone looking,' he said. 'We're doing everything we can – we'll find her.'

I wished I believed him.

'I need you to look at these, Sir,' I said, taking the photographs from the printer. 'I'm certain we're looking for someone who has done this before, who has a type,' I paused, as I slid the corporate image of Kylie towards him.

'Laura Lamb?' he said.

'I shook my head, 'No, a woman called Kylie Roberts, found wrapped in polythene in a fishing hut on the Isle of Sheppey. 'I'm getting the files sent over.' I took a breath. 'I think he is the man who has my sister.'

Tomlin's face was a mask of concern. He took the images and sheets of paper and then said, 'Why don't you go home? I promise I will ring if we have any news.'

'I don't want to be on my own,' I said, and when the words came out they were as much a surprise to me as they were to Tomlin.

'I can organise a family liaison officer to stay with you,' he said. 'There's nothing we can't manage here. I promise you–'

I looked at the sheaf of papers on his hand. 'He has a type.' I repeated.

Tomlin, to give him his due, waited and listened. 'I do know that it's not evidence,' I said. 'I've got nothing to prove the theory, but there is a strong similarity between the cases and the physical resemblance between at least four of the victims. And Kathy fits the profile.' I paused again.

'We'll go over it all, I promise you. But now I want you to go home,' he said.

I was about to protest but he held up a hand. 'We are doing everything we can, Mel. I've called in extra officers, we're all over the town, every shed, every outbuilding, every house is being searched. If Kathy is here, we'll find her. Now go home. Are you okay to drive yourself or do you need someone to drive you?'

'I'll be fine,' I said.

I didn't want to go, being at home would take me away from the search and the first-hand immediate knowledge, the frustrations and the progress that came with it, and that was what Tomlin was trying to protect me from.

'I'll send a liaison officer,' he said, as I picked up my coat and bag. 'And we will let you know as soon as we have anything. I promise.'

I found that I couldn't look at him, couldn't meet his eye.

As I got to the door Mike came over. 'I'll drop by later with an update,' he said, touching my arm. I nodded, not able to meet his eye.

Chapter Twenty-One
Light

Outside the day was already darkening. I made my way across the car park feeling the chill after the airless warmth of the office. As I reached my car I pulled out the remote and pressed the button, I heard the clunk as the doors unlocked and the lights automatically came on. *The lights came on.* The idea fired a thought and the thought caught light. At Laura's flat when we had been searching it the lights had come on as the daylight faded.

'*We go all over the country.*' Jimmy had said. *We're working with the technology boys – they're all singing and all dancing these new houses.*'

I stood stock still as the pieces fell into place.

Anya Vassali had been staying in a state of the art architect designed house. Lisa Rhodes was going to look at a new flat in a prestigious new warehouse conversion. Kylie Roberts had worked for an estate agent. Carly Brand was having technical issues with the internet connection at her flat and had left to travel to a satellite office. There was a connection.

I turned and hurried back into the police station, taking the steps two at a time. As I got to the incident room Mike looked up in surprise. 'What is it?' he said. 'I thought you were going home? Are you okay?'

Tomlin had spotted me too and came across looking anxious. 'What's the matter?'

'Where did Jimmy say that he had been with the company he works for?'

Tomlin pulled a face. 'York, I'm not sure of the other locations, but I can get Rowe to pull up the footage,' he said. 'Why?'

'I think I've found the connection. We need to find out what the company is called that Jimmy works for and where they've been over the last three or four years, and then map the sites.' I had my coat off and was heading back to my desk.

'I sent you home,' Tomlin said grudgingly.

'I know but I think I might have found the link. Smart houses,' I said 'Integrated systems.'

I pulled up the files from the earlier victims onto my computer screen, as I typed DC Rowe came back in with a list of the places Jimmy had mentioned. Reading, Harrogate, Southampton, Denham Market, and then between us we mapped the dump sites for the earlier victims – none of the sites were more than an hour's drive from where the bodies had been found, and four of the five were much closer, one of those being Laura lamb.

Tomlin looked at the pins and nodded. And then turned to Mike Carlton. 'I want you to go and bring Jimmy Grenard back in.'

I turned back to the terminal and did a search for the new estate that was being built just outside Denham. The main contractor was listed along with various partners. 'ISFH Technology Partnership' was listed as providing *seamless integrated systems* for the executive specification homes. *'Total control at the touch of a button as well as remotely from your smart phone.'*

Rowe, at the next desk, was ahead of me and already trying to find out where else the company had been working.

She scanned through the text from their website. 'Here we go. They provide whole systems and also offer on-site maintenance and dedicated servicing nationally for everything from a single dwelling through to entire new build housing estates and tower blocks,' she read. 'Says here that they specialise in working on heritage properties. They won some kind of award for work done

258

on a historic mill in Yorkshire that was converted to flats and a warehouse in York.'

She turned to me. 'In York.'

I nodded. 'And Laura's flat was in a converted medieval building. I've got a number for the management company in King's Lynn. I met their concierge-'

Rowe clicked back to the case notes that were logged onto the system. 'Here we are,' she said and tapped the numbers into the keypad while I turned back to the information on my screen.

Rowe asked questions and nodded and asked more. I waited. She wrote something down. I waited. She thanked them and hung up and then dialled another number and asked the same questions. After five minutes she hung up and turned to me.

'The management team for Laura's building have a service contract with IFSH. They were the company that installed the original system when they did the conversion. Laura Lamb bought her flat off plan. She was one of the first to move in while the system was still being installed.'

I felt my heart tighten in my chest.

'We need to know the name of the engineers who installed the systems in King's Lynn and who has been there to service it.' I said, 'And we need to know who they've got working on the estate in Denham.'

Rowe nodded, and called IFSH. After what seemed an eternity on hold, she said, 'They're checking and have said they'll get back to me.'

If we were saying that our killer was connected to Laura's flat, it still isn't quite enough - one link to one woman is not enough to persuade anyone that the murders are being carried out by the same person. The way they were wrapped and posed after death was another similarity that indicated the same perpetrator but again without evidence it wasn't definitive proof.

I scrolled through the witness statements from the other cases to find the one that I was looking for. 'Anya

Vassali was staying in a state of the art architect designed house. Anya told the postmistress that she had to go back to meet someone. What if she was going to meet a service engineer for the house's integrated systems?' I said. I knew it was a stretch. I knew it.

Rowe nodded and picked up the phone. 'What's the architect's name?'

'Jack Fending,' I said.

'It's just a phone call,' Rowe said. 'It will take five minutes to verify. What's his number?'

I read it out. She tapped the number in, introduced herself and asked the questions. She made notes. I could hardly bear to listen. When she hung up Rowe said, 'Apparently there had been a problem with the central control unit, he thinks it was while Anya was staying there but can't be sure, although he said he would check his diary as it's the kind of thing he would have made a note of. He knew an engineer had come out at least once. Fending wasn't expecting him back as the problem appeared to be solved. He didn't use IFSH, he used another company, but he got the impression that the engineer was self-employed. He gave me their number, I'll ring them.'

I nodded.

'There is a possibility that he might have worked for other companies,' said Rowe, covering the receiver.

She was right, but a part of me had hoped that there would be a direct link back to IFSH. I took a breath and tried to steady the little flutter of fear. I felt certain that this was the answer, and then I wondered if perhaps this was how Rachel Purvis had felt. Hadn't she been certain that the murders were linked too?

It felt like things were moving, getting faster, getting closer, rushing towards me and I felt dizzy and sick.

One of the local PCs came over and said, 'DCI Tomlin wanted you to know that we've got Jimmy Grenard in interview one. He's being interviewed under caution.'

I nodded, thanked him, wondering as I got to my feet if I had been mistaken, what if I had just led the team to my brother-in-law? Was he the one we were looking for? What if he had been killing Kathy again and again because until now he couldn't bear to kill the real thing. What if her walking out on him had been the last straw? The thought stuck in my throat. What if Jimmy had murdered my sister?

I thought about him turning up at my door a few nights earlier reeking of booze and wondered if that was real or if Jimmy had just been making the effort to give himself an alibi. And then there was what Jimmy might say in the interview, what he might tell Tomlin about our relationship. How would that look?

I felt my colour rising, while at the same time wondering how I could be so fucking shallow when Kathy was missing and in danger. Except of course that, what we had done back in Ross-on-Wye, gave Jimmy a motive. And me.

Rowe meanwhile was still on the phone. Now that we had Jimmy, I joined her. It took half a dozen phone calls to confirm what I had suspected. Now I knew what we were looking for the pattern seemed obvious.

Carly Brand's body was discovered in a derelict building next door to a building site where IFSH were working. Her building had been having issues with the computerised security and lighting systems, and they had sent an engineer from the IFSH site to sort it out.

The engineer had been to the building three times in six weeks. The building manager said it was usually reliable but he had been relieved that there was an engineer working on another project so close and had been able to come to put it right. Conscientious he said, the man had kept coming back to check up and ensure that the system was working properly.

The flat that Lisa had been viewing had a centralised computer system that controlled the heating and lighting in the flats and the public areas. It had been installed by IFSH.

An engineer had liaised with the estate agents that Kylie worked for to arrange access to various properties that had smart systems installed. Yes, sometimes he rang to organise site visits, yes sometimes he arranged for her to drop keys off so he could have access. The young woman I spoke to thought it was a company with a name like Fish but couldn't be sure, but would see if she could find out and get back to me.

What we needed was the name of the engineer. Rowe called IFSH again; they were polite and helpful and apparently still trying to find the information. How hard could it be? The receptionist said that they were a small company, always busy, always in demand with more work than they knew what to do with.

I called up Geraldine Sloane to start a social media search, starting with Jimmy and the company itself.

I went in to brief Tomlin on what we had.

'That's good work, Mel. Look, if you want to hand it off and go home now, everyone would understand. We can take it from here. We've got the connection – we can chase it.'

'We just need a name,' I said. 'Jimmy is working with these guys. He has to know who it is.'

Tomlin picked up the notes Rowe and I had made. 'Let's talk to him then, shall we?'

I left Rowe working the phones and went into the side room where I could observe the interview. Jimmy looked confused when Tomlin opened the door. 'Have you found her?'

'You understand you are still under caution, Mr Grenard?'

Jimmy looked stunned. 'What the fuck? Do I need a solicitor?'

'I don't know,' said Tomlin calmly. 'You tell me.'

'I don't understand.'

'What we need from you, Jimmy, is a reason not to arrest you in connection with your wife's disappearance.' His tone was calm, almost icily so.

Jimmy blinked. 'What? Surely you're not serious?'

'Where did you go after Kathy left the pub on Thursday evening?'

Jimmy swallowed hard. I could feel his resistance.

'Did you take her somewhere? Maybe you had a row, maybe she wouldn't listen?'

Jimmy's face contorted in pain. 'I wouldn't hurt Kathy. I already told you that, I couldn't.'

'So where did you go?'

Jimmy took a breath. You'd have to have been dead not to see the struggle going on in his head, finally he said in a soft almost inaudible voice. 'I was meeting someone.'

'Someone?' encouraged Tomlin.

'This is really hard,' said Jimmy. 'I don't know if I can—' I could see the panic on his face.

'Jimmy,' said Tomlin. 'We need a name.'

The word came out in a rush. 'Her name is Liz, Liz Hartman.' He paused. 'She's the boss's wife. I went out of the pub and met her. She told Richard she was picking up a takeaway.'

'And she'll be able to corroborate this?'

Jimmy blanched. 'She's married to my boss.'

Tomlin sighed. 'Do you know where Mrs Hartman is at the moment?'

'At home I should think. Her old man always rents a house where we're working so they can be together, he doesn't like to leave her on her own.'

Tomlin glanced at Jimmy. 'And how did you arrange to meet her?'

'You read the text. Monday afternoon I told the guys I work with that I was feeling rough, and nipped round there to see her. We'd emailed last week when she had got herself settled in the new place. She sent me the address. Thursday night, Richard was driving to Cambridge for some meeting or other. She said he wasn't likely to be back until midnight. I went to talk to her, told her about Kathy, grabbed a pizza and then came back to the pub. I suppose I was gone about half an hour, forty minutes tops. We sat in her car. Talked.'

Tomlin nodded. 'Okay. I'd like Mrs Hartman's details. And now what I want is a list of the people you work with and a list of the contracts you've worked on where you've been subcontracting for IFSH.'

Jim frowned. 'Seriously? Why? I just said I was with Liz, she can tell you. I mean there is no way the blokes know anything. Christ, Hartman will kill me if he finds out.'

Tomlin pushed across a piece of paper and pen. 'Their names.'

Jimmy nodded and picked up the pen.

*

DC Rowe opened the door to the observation room and stepped inside. 'Scuse me Sarge but IFSH have just sent us a list of workers they have on site in Denham. They employ administrative staff but all of their fitters and engineers are sub-contractors or self-employed. They've given me the name of the main subcontractors working on the installation at Denham. Richard Hartman. He's the guy providing plumbers and carpenters, basically the building side, and then there are the installation engineers. There are two of them, Polish guys,' she glanced down at the sheet of paper in her hand. 'Aleksander Wiśniewski and Tomas Kowalski. Aleksander Wiśniewski is the lead engineer.'

I nodded. 'Let's go with them first. Can you run those names?'

Rowe nodded. 'Do you want me to ring the subcontractor, Richard Hartman?'

I considered for a few moments and then shook my head, 'No, we don't want to spook any of them.'

Tomlin was still in the interview room where Jimmy was compiling a list. When he was done Tomlin got to his feet and came out into the main office. I stepped out to meet him.

Tomlin glanced down at the list. 'I need to talk to Tom Green about man power. We need to get all these men picked up and get someone to confirm your brother-in-law's alibi,' he said and headed off toward Tom Green's desk.

It was late Friday afternoon. The reality was if we didn't get to the building site fast and pick up the men soon they would be off site and on their way home for the weekend. It was already almost totally dark. The chances were that they had already left.

It seemed like seconds after Tomlin had spoken to Tom Green that people were on the move and hurrying outside.

I glanced back at Jimmy still sitting in the interview room; I have never seen anyone look more alone. I went back to my desk, and then there was stillness, waiting. I could hardly bear it.

While we waited Rowe and I ran the names. We started with the engineers.

Aleksander Wiśniewski came back as a computer engineer from Warsaw with a string of letters after his name, and was currently working as *part of our highly skilled subcontracting team,*' for IFSH. We found a picture of him on their website. He was in his mid to late thirties, tall and slim with a great shock of thick blonde hair, and dark eyes. Tomas Kowalski was thicker set with beetling brows and a paunch. He looked to be around the same age but with dark slicked back hair and sideburns.

Half an hour after officers had gone off to the building site, there was a slight rumble downstairs, and then a clamour that echoed through the building as officers brought the IFSH men in from the building crew. The men were still in work clothes, boiler suits and high vis vests, heavy jackets, boots. They had loud voices and all had an air of surprise and indignation.

A PC had also brought in Liz Hartman. She was downstairs in another office. The duty staff began the job of processing them. And I could only observe.

It quickly became apparent as the duty sergeant crossed the names off the list given to them by Jimmy Grenard that one of the men was missing, and not only that but while we had seven men on Jimmy's list one of the men from IFSH's list wasn't there either. The officer went through the names again. There was no sign of Aleksander Wiśniewski, and when asked they denied all knowledge of knowing anyone called Aleksander Wiśniewski. Their engineer was called Lennie Novak – the seventh member of their team, and he hadn't been on site all day.

Richard Hartman, their boss, said Lennie had phoned in that morning to say he had got some kind of a bug, and wondered if he had caught it off Jimmy, who had been off sick on and off all week. Lennie was their lead engineer. Hartman said he often had to go and do installations, repairs and servicing that weren't related to the main job but he was a good man, worked all hours.

The only good thing about that was that if Novak was our man then he wouldn't know that we were hunting for him. The bad thing was that he had a whole day to cover his tracks and move on.

I kept looking up at the clock, willing the hands to slow down.

The men's stories dovetailed: Lennie Novak drove a white Mercedes van in which he stored the specialist parts and spares for the systems as well as his own tools, he lived off site in a caravan which he took from job to job. No one knew that much about him. He was a quiet man. He didn't socialise much, the odd beer after work but not much more than that. And yes, he often went off site to service or repair other systems that had been installed by the company. No one knew where his caravan was parked. No one knew where he was.

I rang IFSH to try and track down Lennie Novak and see if we could find a home address. The woman I spoke to sounded slightly guarded. Yes, they used Novak occasionally. No, they weren't able to furnish a home address for him. He was paid through a company. She gave me the company address. DVLA had no record of a vehicle registered in that name, and although Novak's bank details checked out the company address was fictitious.

An alert was put out to be on the lookout for a large white Mercedes van towing a caravan and being driven by a single white male. Realistically in Norfolk those were not rare. We needed more.

We had been lucky to have found the men at the site at all. The weather was so bad that they had been planning to leave early. Another few more minutes and we would have missed them. The construction site would be closed at five for the weekend with just a skeleton security staff in place. The show homes would reopen the next morning at 9 am so that the developers could show people around, but the rest of the site would be shut off.

While the initial interviews were helpful, the truth was no one had any idea where Lennie Novak was and we had very little to go on to help us find him.

'Let me talk to Jimmy, Sir,' I said to Tomlin, 'Please, we need to find out what we can about Novak. Jimmy knows me, he'll talk to me. It has to be worth a shot, hasn't it?'

Reluctantly, Tomlin agreed.

Jimmy was hunched over the table in the interview room, all his usual swagger drained away. He was the colour of milk; he looked cold, old and desperate. As I walked in relief washed across his face.

'Oh thank God, Mel, what the fuck is going on. Is Kathy here? Where was she?'

I motioned him to sit back down. 'We haven't found her yet Jimmy. I need you to help me.'

'Anything,' he said, his voice cracked with emotion. 'That other copper said they thought I'd done something to her. I wouldn't, you know that, I wouldn't-'

Only break her beautiful loving heart, I thought miserably, looking at him.

'It's not about Kathy, I want you to tell me everything you know about Lennie Novak. What do you know about him?'

Jimmy shrugged. 'Nothing really. He never says very much.'

'Has he got a family?'

'I don't know. He never talks about them if he has.'

'And was he in the pub the other night when Kathy came in?'

Jimmy considered. 'Yes, he was. What's all this about? We were just having a drink.'

'And was he with you all evening?'

I could see him considering. 'No, he wasn't but that's pretty much par for the course for him.'

'Okay and what does he drive?'

'A Mercedes panel van. I don't know what the reg is but it's fairly new.'

'And is that a works van? Maybe with decals or a logo or something?'

Jimmy shook his head. 'God no, he'd hate that. He always keeps it totally spotless. If you look inside it, it looks like it's brand new. He always covers the floor in polythene so he doesn't get boot marks all over the floor. All fitted out so he can strap stuff down, tie stuff in, so nothing moves.'

'And he brought it onto site?'

Jimmy nodded. 'What is this about, Mel? Why are you looking at Lennie?'

'And you're sure you can't remember the registration.'

'No, but I'd have thought security probably have it. You can't just drive onto the site, you have to sign in.'

I nodded. Time was of the essence. 'That's good. I won't be a minute – and I'll be back, I promise,' I said and stepped out into the corridor to pass on what Jimmy had told me to Mike. Then I stepped back inside.

'I don't understand, what's Lennie got to do with any of this?' Jimmy said.

'That's what we're trying to find out. What do you

know about him?'

'Lennie?' Jimmy shrugged. 'Nothing really. He's not much of a people person, just does his job, does it well. He's really thorough, conscientious, barely talks to anyone. I mean he's civil enough but not really friendly.'

'But you socialise?'

'We have the odd drink after work. He never stays the distance, just has a beer and then goes back off to his caravan.'

'And was he definitely in the pub the other night when you met Kathy?'

'Yes, what is this? Do you think Lennie is involved in this?' Jimmy said.

'Let me ask the questions, Jimmy. What about his caravan? Where does he keep it?'

'Dunno. I don't think I've ever seen it.'

'But do you know where he's parked up?'

Jimmy shook his head. 'No, not a clue. He's not someone who likes mixing. And he does other contracts servicing other systems, so sometimes he's gone for maybe for a day or two, sometimes a week and then comes back. I can see a caravan is a sensible choice if you're on the road all the time.'

'Okay, and you don't know where he's parked it?'

'No, but if you want to know more about Lennie you should really ask Tomas, they worked together all the time.'

'Okay, we will. Do you know someone called Aleksander Wiśniewski?'

Jimmy looked blank. 'No, never heard of him. Who is he?'

I took a breath wondering how much I should tell him, and in the end decided we were at a point where we needed something, anything and it was worth the risk. 'He is supposed to be the lead engineer on the job you're on at the moment.'

And for an instant, the briefest second I saw something on Jimmy's face, which I seized on. 'What is it?' I said.

He took a breath. 'I don't know anything about this bloke specifically but,' he stopped. 'You really need to talk to Tomas, he would know for certain.'

'I'm talking to you, Jimmy. Please, tell me, what is it?'

'I've come across it before on other jobs. I don't know about Lennie, but say you've got this shit hot bloke with all the right qualifications, all the certificates and the full pedigree for something. A specialist. When you price a job that's who you price in on the quote for doing the work. It gives credibility and bumps the price up, but it also looks like you know what you're doing and the customer trusts you've got the best person for the job. But then-'

I looked at him. 'But then?' I prompted.

'You send someone who can do the job, probably just as well as the other bloke but who maybe hasn't got the right bits of paper, and you charge the higher rate, as if you were sending the qualified bloke. You pay the other bloke who hasn't got the qualifications half the money and pocket the difference. I'm not saying that is what is going on here, but I wouldn't be surprised, and it would explain why this Aleksander bloke isn't on site.'

'When he was pissed one night Tomas told me that Lennie had told him he was some sort of Professor back home, but we've never found out where back home is exactly. He's never really seemed a good fit for a building site.'

'And also,' Jimmy stopped. 'Tomas'll tell you the same thing. He came over here for the work, he's a good guy, a real grafter, Tomas, but once he said he didn't think Lennie was really Polish. Lennie can barely say half a dozen words in Polish. Anyway, Tomas made some joke about it, and said the words he did know sounded like he learned it out of a book. They had a real ding-dong about it. It's the only time I've seen Lennie lose his shit over anything, Lennie said he'd spent a lot of time abroad with his parents when he was a kid – but you could see he was really pissed off about it.'

I made for the door, someone needed to talk to Tomas.

'Oh and wait,' said Jimmy, as I was about to go. 'I think I've got a photo of him if it'll help. On my phone. Last job we went on we went out for a Christmas drink. Even Lennie couldn't turn that one down. We were in a bar. If I can have my phone I can show it to you.'

'I'll get someone to bring it in for you.'

'Can't you get it?'

I turned and shook my head. The truth was I had what I needed from him. Now I needed to find Lennie Novak and Kathy. I slammed the door shut behind me.

'We need to get in touch with the security team on the Tile Farm site,' I said to Mike, as I headed to Tomlin's office.

A few minutes later uniformed officers were on their way to Tile Farm and Tomlin and Mike went in to question Tomas. And I waited.

Outside it was full dark now. Fog hung in the jaundiced yellow orange lights of the car park. It was bitter cold and dark and I wondered where Kathy was.

More than anything I wanted her to be found and to be safe. I wanted her to moan about the yoghurt and complain that I'd eaten the bread, and the thought of it bubbled up into the back of my throat, making it impossible to swallow.

A while later Tomlin and Mike emerged from one of the interview rooms; Tomas confirmed that Lennie Novak was doing the work Aleksander Wiśniewski was supposed to be doing. Rowe was back on the phone to IFSH to see if they had details of which contracts Lennie Novak had worked for them.

Uniform phoned in. The security guard on the building site had the number of Novak's van.

It had last been on site that morning at 6.15 a.m. Six-fifteen am, well before anyone else was on site, well before he had rung in sick. The guard had thought it was odd as in the winter work usually started at eight, but

271

Lennie said he needed to come in and drop off some equipment for the rest of his crew as he had another job to go to and wouldn't be in for the rest of the day. The guard had let him through, Novak had headed down to the storage containers at the back of the site, which were tucked away near the old farm buildings, and had left around twenty minutes later.

I watched Mike as he relayed the message.

At least now with a registration number we could find the vehicle more quickly. But what had Novak been doing on the building site at that time of the morning and had he had Kathy with him?

DC Rowe was busy tracing the name and address relating to the registration number. I sat down at my desk. My phone rang and for a wonderful blissful second I thought it was Kathy, and then I realised it was Phil Hurst who had found the tracking device on Laura's car. I hesitated and then took the call.

'Mel?' he said. 'I heard about your sister. I'm so sorry. Is there anything I can do?'

I took a breath. He was the last person I had expected to hear from. I sniffed back the tears that threatened. 'Just don't be nice to me,' I said.

'Do you want me to come over.'

'You're working.'

He laughed. 'That wouldn't stop me. Anyway I'm just about to clock off. I could be there in an hour.'

'No, you're fine. We're just waiting — we've got something.' I didn't say anything else because I wasn't sure what exactly it was we had.

'If you need me, I'm here,' he said. 'You want me to ring you later?'

'Yeah, yes that would be good,' I said and hung up.

*

Tomlin brought us all in for a briefing so that the rest of the team could be brought up to speed. He ran through the new information and recent discoveries. My sister's picture had been added to the boards along with the photo we had lifted from Jimmy's phone of Lennie Novak. The other small blonde women now sat to one side of Laura's image with question marks by their names.

Novak was tall and well-built with a shaved head and a body builder's physique. He looked to be in his late thirties. In the photo he was a few inches taller than Jimmy which would make him six feet two or three.

I found myself a place at the back of the room.

'We've issued an alert for the vehicle and driver,' Tomlin said. 'We've got nothing to hold any of the other men on. I intend to keep Jimmy Grenard and Tomas here for the time being to help if we need more information - both men have agreed to cooperate.

'Given what we know about Novak's movements over the last few hours, I want to get a team together to conduct a search of the building site and the farm buildings, as well as double the efforts to find both Novak and his caravan. If we assume that his methodology is the same for all his victims then we may still have a window here. The evidence suggests that Laura Lamb was kept somewhere overnight. We know he killed her in the hours just before taking her to Isaac's farm. I think at this point there is a still a very good chance that we can find Kathy Grenard alive.' He didn't look in my direction as he spoke.

DI Foreman stepped to the front. 'We're calling the officers in off the house to house, and while I understand what you're saying, given the weather conditions and the fact it's pitch dark out there I'm not sure what we can reasonably achieve searching at night. It's a huge site, there's no light - I agree we should get some men down there, but there is no way we can conduct a full search until tomorrow morning. It's too dangerous. I mean what can we see without floodlights? You might be lucky but the likelihood is we'll be just shambling around in the dark.'

He glanced across at me and then back at Tomlin.

'I'm sorry,' he said. 'But it's just not practical. I think we should check the storage facilities because that's where Novak said he was going, but much more than that I don't see as feasible. In reality we have no idea where Novak went on the site. Or why. It's a big area, in twenty minutes, unobserved he could have gone anywhere. I'm assuming the guard didn't watch him or go with him?'

Tomlin glanced at Mike who shook his head. 'There was no reason to – he was known to work on the site. They knew he came and went off to other jobs. The security guard had been on his rounds and was waiting for the shift to end. He assumed that Novak went down to the storage containers where the crews keep their gear. Those are floodlit for security reasons and Novak said he was just dropping something off.'

Foreman nodded and Tomlin spoke. 'Then we should start there. I appreciate what you're saying. DI Foreman. So, we need to do what we can tonight and then initiate a full search first thing as soon as we've got the light.'

There was a rumble of agreement from the officers. It was decided. I had no input, technically I wasn't even meant to be there. I felt sick to the pit of my stomach and stuffed my hands into my jacket pockets to stop them from shaking. I wanted them to search every last inch, dark or not.

DC Rowe had found details of the van from DVLA. 'The van is registered to an Ann Louise Fielding. She is also the insurer. Leonard J Novak is the other named driver. We've got an address in Birmingham for Ann Fielding. Just one thing.' Rowe passed a printed sheet of paper to the front and then continued, 'I took this from her driving licence. Ann Fielding is small, blonde,' she said. 'I've been through the electoral roll and she appears to live alone. But on a previous census she was shown as living with a Leonard John Novak. I'm trying to see what else I can find.'

'Good work, Rowe. Can we get onto West Midlands and see if they can get some officers round to Ann

Fielding's address asap?' said Tomlin. 'We'll need to speak to Ms Fielding. There is also a slim chance that Novak may be heading there.'

Rowe nodded, and headed back to her desk.

A plan was actioned, a search arranged, updates on the details for Novak's vehicle given out, and now we had a photo from Jimmy's phone he should be easier to find. There was nothing else I could do now.

I sat quietly as the jobs were sorted and the plans arranged. I knew without being told that a line had been crossed. I was no longer a police officer on the Major Investigations Team, I was the sister of the victim and I shouldn't be there.

I knew that the others couldn't speak freely in front of me, couldn't say what was on their minds, and although I knew what they are thinking they couldn't say it aloud while I was in the room. Tomlin said that he believed that Kathy was still alive. I hoped he was right but I sensed he was in the minority. To let them do their jobs properly what I should do was go home and let them get on with it, but I also knew that this office was where any news would come in first. This was where I would find out what was happening and where Kathy was. I stayed resolutely where I was.

Tomlin came over and sat down alongside me. I knew what he was going to say even before he opened his mouth.

'You've done as much as you can here, Mel, you have to leave it to us now. I'll send an officer from Family Liaison to sit with you. Go home. Please.'

I nodded but didn't move.

'Don't make me order you.'

'I want to be here,' I said, in a voice that was barely above a whisper. I was afraid I might cry.

'I'll keep you in the loop every step of the way. I'm going to get someone to take you home now. Okay?'

I was thinking about resisting but in the end just nodded.

He was right. I was in the way here. I had found the

link. I had seen the pattern, but now it was up to other people to follow it up and find Novak and Kathy. I went over to my desk, Sophie Rowe was off somewhere else so I picked up my bag and coat and walked out of the office.

I could feel the eyes of the other officers following me and made an effort to walk with an air of confidence. As I got to the front door of the police station and stepped out into the car park Rowe hurried out behind me, wrapped up in a padded jacket.

'You should be upstairs,' I said. 'I'll be fine to drive myself home.'

Rowe shook her head. 'No you won't. Boss's orders and I'm staying with you until Family Liaison gets there. Give me your keys. You'll need to direct me.'

We drove slowly through town. Sophie said all the right things, things I'd have said if the situation were reversed. Things about everyone doing all they could. Everyone pulling together. Every possible place being searched.

Kathy's car was still parked in front of my garage so we parked up by the maisonettes and walked to my place.

There were lights on in the houses around the courtyard but my house was in darkness. I realised that there was part of me that still hoped, by some miracle, that Kathy would be there waiting for us, totally oblivious to the fuss that she had caused.

Inside the house everything was as I had left it. Rowe followed me inside. 'Do you want to take my car back?' I said, turning on the hall light.

Rowe shook her head. 'No, it's fine. A patrol car is coming to drop the FLO off soon so I'll get a lift back with them.'

'Do you want tea?' I asked. So British.

She nodded. 'Yeah, that would be good. Is there anything you want me to do?'

I knew if I asked her to find my sister we might both cry.

I opened the fridge to get the milk out. Inside was the food that Kathy had bought, the open packet of yoghurts, and the hummus.

'Shit,' I said, shutting the door. 'I don't know if I can do this. Where has he got her? Where is he?'

And then I started to shake and cry, tears not of grief but of fury and impotence and blind rage. 'There has to be something I can do.'

Rowe touched my shoulder. 'Be here for when she gets back, Sarge,' she said. 'Here come on, let me make the tea.'

I didn't want to go into the sitting room and see the neatly made makeshift bed on the sofa but there was nowhere else to go. As we stepped into the room Rowe's phone rang. She stepped outside to take the call and then coming back in said, 'If you don't mind I'll take you up on the offer of your car.'

'Why, what's happened?'

She hesitated.

'Tell me,' I snapped.

'A caravan has been reported on fire on a piece of waste land just outside Denham, the farmer says a man who called himself Lennie had asked if he could park it there while he was working in the area.'

'I'll drive,' I said. 'Have you got the address?'

For a second, just a second I saw that Rowe was considering saying no and then she said. 'I'll drive, you navigate. The details are on my phone.'

'Do you know how much damage was done?' I said as I locked up and we made our way back to the car.

'Pretty extensive from what they said. Looks like someone used an accelerant. But they'd taken the Calor gas tank off so it was just fire-'

As we pulled away from the kerb Rowe's phone rang again.

I answered it. It was Mike. 'Hi Rowe, are you still with Mel?'

'It's me, Mike,' I said.

'We've got him,' he said flatly. 'Traffic have just

277

picked him up heading North on the A17 to pick up the A1. They're bringing him in now.'

'Is Kathy with him?' I asked.

I heard the beat, the moment and knew what his answer was. 'No, I'm really sorry, Mel. Just him in the van.'

I glanced across at Rowe. I knew she had been hanging on every word.

'Thanks for letting me know, Mike. Rowe and I are going to the caravan fire. I'll see you back at the station.'

'Stay safe,' said Mike, and hung up.

'Do we know if there was anyone in the caravan?' I asked.

She shook her head. 'No, but the fire crew is still damping it down. It's going to be awhile.'

Once we were out of the estate Rowe hit the blue lights and we headed out through town on the Lynn Road to the A10 North to King's Lynn. Five or six miles out of town we turned off to the right and followed a maze of narrow lanes down to a semi-circle of rough scrubland a few dozen yards back from the verge, almost completely obscured by bushes. Unless I had seen the fire tender and the patrol car parked on the verge I would have driven straight by. In the lazy rolling lights of the police car I could see the towering pylons a few hundred yards away that strode across the landscape like giants.

We got out of the car and headed into the bushes. Deep in the scrub, now no more than a burned-out shell was what remained of what once had been a large touring caravan. It would have been invisible from the road. Firefighters were busy rolling up hoses, two men were still playing water onto the smouldering pyre.

I looked round at the sea of mud, water and debris. Fire crews respond to fire. They trash potential crime scenes. Big boots, gallons of water, the destruction of the physical evidence with axes and grapples to drag burning material away to extinguish it. To one side of the small clearing was a heap of the caravan's contents that had been dragged out from the interior.

If this was Lennie Novak's caravan then there was a chance that we would be unable to recover any useful information from the scene. We were dependent on what had been protected from the heat by falling debris or had escaped the worst of the flames.

I introduced myself to the patrol officers and then the fire officer in charge of the scene came over to give us an update.

'We got a shout from the farmer who saw the flames. He thought the bloke who owns it might still be inside, said he came and went at all sorts of odd hours. And we were obviously concerned about the proximity to the overhead cables specially if the gas bottles went up, but when we got here the gas bottles had been disconnected and were over there on the side of the road and the storage compartment had been wedged open, presumably so anyone coming here would realise it wasn't likely to blow up.'

'And he didn't want to kill anyone,' I said. Only women who resembled someone he had once lived with.

Getting closer I got some sense of the extent of the destruction. And something else. In amongst a pile of debris that the fire fighters had dragged out of the burning van was a single high-heeled shoe. Charred but recognisable. A small midnight blue shoe with a tiny diamanté trim, a match to the one I had seen in the pub car park. Kathy had been there, in that van, in amongst these bushes where no one could see her or hear her.

I turned to Rowe. 'Can you get that bagged,' I said, all business now, trying to keep the fear out of my voice, trying to stop my knees from buckling. She did a double take and then saw what I saw. Before she could speak, I said. 'It's Kathy's. We need SOCO out here as soon as they've got it cool enough to work on.'

*

279

Lennie Novak sits in the interview room at Denham Market police station. He is dressed in a white disposable paper suit as his clothes have been taken into evidence. He looks remarkably calm. He is very still. His eyes are closed. His arms are crossed and his chest rises and falls slowly, almost as if he was sleeping. He has declined legal representation.

An extensive search of the storage containers and at the building site have turned up nothing, but SOCO have found hair on the floor of the van on the polythene covering, which using an expedited analysis will show that they belong to Kathy. A search of the debris from the caravan has already turned up the remains of two tracking devices of the same make and in similar cases to those found on Laura Lamb's car.

And there is something else, a charred water damaged photograph in an ornate silver frame.

The photograph is of a young woman on her wedding day. She is laughing. We can see her face through her veil, her eyes are bright, her expression knowing and mischievous, almost teasing. She has her hands up, palms towards whoever is taking the picture, as if she is fending the photographer off, although her expression suggests something very different. The young woman is beautiful in a girl-next-door-kind of way. She looks a lot like Laura Lamb, and Anya and the others, but I think as I stare down at the copy they have given me, that most of all she looks like Kathy.

Now that we have a name we can place Lennie Novak's Mercedes van in the vicinity of the abduction and dump sites of the other victims that we have on my list. The house in Birmingham is empty. There is no trace of Ann Fielding or her children. Neighbours say they think that the family went back to Poland. No one has reported her or her children missing.

In amongst the debris of the ruined caravan SOCO finds an earring that belonged to Laura Lamb but other than the shoe there is no sign of Kathy. The consensus on the team is that there are likely to be other victims that we haven't found or identified beyond those on the list. Novak travelled extensively throughout the UK.

The door to the interview room opens and Tomlin and Rowe go in to question Novak.

He nods to acknowledge their arrival. DC Rowe starts the recording and then reads him his rights. The questions are simple to begin with. Yes, he is Lennie Novak. He speaks with an accent that is difficult to place. Yes, he has been working for IFSH on their integrated systems.

'The internet of things,' he says with a quiet self-assurance. 'It is the future.'

His answers are brief, almost as if it is too much of an effort to reply.

Tomlin asks him where Kathy Grenard is. He shows him a photograph of Kathy and of the others, but his main focus is on Kathy. If she is still alive then we need to know where she is. Tomlin shows him a photograph of the shoe. Novak declines to answer. Tomlin asks him again.

And then Novak looks up as if he knows that I am watching him from the observation room.

'Taking the last one was a big mistake,' he says, staring straight at me. 'I should not have been so greedy. Greed made me careless. It was too soon. There was no time to plan.'

Tomlin nods as if this is the most natural thing in the world. 'So where is Kathy? You can still help yourself, Lennie . All you have to do is tell us where she is. Is she still alive? We can help you.'

Lennie Novak turns to him and smiles. 'No one can help me. I have nothing more to say,' he says.

'Can you tell us about Ann Fielding?' asks DC Rowe. She pushes a copy of the photograph in the frame, sealed in an evidence bag, towards him.

Novak looks down at the picture, his fingers reaching out to work over the outside of the bag, tracing her face, and then he looks up at DC Rowe, with the sleepy predatory eyes of a lizard. 'My precious Annie. I love her you know, my Annie. They all came after Annie,' he says. 'All of them.'

*

A Family Liaison Officer drives me home. Her name is Beverley. She makes me scrambled eggs and a mug of tea. We sit in the kitchen, at stools by the breakfast bar, because I can't bear to go into the sitting room. She talks about her garden.

It feels like I am watching myself from the outside. I find that my mind refuses to look at the truth for more than a split second at a time. It feels like holding my hand too close to a fire, if I hold it too close it will burn me too, so I keep testing the heat and then pull away again and again. I am exhausted and don't imagine I will be able to sleep, but I do. When I wake up for a few seconds I think I must have been having a terrible dream but then, two seconds later I remember that it isn't a dream after all. When I come downstairs Beverly has folded up the sheets and blankets and put them away in the airing cupboard. I don't know where she slept.

*

At first light the next morning a full search team begins combing every inch of the Tile Farm building site just outside Denham, every shed, every trench, every shell of a house, every square yard of the derelict farm, every footing, every building, every vehicle, every last inch.

A team of ground workers turn up at nine and are kept off site in the canteen. Half an hour later a mixer lorry full of concrete turns up. He tells the officer on the gate that he has to pour it or it will set. It's the reason the ground workers are in on a Saturday morning. Behind the cab the great drum turns and churns, keeping the concrete moving so it doesn't harden. It sounds like the sea rolling in over a pebble beach. They need permission from the search director for the lorry and the ground workers to come onto the site and work.

The driver wants to know what the problem is, he was there Friday morning first thing, and he and his mate had pumped two full loads into an old well that had been on the farmyard. It was half full of crap and water, just there under a thin metal manhole cover, bloody dangerous, thirty foot deep at least, a bricked lined tube. They'd been back and forward all day, filling it up, that and the cellars that ran under the farm house over on the far side of the new estate. 'So,' he wants to know. 'What was the problem now?'

The concrete wouldn't be set yet, not in this weather but he had come with the last load to cap off the well and the cellar. Apparently it was going to be a children's play area when it was done.

Tomlin and Foreman who have been on site since first light are hot and wet inside their oilskins, hair slick with sweat as they work alongside the rest of the searchers, and can only speculate what was in the well and the cellars before they were capped off. There is no way ground penetrating radar is going to go that deep. The search teams work all day until the light fails. The searchers find nothing.

*

Once he has legal representation Lennie Novak's solicitor informs us that Mr Novak would like to confess to the murders of Anya Vassali, Kylie Roberts, Carly Brand, Lisa Rhodes and Laura Lamb. He is prepared to gives times, dates, anything we need. He has no comment to make regarding the whereabouts of Ann Fielding, nor the disappearance of Katherine Helen Grenard. It is all that he says, after that Lennie Novak says nothing.

Chapter Twenty-Two
After

The new houses on the Tile Farm estate spring up like mushrooms. Every week lights go on behind the windows for the first time. There are cars on the new driveways, shrubs and flowers planted in the tiny front gardens. Families starting new lives in new homes.

I go there every week, I just walk, I don't linger. The main farm house has been converted into luxury apartments, and the outbuildings into houses, they're not quite finished yet but close to it, between them they frame a communal garden. The play area the developers promised is almost ready. New trees have been planted around the edge, topping a low grass bank out beyond the play safe surfaces and brightly coloured swings and slides. The little trees are just about to come into blossom.

*

I'm still finding it hard to believe I will never see Kathy again. Grief is like something alive, an animal, coiled, raw and cold inside me. Sometimes it is angry, sometimes it fills me with so much frustration and fury that I don't know what to do with myself, and then it dozes and I think that maybe things are getting better, and then it uncurls, taking me by surprise, roaring through me, and I cry until it feels like I will never stop. Sometimes I find I'm crying without realising it.

Ground penetrating radar has been unable to find any trace of a body in the cellar at the old farm house. In the area around the well the shaft is too deep, the heavy clay soil too water logged for the equipment to give any meaningful results. Some nights I dream I am drowning in ice cold, liquid concrete, the breath being crushed out of my chest under a weight I cannot shift.

*

Lennie Novak is currently on remand awaiting trial, charged with the murders of Anya Vassali, Kylie Roberts, Carly Brand, Lisa Rhodes and Laura Lamb. There is insufficient evidence to charge him with the murder of my sister, Kathy, despite her shoe being found at his caravan and the trace evidence in the van. He still refuses to tell us what he did with her.

*

Tomlin convinced me to take compassionate leave, as well as the mandatory counselling. The rest of the team, aware of how it feels to be out of the loop, have rung or dropped by to keep me updated on progress, not often, but enough. I know they can't tell me everything, and I know they won't tell me everything. Phil Hurst has been round too – the casual, good sex guy from the Forensics Team. He didn't ask me anything, didn't try out any of the words that are supposed to be comforting, instead he turned up on my doorstep with wine, chocolate, a takeaway curry and his Netflix password.

I don't want to be away too long from the job, the longer I leave it before going back, the harder it's going to be, but Tomlin is right, I do need some time away. I'm glad Novak is in prison. His confessions have been detailed and precise. He will get a full life term with no chance of parole. I want him to be convicted of Kathy's murder, but he is still saying nothing about her or any of the other women that DS Rachel Purvis is convinced he murdered, including his ex-partner, Annie Fielding. Rachel Purvis and I have spoken a lot over the last few weeks.

DC Rowe came round to tell me that local officers in Birmingham have traced Annie Fielding's children – a boy and a girl, Billy and Freya, aged eleven and twelve. They're alive and well, and living with Annie's mother and father, Eileen and Frank Taylor, in a neat little semi in Solihull. According to Mrs Taylor, Annie and Lennie Novak were never married. The photograph found at the caravan was of Annie's wedding to someone else, a man called Jack Fielding. The wedding photos, according to Mrs Taylor, had been taken by Novak – at that time a family friend.

In her statement, Mrs Taylor told officers, 'Annie's marriage to Jack lasted about three months, then she ran off with Lennie. She had been seeing him all along, I reckon. She should never have got married. I said to her, "Are you sure?".But she'd got the dress and everything booked. I knew then that it wasn't going to last. I know Lennie's quiet and doesn't say a lot, but he thinks the world of Annie, completely idolises her. It's a lot for me, you know, what with the children and my Frank. She always was a handful, Annie, never could settle to anything. Lovely girl, do anything for anyone but trouble, you know.'

Officers noted that Annie's father, Mr Frank Taylor, had limited mobility, chronic leg ulcers and required oxygen. He seldom left the house. I imagine Mrs Taylor as a small threadbare woman, trying hard to keep it all together. Mrs Taylor said in her statement that she hadn't seen Annie in approximately eight years.

'She came round one afternoon and asked me if I could have the kids for the weekend. She said she needed a bit of a break. Annie told me she and Lennie were going somewhere nice. Somewhere really special that he'd got planned for her. Not that I believed a word of it. He'd already let me know he was working away. I thought that she was planning to go off with someone else. She always has been flighty. When the going gets tough Annie is up and away. I warned Lennie what she is like. I could never see her settling for family life. I wish she would just get in touch though. It's not right, is it? Lennie sends me money. I don't believe what they're saying about him. It can't be right. He is such a good man.

*

Despite a nationwide appeal, as yet there have been no reported sightings or information relating to the whereabouts of Annie Fielding.

*

'Here you go. Piping hot. Do you want to budge up a bit on that blanket?'

I look up from the wall where I've been sitting. I've been staring, unseeing, out towards the sea, out over the sandbanks and the boats on the quay at Wells-next-the-Sea. We're having a day out on a bright, late spring day, which apparently is just what I need. To be honest I'm not arguing; some days now there are the tiniest chinks of light in the darkness. Phil Hurst is making his way back towards me with a carrier bag in one hand and two cans of drink clutched precariously in the other.

He's smiling and I find myself smiling back. We've been seeing each other regularly for a while now. He says I'm only after him for his Netflix subscription. It feels good. No one is more surprised than me.

As he is unpacking the carrier bag, the phone vibrates in my jacket pocket. Instinctively I take it out and read the name on the screen. It's Jimmy. I hesitate for a split second and then decline the call. I'm not ready for the conversation with Jimmy yet.

'Do you want ketchup?' Phil asks, reaching into the bag

'Yes please, and salt and vinegar.'

287

Phil grins, and I turn my attention back to him and the fish and chips.

The End

Printed in Great Britain
by Amazon

84078222R00169